Holiday

Stanley Middleton

W F HOWES LTD

This large print edition published in 2009 by
W F Howes Ltd
Unit 4, Rearsby Business Park, Gaddesby Lane,
Rearsby, Leicester LE7 4YH

1 3 5 7 9 10 8 6 4 2

First published in the United Kingdom in 1999
by Five Leaves Publications

A CIP catalogue record for this book is available
from the British Library

ISBN 978 1 40743 354 7

Typeset by Palimpsest Book Production Limited,
Grangemouth, Stirlingshire
Printed and bound in Great Britain
by MPG Books Ltd, Bodmin, Cornwall

FSC
Mixed Sources
Product group from well-managed
forests and other controlled sources

Cert no. SGS-COC-2953
www.fsc.org
© 1996 Forest Stewardship Council

To Miriam and Selwyn Hughes

CHAPTER 1

Light shimmered along the polished pews as the congregation heaved itself to its feet, hailing the Lord's Anointed. Grain arrows waved darkly in the wood under the coating of shellac, the brightness of elbow-grease. Brass umbrella-holders gleamed, but the metal rectangle to house the name of the pew's occupier had been allowed to blacken in disuse.

Edwin Fisher glanced at his hymn book as he listened to the voice of the woman next to him. 'He comes,' she sang, 'with succour speedy, to those who suffer wrong. To help the poor and needy, And bid the weak be strong.' Her voice pierced, and she enunciated without inhibition so that a boy and a girl two rows forward turned round to stare at her. Their mother gently handled them back to propriety.

Fisher hummed, not opening his mouth. The walls of the church stood white, thick, while the narrow, pointed windows were leaded into small diamonds of cleanish glass. Above his head the gallery stretched, supported on metal pillars in regency blue. Typically, he smiled to himself, the chaste colours of the late eighteenth, early nineteenth centuries applied, not without success, in this Victorian building intended for dark browns and country cream. The woman next door lifted her head as sunshine caught the hair of the small boy who, now climbing on to his seat, leaned against his mother, tried to finger her hymn-book. 'Love, joy, hope, like flowers, Spring in His path to birth.'

The congregation, Fisher guessed from the rear, were almost all middle-aged or elderly, and the majority women, in flowered hats, bonnets of convoluted ribbon and pale summer coats. Holiday-makers enjoying a full church, hearty singing, a popular preacher. There was, he noticed, no choir to speak of; two girls, an old lady and a grey-haired man occupied the stalls in front of the organ. Fisher did not like this: nonconformity as he recalled it demanded a large, fractious choir, bossy with prima donnas' whispers, to drill the congregation's singing into disciplined enthusiasm. The members here must be themselves on holiday or at home in the boarding houses laying the tables, basting joints.

The sun-bars angled down packed wild with dust-specks so that the air danced alive with energy between the areas of dim cleanliness. The congregation voiced the last verse with vigour, lashing the organ on, praising God in his tabernacle. 'The tide of time shall never His covenant remove; His name shall stand for ever, His changeless name of Love.' Silence settled heavily; the minister adjusted his hair, his preaching bands and the sleeves of his gown. Thus prepared, he pronounced the benediction and as the organist had gulped a final amen people flopped into their seats covering eyes with their right palms.

Edwin Fisher looked about.

Sunlight now dazzled as if it were reflected from the sea outside. The congregation was moving sluggishly, fingering silk scarves, exchanging bright words to the accompaniment of the B flat prelude from Bach's Short Eight. Fisher was first from his back seat to the door where the preacher, shorter, less impressive than from the eminence of his pulpit, smiled and shook his hand. Outside light whirled as if the whole morning were one huge glassy fire fanned by the scuffle of wind into incandescent brilliance. Bankside Methodist Church. Dull gold letters. Morning and Evening, preacher, Rev. J. Parkinson Dewes, M.A., B.D.

The streets were quiet.

Presumably those for the beach had made their way there two hours back and were not returning for lunch. The contemporary pattern. Breakfast, into the car or down to the seaside, and not back before six for evening meal and television. So his fantasies about choir-singers bent over gas-stoves meant little; perhaps such dusted then, scraped mountains of spuds, weeded garden-paths or rested their bones with Sunday newspapers.

In spite of the sun the wind nipped at street corners in this east-coast town. On a main road now Fisher eyed an open stationer's shop with its racks of cards, gaudy paperbacks, union-jack carrier-bags, buckets and spades. He loved this place with its covered arcades of metal, as if the industrial revolution had turned itself soft, displaying milder arts. He'd pushed here as a boy, wide-eyed, escaped from his boring parents amongst the panama hats and whitened plimsolls, listening to expansive talk, envying the means of generosity, delighted with girls, above himself.

Whistling, he decided against the beach, made for a pub.

The lounge, at three minutes past twelve, was empty, momentarily dark, and warm. Backed by shelves of bottles, each reflected in the mirror behind, the barman pulled a white coat over his shirtsleeves. He served Fisher without hurry, remarked on the sunshine and temperature before moving across to the other counter. Here it was as quiet as the chapel, but gayer, bitter; no place of worship boasted a plush carpet. Sipping his ale, Edwin Fisher considered the afternoon.

First, he must eat, but where? A sausage roll with his beer, or out to starched tablecloths and tips? When he'd visited this place as a boy, they'd called at the swing-chair weighing machine on the prom as they'd made their first trip to the sands. Vaguely he recalled his childish annoyance at the ceremony: mother first, then himself and his sister, finally father, and the weights inscribed on small cards while the old man chaffed the attendant who was all affability for sixpence. Fisher remembered the brown monkey's face with its white streaks of eye-creases. And on Saturday morning, that day of sad exodus, they'd line up again, have the new weight recorded and subtract, they hoped, first from second.

These days everybody slimmed, sucked fruit, ate steak, eschewed ice-cream and beer. In those years of rationing, one did well to gain; to be fat was to be healthy. Fisher thought of his father, thin as a rake, swinging his tennis-shod feet from the chair of the weighing-machine as he groaned, 'Put another pound on, for heaven's sake. They'll think I'm pining away.' And his wife would reply slyly, behind her hand, 'Not with all that noise, they won't, Arthur'.

Edwin had hated his parents then, for the shopkeepers they were. Obsequious, joking, un-educated, the finger-ends greasy from copper in the till, they drew attention to themselves. When the retainer ushered his rabble round the stately home, Father Fisher asked the first fool question, chirped the witless crack, was rebuffed in all eyes but his own with the guide's calm, 'No, sir. With respect, I don't think that could be so 'ere, sir.' Yet the old idiot had brains; he made his shops pay; he'd left his children tidy sums. And he'd read, though with a mind bent, young Edwin had decided, on trivialising.

5

'Did you know, our Edwin, that Beethoven did multiplication tables on his death-bed?'

'No.'

'Well, he did. It says so here.'

'What does it mean by "did" them?' The boy was pushed into disguised objection.

'Did?' His father peered at the magazine or library book. 'Don't say. Learnt 'em. Or used 'em, I sh'd think.'

Back to his browsing. Not a thought of the music. The only Beethoven he could recognise was the Minuet in G that Tina plinked on the piano. If Edwin listened to the radio concerts, his old man complained.

'Can't you turn that thing down? It goes through you. Anybody can see you haven't done a day's work, or you wouldn't want that racket.'

'It's Beethoven.'

'No wonder he went deaf.'

Fisher never sorted out his father's views on education, and could make little sense of them now. Both children went to university, and though Arthur grumbled about expense he paid up. Nor did he seem to envy their expertise. His magpie mind stored snippets of information with which he gleefully caught his offspring out, but he never attempted to organise or coordinate his knowledge into a system. His favourite reading, his son told him in moments of exasperation, was a set of children's encyclopaedias.

'Why not?' Arthur would say. 'Interest's interest.'

His mother successfully taught herself what they were about, and could talk easily of 'O' and 'A' Level, university entrance, moderations, class of degree. When he thought about the matter now, Edwin wondered what sort of picture lay behind Elsie Fisher's correctly chosen phraseology. But he'd never fathomed her, even when she was alive. Comfortable, cheerful, one would have guessed, not ambitious either socially or intellectually, she'd driven her husband on to pile away money and her children to become well qualified. A regular attender with her family at the Methodist Church, Vane Street, she'd never mentioned God or displayed herself to her family on her knees praying for guidance. Secretive, she'd lived openly; a plain women who'd serve in the main shop, who would hold no office however undemanding in the church, she'd slave-driven her children and her husband so that they dared report only success to her. Even that she never praised fulsomely, but they learnt to look for a narrowing of the eyes and a slow nod to denote approval. Sometimes she'd say as when Tina passed for the high school,

'If I were you, Arthur, I'd give them half a crown.'

'Both?' Assumed grievance.

'They'll learn to appreciate each other.'

'If Ted's naughty', Arthur'd say jovially, 'I s'll have to smack the pair on 'em on that reckoning.'

'If what she's done isn't worth five shillings to you, then don't give it. I'll find it from the housekeeping.'

'And cut my teas down.' Smiling under tooth-brush moustache.

He invariably shelled out.

At thirty-two Edwin Fisher admitted his emotional immaturity when he thought back to those days, in that he felt again the embarrassment, the shame, the yearning to be elsewhere or some other body, which had constantly nagged him miserable. In his mind now he admitted his parents' virtues; they were both compulsive workers, both knew a deep love for their children which they had no means of expressing to the clever, class-jumping offspring. Now that both were dead, he saw this, wished it otherwise, but failed to nail himself down to reason. Perhaps it was some fault in him. When he met his sister, a doctor married to a doctor, he began to build his barricades again, as though they shared some secret, desperate hostility. Not that she admitted much; distant, tweedy, sensibly detached, she regarded his approaches with amusement, but let them spend more than thirty-six hours together they quarrelled, not out of principle, but from buried habit. They were, he decided, still fighting for their parents' affection.

Through the open window at his back he heard the shouting of children, the sharply raised voice of an adult. Curious, he decided in the end not to stand to find out the cause. Make your mind up when it's too late; that was his line. He sipped his beer, exchanged three more words with the barman who returned flourishing a torch, examined the polish on his shoes and made for the door. He'd do without lunch, buy a pound of apples, walk. On Sunday? Anything could be bought at the seaside in summer. He pushed towards the beach in the day's brightness.

As soon as he'd left the pavements for the soft, paper-littered sand he knew he was where he did not want to be. Nothing for him here but this wide stretch of fine dust, this shallow sea ten minutes' march away and people in deck chairs, on rugs, behind gaudy wind-breaks, lying stripped and red, oiled in the sunshine. He'd take his shoes off, roll his trousers and paddle ludicrously as his father had done twenty years ago. Even when the old man had dabbled in the edge he'd kept his trilby hat on, preserved his respectability by attracting ridicule. That wasn't true. Arthur Fisher had noticed nothing untoward in his behaviour, because there was nothing except in the mind of his jumping-jack of a son.

Edwin sat, emptied his shoes, fingered them on again. Here sprawled a man who'd left his wife, if that was the word, who had thus entitled himself to histrionics, to an emotional extravaganza, but whose person had decided to perform it again through his father's antics. He stood, pulled at his jacket, slapped the pockets, told himself he'd forgotten the apples and made for the promenade.

The sun struck warm through his jacket in spite of the wind. Suddenly he walked livelier, stretched

9

taller, recognised optimism. He'd like to speak to somebody, exchange afternoon banalities. The road leading to the beach, sprinkled with blowing sand, had become crowded, bright with swirling frocks, puffed-out chests, families with objectives. Nobody had a word for Fisher. No dirty old man, chuntering into his moustache, dragged his raincoat about him to beg for a match, a fag, the price of a drink. The people exchanged no confidences amongst themselves; a woman screeching about her sunburn was the exception.

Catching sight of himself in a shop-window he paused to admire the upright carriage, the thatch of hair, the distinction of nose, delicate hands. He did not posture long, but the moment did him good. For a dozen steps along the road he felt himself somebody, a noteworthy, though the scores passing paid him no attention.

He'd walk along the promenade; he'd take a bus; he'd buy a paperback and read it in a shelter along the front. On holiday. A free man. Without burden of wife, without children, a child. Now he swore, angrily, sourly, out loud, he thought, but no-one heard, turned a head, registered disapproval as he moved on.

'Piss off.'

The sentence stopped him. A red-faced man had spoken to another who'd shrugged. Both wore raincoats. Both seemed sober, with hands in pockets, middle-aged artisans without axes to grind. Ten seconds before Fisher six yards away had noticed neither, but now there seemed a stoppage in the movement of the crowd, because of the fierceness of the delivery.

'You heard what I said.'

The expression on the face of the second man did not change. He might have been mildly interested, but unembarrassed, not cowed. He nodded, sucked his thumbnail briefly, replied,

'Please yourself.'

'I shall.'

Neither moved; the few near them stood frozen; beyond that the frocks and slacks flapped forward to the sea. The first man swung away in a clumsiness of anger so that he cannoned into Fisher, mumbled an imprecation or apology, pushed away muttering. The second took his hands from his pocket, turned townwards, but without hurry. Fisher followed him for want of occupation. A hundred yards on, the man posted a letter, stooping to read the time of collection. The humdrum action surprised Fisher, who expected nothing ordinary of somebody who'd drawn attention to himself in the open street. Had he made some obscene suggestion? Or begged humbly? Did the two men know each other so that their exchange stemmed from earlier quarrels?

Fisher drew alongside.

In this street, Carlin Avenue, hardly a soul moved. Curtains were drawn on one side against the sun; lime trees flourished. Silence with vigour.

'Lovely day, now,' Fisher said.

'Uh.' A not dissatisfied grunt.

'Wind's a bit on the cold side.'

'Um.'

Both syllables sounded friendly enough, belied truculence. Fisher, past now, could only press on. When next he looked back the man was lighting a cigarette; a minute later he'd disappeared, into one of the houses. Face wry, kidding, codding himself Fisher found his way diagonally to the main shopping street and thence to the promenade. Here he walked more briskly and considered the morning's visit to the chapel. He'd no religious belief, no nostalgia, he told himself. A monkey's mischievous curiosity had pointed him there and disappointed him at his lack of response. What he'd expected, what anybody expected, was now beyond him. A verse demanded attention, annoyingly.

Whether I fly with angels, fall with dust,
Thy hands made both, and I am there.
Thy power and love, my love and trust
Make one place everywhere.

He repeated the lines aloud; called them out again, modifying his stride to their rhythm. People passed, brightly, whipped by the wind, eyeing him, ignoring. George Herbert, he thought, as he wished for equivalent faith. In the seventeenth century Edwin Fisher would have believed, but grudgingly, in tatters, a sullen assenter, up with no angels. So Herbert.

Suddenly, as a gust lashed, half pivoting him, and tippling the hat from the head of a pater-familias, Fisher laughed, out loud, without reserve, as if the wind had thumped the sound from him. Then he ran, caught the spinning rim as it came up to him, and returning it, walked off cheered.

CHAPTER 2

In his digs Fisher occupied Sunday evening at the bedroom window.

He'd half considered the furniture; polished veneer with curling scrolls at bed end and wardrobe door. The place was clean, and he'd plenty of room. Outside, he saw similar houses, red roofs with chimney-pots and disfiguring aerials, white windows where other visitors stood at washbasins, rubbed calomine lotion into their cheeks, slipped into finery. Dressing for dinner, one week of the year, they prepared for chips and chops, salmon salad, brown windsor, ice-cream.

He could hear footsteps, the occasional shout of reprimand that denoted children. Who came to these places, now that the package deals to Ibiza or Tangiers were so cheap? The conservative? The family man and dependants? The almost poor? He stopped the questions, began to lecture himself. He'd no right to this superiority. Let them crook fingers at coffee cups and boast of their cars, or be uncertain whether to laugh at or slap their boisterous kids they'd be better than he. Better? Humans? Even if they'd robbed the gas-meter to give themselves inclement indigestion at six-thirty in the evening.

He stood at the window, eyes above the lace curtain.

Outside it was bright still, and calmer. On the dressing table he'd put his writing case, which lay open. Perhaps, not this day, he'd write to his wife, a mild letter of description, with no mention of himself, no recriminating, merely a message so that she knew where he was, and in her anger at him could learn what this house, this street, this seaside was like. He'd not apologize or sulk or shout, but put down physical facts about rooms and holiday artisans and lilos until she screamed.

Downstairs a gong rumbled; footsteps drubbed the stairs.

He sat at a small table on his own, in the corner furthest from the window, under a tall hat-stand. His courses were brought by a smiling fourteen-year-old in a blue overall matching a headband. The meal was hot if tasteless, and undisturbed by the other guests who, brick red, seemed too tired for badinage. Even the children ate soberly, though one was whipped away to bed by a harassed mother before the main dish had been served.

One couple said 'Good evening,' but there conversation stopped. Over coffee two tablesful demonstrated that they came from the same town, the same street but as soon as they became hilarious Fisher drained his cup and went upstairs.

He cleaned his teeth and read for twenty-minutes

E. T.'s memoir of D. H. Lawrence, sitting comfortably in a cane-chair, feet up on the end of the bed. Then he pulled his raincoat from the wardrobe, went down where in the small front garden the middle-aged couple from the next table stood hatless to inform him it was a fine evening, and to inquire if he was walking far. He did not commit himself, since he did not know, but the three sociably grouped themselves for a few minutes round a rose-bush, admiring the dark-red flowers, guessing, not hopefully, the name.

Not displeased with the encounter, Fisher spent the length of the street trying to place the man's occupation. Then he made swiftly for the promenade, the beach, which, littered-thick, stretched deserted. He walked unsteadily in the sand because there was no purpose in this, nothing to see; already one or two men with pointed sticks speared crisp-bags and ice-cream cartons which they crammed into sacks.

The sun behind the promenade hotels threw long shadows, as an evening wind smartened the cheeks. Down by the sea's edge, which he shared with a dog and a courting-couple, Fisher pampered himself, enjoying his hesitancy, unsure of what he wanted. He set off to walk northernwards along the coast, but half an hour of this convinced him he wished to do something else, so that he turned inland, past a caravan park and on to a flat road between bungalows and shacks. As soon as he found himself near the town's centre, he turned into a back street pub, and ordered beer.

Here the walls were hung with bedroom mirrors and strings of fairy-lights; each table was glass-topped in green. With displeasure he realised from behind his jar that he recognised the man entering opposite, parking himself with back to the cush-ioned settle. David Vernon, his father-in-law.

Preparing to speak, Fisher eyed the other, who stared back without interest, as if he'd no idea whom he watched. Round marble-green eyes in a red face, Vernon looked like a cornet player at rest after an athletic solo, excited still, but recover-ing. Nothing in that, Fisher knew; Vernon played the violin with style, and his bucolic expression denoted no yokel's simplicity. In the end, the older man nodded, but briefly, suggesting nothing, giving nothing away.

Fisher felt he should move; the place was not yet crowded, but in the end it was his father-in-law who stood, shuffled across. Smart golf-cap, white military-style mackintosh, checked tweeds, polished brogues, but no walking stick. The man made a performance of sitting down, pushing his stool, puffing and blowing, raising the tails of his coat.

'You're the last man I expected to see,' Vernon said. Fisher returned no answer to that. 'Not a bad little pub this. The landlord knows how to look after his beer.'

'This is quite good.'

Both lifted, and sampled. Both replaced glasses

17

on mats together. Vernon jerked on his belt, dug chin into collar, said,

'I was sorry to hear about your business.'

'Yes.'

'Not my affair, mind you.' The slight Welshness of his accent clashed with the bucolic English face. 'If you and Meg can't get on . . .' He shrugged, pouted, saddened his expression. 'Is it final?'

'I should think so.'

'Pity. I'm not claiming it's your fault. She's got something to answer for. One thing puzzled me, though.' Did it, Taff?

'Uh?'

'Why didn't you come to see me?' Now Vernon sat upright, shoulders back, officer on parade. 'I'm not saying I could have sorted this out for you, but I've a wide experience of matrimonial cases. As you know.'

'Seemed no point.'

'What does that mean?'

'I've heard you say that once you became involved, yourself, with your client, you were lost, couldn't stand it, couldn't live with it.'

'I see.' Vernon bit his lip so that for a moment Fisher saw the young, thinly handsome solicitor of thirty years ago, the smartly intelligent scowl, the impression of undivided alertness.

'It's your own daughter.'

'So I'm emotionally in . . .' he changed the word, 'entangled,' liked it, repeated it vibrato 'entangled.' Jaggers' bite at thumb now. 'Yes. Yes.' He picked up his pot, but did not drink. 'Where's Meg?' he asked.

'At home, for all I know,' Fisher answered.

'And you?'

'I've gone to live with a colleague, share a flat.'

'Does he know why? I take it the colleague is a man.'

'Yes. A man. He knows I've left my wife. I told him.'

'You sit and talk about it?' Vernon insisted.

'No.'

'People do, you know. Intelligent people. University teachers.' Jibing now. Uncertain, getting his own back.

'They do.'

'Just as some well-to-do solicitors spend their Sunday evenings in back-street pubs in sea-side towns.'

Vernon, not nettled, tapped his paunch.

'I was tired. So we decided on a fortnight here. In the Frankland Towers.' Most expensive. 'Irene went to church, but I didn't feel like turning out. I didn't fancy swigging with the plutocracy. So I settle on the first little workmen's pub I see. And whom do I meet there? My lapsed son-in-law, Edwin Arthur Fisher, Master of Arts, Master of Education.'

He drank, apparently pleased with himself for levelling the game. Fisher looked on him with something like affection, knowing this chitter-chatter was typical of the man and a camouflage for his intelligence. When first he'd courted Meg,

19

the father had invited him to play chess, and then, welcoming had fought hard, hating setbacks. That a grown man, stolid as a farmer, could so drive himself to win an unimportant contest, had amused and then frightened Fisher. Vernon had to establish superiority over his new rival, if only at chess. He could have squashed his opponent at bank-balances but that would have been nothing; intellectual victory, with best ivory men, alone had validity with this young academic dumped on him by his daughter.

'Haven't you been round to see Meg then?' Fisher asked.

'What do you think?'

'You have.' Fisher took spectacles from his pocket. 'Did she say anything?'

'Ah, that's a question, now, isn't it?'

'Look,' Fisher said. 'I don't want to make a meal of it. I've left her for good, and I think she knows that, and wants it. But I was married to her for six years, and that means something. If I could do anything for her, without going back or saying anything in person, I'd do it.'

'How's she managing financially?'

'I'm continuing the mortgage and my solicitor's arranging monthly payments.'

'I'm not acting for her.'

'I wondered.'

'She's an odd kid.'

They drank in silence now the pub seemed fuller of noise. Fisher set up fresh pints, and sitting said,

'D'you know, I'd considered what I'd say to you if we met.'

'Well, boy,' Vernon answered, 'we're rational human beings, aren't we? But Irene's furious. She saw your marriage as perfect.' He grinned, with mischief. 'Perhaps she thinks Meg'll be back, inflicting herself on us.'

'Not much fear of that.'

'You think not. Well, now. They didn't get on; that is for certain. She's a selfish bitch.'

'Who?'

'Naughty, naughty. You pays your money. Still, I was a bit surprised that it was you who went. If she'd have flipped off . . .'

'She knows which side her bread's buttered.' Fisher.

'Will she get a job, then?'

'I imagine so.'

Again, they listened to the clatter of the pub. In the far room a piano clinked into hits from the musical comedies. Vernon, not without malice, hummed a snatch of 'Love will find a way.' In spite of his military appearance, his intelligence, Vernon's tastes were simple; a drink, a television serial, Messiah at Christmas, hymn-singing half-hours on radio, watching some clever sod's struggles in difficulty. On some good-badness scale how would one mark him? Though he was selfish, the trait wasn't apparent. He did not scatter money about, but he was not obviously mean. He cared nothing for his wife and daughter; he never acted cruelly. He was an atheist who attended the parish church twice a month.

Now he sat, rubicund, bucolic, in a backstreet pub enjoying his evening drink and his son-in-law's discomfiture. Fisher had no proof of this; he suspected that if he'd announced a reconciliation with Meg, Vernon would smile because he'd torment his wife with the news and guess, rightly, the date of their next major rumpus.

'Penny for 'em,' Vernon said.

'Eh?' Hard to hear in this din.

'What are you thinking about?'

Fisher looked at the group of middle-aged patrons pulling up to their table, shedding caps, headscarves, coughing, ready to snatch shining drinks from the tray to toast each other.

'You,' he replied.

Vernon shook his head. The meat-faced leader of the new arrivals raised his glass, having handed out the gin-and variables to his ladies, and said,

'Here's to all of you.'

Cheek dimpled, Vernon raised his glass to them, bowing with ceremony. This courtesy was well-received. In half-an-hour's time he'd be explaining some point of law to them, with half the room agog, silent at his words.

'And yours, sir.' Meat-face.

Fisher gulped his beer away, wished Vernon good-night and made for bed.

CHAPTER 3

Early next morning Fisher was up for a walk.

He'd woken uncomfortably before six and having shaved to the seven o'clock news on his transistor set, had shined his shoes and set out. Again there was an appearance of ceremonial to be kept up. His father had always taken him out for a trot on the promenade, a newspaper and a few improving words to the swing of a walking-stick. The old man had been energetic; one granted that. As the pair gathered speed, and Fisher seemed to recall running quite desperately to keep abreast, his father would draw his attention to the clean air, the ozone, the smell of bacon frying, the morning sun's sheen on the great windows of the sea-front hotels. He'd gesture with his walking-stick at the sand and reach some conclusion about last evening's weather; they'd consult the tide-clocks and try to make head or tail of them, or the two-day old graphs of sunshine. 'Finest hour of the day,' Arthur Fisher would intone, handing his *Journal* with its inch-high headlines to his son. Edwin had not liked that; he was no dog. Besides if the paper were creased or rucked by a small sweaty hand, there'd be trouble when father, brushing his moustache bushy, sat down to page one and a few comments before the breakfast-gong.

Now Fisher walked smartly, swinging *The Times*.

As he'd bought this, he'd suddenly surprised himself making conversation with the stallkeeper in his father's manner, friendly, hectoring, patronising. He'd totted up the change aloud, inquired about the wind's direction, interpreted a sleepy reply and drawn the man's attention to the photograph on the front page of a picture-daily. His dad had never worried himself about response; these dummies were scattered round his road to be harangued, or punned over. When Arthur Fisher holidayed, the whole world joined in, whether or not it noticed.

This morning the sea glittered in splodges, ridges of shifting gold. The wind dipped from the east as the gulls spread wide wings and cawked. An artisan hurrying to work, leather snap-basket in hand, ignored Fisher's cheerful greeting. Two girls on the far side of the road, skirt-ends lively, scurried prim-faced, one holding her hair in place with a spread right hand. The promenade was empty, and Fisher, tapping the metal railings with his newspaper had nothing to say or nobody to say it to. He lacked a son to race alongside him, to know the difference between a holiday father and a workaday, to admire, to be the recipient of convictions that would have evaporated with the day's light.

His son had died.

Donald Everard Vernon Fisher was dead, had never visited this place, had not done much beyond crying for his mother and then, when she had needed him most to keep her sanity, and her husband, had failed to live.

A slap with *The Times*, a quick turn on the heel dismissed the dead.

At breakfast the young married woman at the next table made conversation. Her children had behaved well, but on leaving their stools had moved toward's Fisher's chair where they stood staring.

'Hello, you young fellows,' he said, deliberately sudden.

The deep voice startled them so that they gasped out loud and ran to their mother, clutching her slacks.

'They aren't being a nuisance, are they?' He guessed she had assumed her most elegant accent, from the expression on her husband's face.

'Not at all.'

'This is the first time they've been away. It's strange for them.'

Fisher examined her fair shortish hair, gay jumper, straight back. She'd beautiful nails, but dyed to resemble black grapes. The husband, high-necked shirt, bushy long sideburns, collected the boys and ushered them upstairs.

25

'Well trained,' the girl said to Fisher.

'So I see.' She was determined to talk.

'It's nice to see the father taking a hand,' the middle-aged man said, from nowhere.

'He's as good with them as I am.'

'Why's that?' Fisher asked.

'Well, he's always done his share, and he can mend things. They've always got a job for him when he comes home.'

This was smilingly approved round the room, so that it seemed that even the children there applauded this paragon of a father. The middle-aged man monopolised conversation, while his wife smirked modestly into her cup of pale tea. Fisher, buttering his last triangle of toast, thought the young woman appeared disappointed at his silence and the other man's loquacity. He, not a bad practice, put the notion into plain words, altered the first verb to 'hoped', the second to 'was' and found himself not displeased. She'd be twenty-five, perhaps. A shop-girl.

She stood, pulled her jersey down, little breasts out-thrust; her eyes were bright blue, large.

'I'll go and see what they're up to,' she announced.

When she'd gone, the middle-aged man's wife commented favourably on the children's behaviour, told Fisher it wasn't often you saw fathers giving a hand like that, and then mischievously, added that her husband hadn't.

'There was a reason,' he muttered.

26

'Oh, yes. I'm not denying it.'

Home counties. Minor civil-servant. Teacher. Shopkeeper. Foreman.

Upstairs Fisher deplored the decoration of his bedroom, picking up, fiddling with a spray of false roses he'd just noticed. This place was dustless, windows bright and curtains fresh from the cleaners, but without taste, a collection of polished, veneered plywood, and cheap pastel plastics. On the way up he'd seen the young father leading the smaller boy into the lavatory, and through the open door next to his own, the mother brushing the elder's bright hair. All the time she was talking: 'And you can make a castle if you like, or a motor-car, or a horse for Tony to sit on . . .' Both the monologue and the moving hand pictured so youthful an energy that he envied her.

He'd nothing to do.

Looking down on the street he watched a family filling the boot of their car. They quarrelled and worked without direction, silently to the watcher, from time to time on the pavement in attitudes of contemptuous amazement. In the end they handed Grandma down, parked her in the back seat, wrapped her legs in a blanket, slammed the door and left her.

Vaguely Fisher approved.

He loved the man in the corner-shop, the fellow who lived six doors up and always cursed the wind, the chaps on the delivery vans, the obsequious butcher. For some reason they represented

27

to him a kind of sanity, an ordered universe; if one of them broke his arm or got the sack, then a star was disturbed. That struck nowhere near the truth. Occasionally, as he glimpsed one of these people at work, he'd feel a rush of affection that would have evaporated inside a minute, completely forgotten until he either saw the person again or tried to make sense, as now of his own personality.

And yet he, Edwin Fisher, lecturer in education, this lover of mankind had walked out on his wife, was glad of it.

When he thought of Meg, now, in this hiatus of a bedroom, he remembered her body, beautifully flaunted, cared for, her face and then, the hate-drawn, spiteful mouth he'd deserted. Again he felt sick anger swill him, humiliation, a pain, almost physical, eating vitals out so that he wanted to hurt in return, to kick at inanimate objects, to restore his manhood by some childish display.

She'd won. He'd not admitted it before this moment, but now in a room he despised, in a town that offered him nothing, he confessed that his wife had won. Immediately his mind began on its usual hundred and one modifications to a thesis, slight qualifications, excuses not be be invented. Of course, if a man upped and left a wife he'd loved, he'd lost something. If he did this while she was still sore with a son's death, he'd nothing to say for himself, but this was not that sort of defeat. She'd managed to destroy in him something he considered of value, his humanity, his sensibility, his himself.

As soon as he started with words, he smiled. 'Put it into baby-talk,' his university tutor had advised him, 'and let's see how the argument shapes then.' Not bad advice for pretentious young jugglers such as he'd been. But not much cop now. Outside in the street the family were scrumming round the car, had in fact returned grandma to the pavement, and were intemperately laughing at the father who in open-necked shirt and cardigan gaped at a bottle he'd dropped, splashing his flannel-legs black as the beer.

Quizzing the mild chaos in the street below, Fisher wondered what Meg was doing now. He could not think that she'd upset herself because he'd left her; she'd hogged her share in the rows between them, and if not with enjoyment then at least unscathed. Like her father, she revelled in a quarrel, shouted, screamed, sulked or kicked merely to get her way, a mistress of tantrums. Again he checked himself. No human being could fight as they'd done, and be unhurt. She'd two advantages over him: she'd more fire and a complete conviction she was in the right. He felt his body flush with hate.

Carefully he turned his mind back to their first meeting.

He'd been standing in the foyer of the Playhouse, superior to the knots of chattering people, the crush at the bar, the coffee-stirring crowd down the steps.

In front of the bookstall, blatantly eyeing him stood a young woman with auburn hair, a great mass, heavily thick down her back. She stared at him; no doubt. Green, wide eyes taking him in. He smiled. She wore a striking full length dress in dark green, with a cape, marked, or marred, with patterns of black lines, straight bunches of fasces. When he smiled she did not look away, made no pretence, merely continued to make her interest in him obvious. While he walked across she did not move, or flounce, showed no sign of approval or otherwise at his action, but waited, stock-still.

'Hello,' he said. He considered himself skilful in these matters.

'Hello.' The voice was very much softer than he'd expected, but she smiled slightly.

'Making anything of Ibsen?' he asked. *A Doll's House.*

'I don't know.' Nothing hopeless in the answer. 'It's perhaps the translator's fault, but it doesn't seem the sort of conversation I hear, well, at home, for instance.'

Her voice warmed to the last four words.

'Now, I think it is.'

'Your home's different from mine, then.'

'I live in a flat, on my own.'

'So do I,' she said, 'but you know what I mean.'

'I don't, to be frank.'

'Don't be awkward, for God's sake,' she said, 'on a Friday night.'

30

A bearded young man in a velvet jacket arrived, presented her with a glass of gin. He looked without rancour at Fisher.

'Cheers,' she said, sipping. He responded. 'I can't introduce you. I don't know his name. I could tell him your name.'

'And yours,' Fisher said.

'Cheeky with it,' Beardy said.

'What do you think of Ibsen's conversation?' she asked.

'Damn all.'

'I think that's rude,' she said. 'He thinks most people talk like the Helmers.' She pointed with a tilted rim of the glass towards Fisher.

'Well, God bless the lad,' said Beardy.

A voice over the public-address requested them to take their seats as the play would be resumed in four minutes' time. They sighed.

'I shall listen carefully in the second half,' she said, slopping the lemon about in the dregs of her drink. 'You've got me worried. I'd convinced myself this was like nothing on earth, and now you say . . .' She really appeared to consider the point. Her shoulders seemed to screw, almost ugly, with the effort. 'Put this glass down somewhere, Malcolm.'

As Beardy turned his back, she announced,

'Meg Vernon.'

For a moment, he was nonplussed, as if she'd spoken in a foreign tongue.

'Edwin Fisher.'

'Pleased.'

Malcolm was back, on escort duty. She bowed her head, old-fashioned, and stepped beautifully away. Fisher, ashamed to stumble in immediately behind them, searched the auditorium. When he found them, Meg's hair seemed darker, less unusual, and she pointed, laughing widely, frivolously. Outside she had seemed serious, not humourless, capable of wit, but almost unhuman. He played with the neologism, because he could handle a little word, occupy himself with it, keep his head while he fought for equilibrium from that three minutes in the foyer when he'd been summoned to a presence. Now she laughed, and bounced, and poked a finger out, and could be criticised.

He saw her a week later, by chance.

Search in the telephone directory had no result, and he'd begun to recover from the impact of the first meeting when he nearly walked past her in the crowded centre of the town.

'Oh, hello there,' he said, turning to touch her arm.

She narrowed her eyes, in the sunshine, slightly untidy, unready for him.

'Edwin Fisher,' he said.

'Have you any more names?' Now she sounded like a schoolgirl or a teaching miss.

'Edwin Arthur Fisher.'

People shoved past them for home at five past five, so that the two were forced apart. He chased her fiercely, under an arcade by a double pillar.

'Come and have a cup of tea,' he said.

She looked at her watch, pinching it between thumb and forefinger, squinting again, and, hitching her shoulder-bag, acquiesced. In the tea-shop, dark with panneled walls and bar-lights, they sat without speaking at a crumb-littered table. Now, make-up unrenewed, face smudged, she seemed at once more approachable and yet complex because he knew that a few minutes' preparation could transform this breathless, dusty girl into the magnificent woman who'd fetched him over in the theatre. She was handsome, with fine eyes, a large mouth and head of dark auburn hair, purpled in shadow, fine and heavy as if cast. One finger had a blotch of ink; the second button of her blouse was lost.

He ordered tea as the waitress swatted the table-cloth.

'Were you going anywhere?' he asked.

'To my flat.'

'And then?'

'Then.' She blew the echo away.

'We'll go to the pictures,' he said, suddenly awkwardly, unlike himself.

'What's on?'

'No idea.' She laughed, said that was silly.

'I don't much mind. I could do with your company.'

'You hardly know me,' she said.

'I don't know you at all.

He began to tell her about himself, his job at

the High School, his ambition to write a play. The waitress arrived; triangles of buttered bread, six assorted cakes on a cake-stand with doyley, tea, milk and sugar in metal containers. Each had a small pot of jam, one dark red, one orange. Pouring out the the tea, she held the knob of the lid under the smirched finger, she paused, breathed in audibly, said,

'I can't go to the cinema with you. I'm not dressed for it.'

The mind was made up and the certainty of intonation made her look older.

'Neither am I.'

'I noticed.'

That held him up, almost shocked him though he could not have said whether it was because she criticised him, or because she thought clothes important. They began to talk about 'A Doll's House', and he enjoyed himself explaining why he found it an important play.

'And yet,' he said, eager, spreading jam, 'there's something wrong with it.'

'Such as?'

'Perhaps it's pre-Freudian. Would she have left him if matters had been right sexually between them?'

'He enjoyed her.'

'Is that it? I don't know. I mean given the position of a woman in those days and their provincial view of petty-crime, she hardly seemed strong enough to make her mind up, just like that, and leave. I know she'd something about her, that she'd borrowed the money which needed some doing for a woman, I admit, and saved her husband's life, but . . .'

'What?'

'To leave three children. Children she loved. For a mere piece of intellectualism.'

'You think like her husband,' Meg said. 'That women are little song-birds or feather-headed spendthrifts. You do. You might think you don't.'

'But a young family . . .'

'Listen,' she answered. 'Nobody would leave children they loved, if they acted sensibly. But thousands do. Lawrence's Frieda. Nearly broke her heart.'

They argued desultorily so that Fisher was thwarted. He was not sure what he felt and guessed that the girl was bent on making fun of him. She'd enjoyed the play, admitted now that the dialogue wasn't too unreal if she made allowances for the old-fashioned translation, but her main objection was that Ibsen was out to act bogeys. Scare her with his horror.

'What do you want, then?'

'Ordinary pieces of life.'

'What's that mean?'

'Quarrels about the rent or the soup. Agreement about what shoes to buy. I don't know. When people come on stage, fit as fiddles and say they're going to die with T.B. of the spine caused by their father's lechery, I begin to think . . .' She broke off, smiling down at her plate.

'That sort of thing happens.'

'I wish it wouldn't. Anyway, I don't want it shoved under my nose. There's enough unpleasantness as it is.'

'But we get pleasure, a marvellous pleasure, don't we, out of seeing men and women face up to, and even be defeated by fearful events?'

'You might. I don't.'

'Why do you go to the theatre, then?'

'Because Malcolm asked me.'

'Though,' he said, 'you knew you wouldn't enjoy it.'

'I'd not seen it before. You never know.'

Now it seemed important to him to convince her, to open her eyes to the poet's art. As he talked, lectured her, hectored, she listened politely enough, even with a show of interest, but with a fixed determination not to be influenced. Her mind she'd made up, for herself. Ibsen and Shakespeare and Sophocles could tear their man, their noble women, to tatters, in the greatest language, and she'd look on as she'd watch a man fly-fishing or a bulldozer flattening a building or a horserace on television. Such things happened, and as I'm here I might as well see what's going on, but I'm not involved, only curious.

'It might be your house they're knocking down.'

'Then I'd be furious. Or sorry, or something.'

'But you wouldn't feel the same for somebody else whose home's being destroyed?'

'Neither would you,' she said.

'Not so strongly, perhaps.'

He argued, and she talked. It was like trying to run a private race against a cripple. She hobbled; he sprinted. When he passed the post, she was elsewhere so that the victory meant nothing, went unobserved. An emotional cripple, that's what this beautiful girl was. He liked the expression but kept his mouth shut. As usual he did not believe himself.

Excited he returned to Ibsen, who hadn't made his Nora convincing. She'd suffered shock, at her husband's self-righteous anger, but that seemed hardly enough to cause her to fly off in the middle of the night, out into a cold, man's world to fend for herself. 'She'd damned soon find out,' Fisher said, finger-nail tapping the table, 'that her husband, hide-bound as he was, priggish, domineering, babyish, wasn't without his virtues compared with some of the men she'd have to deal with.'

Meg picked up her gloves, not quickly, said they should leave. They did not speak again until they were out in the street.

'What's the programme?' he asked.

'I'd better go to my flat.'

'I've only just found you.'

'That sounds like a bit from your friend Ibsen,' she said cruelly. He laughed at that, because she was right. He judged this meeting to be crucial.

'I don't mind what we do,' he said, 'so long as we do it together.'

'Commit suicide?'

'Is that what you feel like?'

'Not at all.'

'I think we should go home, dress up, and go out drinking.'

'Do you know what my father would say to that?' she asked.

'Uh, uh?'

'Is that all your education has fitted you for? To get drunk?'

'And what do you say?'

She snatched her gloves off, half in pique. Now the two of them had crossed the road in a crowd, stood in front of the Council House, motionless among people who stumbled, raced past.

'You've not answered my question,' he began. In no hurry, she wrinkled her face, as if genuinely troubled, needing his assurance. He could not offer it. On a sunny evening he needed to worship, not advise.

'Is something wrong?' he asked.

'You hardly know me.'

'I'm proposing to remedy that.' Immediately he regretted his flippancy. The Council House clock struck the hour with impressive noise, vibrating in the flagstones.

'Six,' he said. 'Tell you what. Let's be back here by eight.'

'I don't know.'

'You don't want to see me, then?' he asked.

'I don't mind. It's not that. Oh, I don't know.' She flailed about with her gloves.

'Here,' he said. 'Eight o'clock. Or somewhere else, if you like.'

Now she stood composed, statuesque, but he would not have been surprised if she had wheeled and stalked off. She nodded.

'Here?' he asked.

'Right.'

'Eight, then.' He held a hand out. 'Goodbye, Miss Vernon.'

Her eyes widened, met his, held steady, looked away. No trace of a smile answered his exaggeration of gallantry. She nodded, jerked the expressive gloves on, pointed, mumbled the number of her bus and made for it.

He watched her, a tall girl, tossing her hair, looking taller.

Against his expectation, she returned exactly on time, beautifully groomed. The square, less crowded, opened to her; men turned their heads and she walked proudly.

'We'll go up to the County.'

'I don't drink much.' She spoke diffidently now as if this small disclaimer implied something else, that she shouldn't be here, that she regretted her promise.

'Neither do I, for that matter.'

When he complimented her on her appearance, making her look at their reflection in the long shop-windows of Market Street she barely acknowledged him. It was as if, in assuming these magnificent and suitable clothes, she allowed them to speak for her. This absent-mindedness of hers worried him in the next months. However interested he might be, or intense, however he exerted himself to amuse or even rile her, she offered him a bare eighth of her attention, and brooded on other matters.

In the hotel she accepted beer; he was content to sit in a corner where he could watch her. There she seemed easier, talked about herself. She was twenty-one, in her final year at a training college, with a job already organized at a junior school in a good area of the city.

'I know the headmistress,' she said, 'and my father's solicitor to the Director of Education.' He could not guess whether she spoke with or without irony. He decided, delighted, that she ought not to be so pale; the skin of her hands which were large and well shaped seemed almost transparent.

'There's something I ought to tell you,' she had said, interrupting an anecdote of his about some clever clowning by the Upper Sixth.

'Go on.'

'I'm engaged to Malcolm.'

Disappointment dried, withered him. He could not be so easily immersed in her.

'He's a lecturer at the college.'

'I see.'

'I attended his lectures on psychology in the first year course. He's very clever. And interesting.'

'You're lucky, then.'

Very slowly she picked up her jar of ale which

she'd barely sipped, held it a moment at her mouth, and then returned it to the table, clutched between both hands.

'It's no good,' she announced.

'What isn't?'

'Between Malcolm and me. The engagement.'

'Do you want to talk about it?' he asked, man of the world.

'I don't mind.' She pouted, shrugged, but minutely, creating no fuss. 'He's boring. And I think sometimes he's silly. For a man who's thirty-one.'

Fisher kept his eyes down, concentrating on his drink.

'It was a great thing,' she said, 'when he asked me out with him. He was a lecturer. And attractive. I lived in a hostel then, and the other girls were jealous. We used to talk to each other about the things he said in his tutorials.'

'What did he?'

'I've forgotten now. Oh, well, once he gave a lecture on how much of human behaviour was instinctive. It was interesting. I'd never thought of it before, and we hadn't done anything about it at school, even in bio lessons. He made it sound fascinating, the way he talked, though it didn't tie up with much.'

'Um.'

'But he's rather silly. And jealous. All caught up with himself. He's everything that counts.' She stopped. 'I oughtn't to talk to you about him. Daddy hadn't anything to say in his favour.'

'Oh.'

'"He's a pretentious, slimy, little shit." That's what he called him.'

'And is he?'

'I think,' Meg said, steadily, 'nobody's perfect. But I've had enough of Malcolm. I shall tell him so.'

'What will he do?'

'There's not much he can, is there?' She did not triumph, merely stated this fact or fiction.

Fisher, delighted, a man again, had emptied his pot, urged her to do likewise, but she refused. She talked on desperately for half an hour until he became unsure whether she meant what she said, or baited him, or perhaps needed his support. At his third pint, she still wetted her lips in her half; he said, clutching himself together,

'Do you know I love you?'

The green eyes settled on him, widened, considered.

'I don't mind you.'

That sounded sufficient for the present, and he took her hand. She pulled off a pair of white gloves so that he noticed she was wearing an engagement ring.

CHAPTER 4

Fisher straightened the shoes at the bottom of his wardrobe. He heard the family in the street drive off, checked that he'd a wallet in his pocket, his pack-a-mack to hand and went downstairs.

'Last out?' he asked his landlady as she hurried from dining room to kitchen.

'I don't think so, Mr Fisher.' I don't spy, she implied. My guests enjoy themselves without my help. 'The beach today, is it?'

'Probably.'

'The glass is high still. I think we're in for some really settled weather.'

He deposited his mackintosh on the hallstand, nodded, and walked for the sunshine at the door.

'Have a good time, Mr Fisher.'

The obsequious use of his name displeased him. As ever, he wondered what she'd report to her husband or the hirelings over the washing up. 'Do you think he's married?' would occupy them to advantage, as she piled the plates and clashed the trays of cutlery. He'd forgotten his newspaper, bathing towel and trunks, but he didn't think to slip back for a second inquisitorial burst of civility.

On the beach he sat watching arrivals. One needed occupation, a family to amuse, a wife to be bored with, a ball to kick round with your mates. Deliberately he searched, moved to a more populous part of the front where he hired a deck-chair as becoming his status, there pulled his shirt off to sunbathe, and lay back.

Finding this unsatisfactory, he sat up, looked about. The young family from the next table already busied themselves behind a red and blue wind-break. Father on his knees dug furiously in the soft sand, while the boys trotted up and down, inter-fering, constantly commenting. Their father's energy seemed expended so that their little forays elsewhere had a point of return; they circled, then dropped to knees, poked a finger into an already collapsing sand pie, laughed, denounced or questioned, staggered up and away. The mother busied herself in an unhurried persistence, unpacking or arranging her bags and carriers, laying articles out for the children. She wore an unattractive bikini and as she knelt up Fisher noticed the red scar of the elastic of pants or tights round her waist. Her belly was slightly slack, un-young, not recovered from her last child-bearing. The bright face was serious as if the whole success of the day depended on her.

Fisher waved; they did not notice.

The sun warmed him, as he slipped in and out of his shirt, now that the wind had dropped.

44

Once he nodded off, but woke comfortably, with plenty to occupy himself with. The little boys licked ice-cream cornets, after which their mother scrubbed mouths with a flannel. Father loped down to the sea, but did not stay in long. When he returned his hair stood on end.

An elderly couple parked their deckchairs at the side of Fisher's. There was no need for the beach was far from crowded but perhaps they'd chosen him out as a suitable companion. He remembered his father pontificating. 'The best thing about a holiday is that you meet interesting people. New places have something to be said for 'em, but it's the new faces.'

'Nature is fine,' young Fisher had chimed in, 'but human nature finer. Keats.'

'That's right.' Arthur's false teeth demonstrated his pleasure. And the old man set out for them, sorted them out, butted into conversations, was snubbed now and then, but generally ended with a catch of three or four 'persons of learning'. Where he'd come across that expression Fisher did not know but by it his father meant able to dispense information that he considered cultural. There was one retired pharmacist who talked about poisons, but tried to keep young Edwin out of earshot; another a schoolmaster, explained Roman burial rites, while another, a military-looking gentleman, was an expert on fossils and produced a handful of belemnites from his pocket, beautiful as bullets.

True enough, the elderly man, after struggling with a mound of kit, remarked to Fisher that the wind had dropped. Within five minutes he confided that they had only just returned from a holiday in Greece.

'And we're here to get over that,' the wife interrupted.

They had educated north-country voices, Manchester perhaps, and sounded honest, robustly so. Their knowledge of Greece impressed; the man had been there during the war, and laced his accounts with Modern Greek phrases.

'We go every year,' he said. 'We've a daughter living in Athens. But it's getting just a bit much for me. We're not sure about next summer.'

'Doesn't your daughter visit you, then?'

The woman continued. Every May without fail; she was married to a high civil servant, but they had no children. It was a great disappointment. There followed the story of Phyllis's courtship, she'd met her husband at Oxford, and ménage in high society. She spoke the language like a native, was often mistaken for a Greek.

'Did she learn it at the university?' Fisher asked.

'No. She knew Daddy was keen on Greece. Perhaps that's why she took notice of Eleutherios in the first place.'

They needed no prompting, these two; insisted that he join them in a cup of coffee, even seemed to have carried down spare cups for suitable strangers. While they talked, he considered these two decent people. At this moment their daughter was in Athens, thinking probably in Greek as she listened to husband, a friend, the radio. How did she make contact with her parents? 'Phone? Weekly letter?

'It was hard for us,' the woman said, 'especially Daddy.'

He pulled a serious-comical face, blubbering his lips out.

'It's a very different thing being interested in a country, spending holidays, and, and, having your daughter live there, marrying. If Daddy hadn't talked about it, and had books, then perhaps Phyllis wouldn't . . . Well, we don't know, do we?'

Fisher put questions, offered comfort, said he saw his sister at most once a year and she lived a mere hundred and twenty miles off.

'We bring a family up, and they split, never meet,' the man said. 'We're odd.'

'Except at funerals.'

They laughed at the wife's wry remark.

'We'd only the one child,' the woman continued, 'and she's none. She's happy enough, and I tell myself that it's not much of a misfortune not to bring children into this world we've got. Made.'

'They might do better,' the husband chided mildly.

'They could hardly do worse.'

Fisher liked the couple with their sharp platitudes. In some small way they seemed alive, keeping their eye on humanity. Through such as these common sense prevailed, against gelignite and napalm, double-talk and pollution. After an hour, of course, he became bored, knew too much. A retired headmaster and his wife, lacking the expected captive audience. When they learnt that he worked in a university education department, they flashed names. Did he know Professors Whitemoor of Liverpool, Thorpe of Manchester, Winstanly of Hull?

Disappointed in himself Fisher left them about three. While they were two strangers, with a daughter in Greece, he could accept their hospitality, admire their bluntness. But now they talked schoolrooms and staff, they became dull, were grey and he excused himself. He concluded, as he walked towards a caravan park, that he liked only the products of his own imagination. That did not displease him; on the concrete slabs, between the caravans and chalets, the lines of jigging bathing suits and nappies, he congratulated himself on being able to distinguish between reality and fantasy.

He had now reached a road, headed townwards when he heard his Christian named called. Obstinately he failed to turn.

'Edwin.'

On this second time he recognised the voice, that of his mother-in-law. He stopped, but could not see her. Mrs Vernon stepped out from a car among a parked row, posed for him.

A handsome women, not unlike her daughter in

colouring but heavier, she had nothing of Meg's vagaries, volatility. She smiled now, announced plummily that she was glad to see him. He made appropriate noises, shook her hand.

'David wanted your address,' she said.

He did not answer that.

'A coincidence, wasn't it?' she laughed. 'Meeting like that. A scruffy little pub, David said, not the sort of place either of you might be expected to patronise.' For a second, he detected a Welshness of intonation, a parody of her husband in the sentence's formality. He dismissed the suspicion; Irene Vernon carried no satire round with her.

Fisher stood, suspiciously. He'd not spoken to Irene since he'd deserted her daughter, and could seen no reason why she should show him affability. She knew what Meg was like, had spent years in contumely with her, but she expected matrimonial cracks, her own and others', well papered over. Mrs Vernon paid attention to appearances; she was English, middle-class, a rich solicitor's only daughter. Her husband could drink in back street pubs, gamble a few quid away at the tables or the courses, make tricky use of information from crooked clientele, play, it was said, with fancy young foreign vaginas, providing the office finances were straight, the Law Society unworried, and her own public pride undamaged. It wasn't much of a marriage, but the joint bank account swelled. Fisher felt he ought to be sorry for the woman, but she showed no sign of needing

49

his pity. The right man had married her, she'd told him often, and they'd achieved a modus vivendi, and though this appeared to allow her husband the pleasure of doing what he liked when and where he wanted, she seemed completely satisfied. Perhaps Meg's tantrums developed from her mother's calm.

'Come and sit in my car', she said. He followed, meekly enough. 'I don't suppose it's any use asking you anything, about Margaret, is it?' No one else called his wife that; Meg, the father's contraction, was not as he'd thought, from the Welsh. Margaret Adelins Savile Vernon.

'I've left her.'

'I know. Could you help us out? A little? You see, she tells us nothing. She swears, and shrugs, but we don't get any sense from her.'

'Not her father?'

'David's both furious, and blind, as far as she's concerned. He'd do anything for that girl, and he can't do anything with her.'

'That's quite witty,' Fisher said.

'It's not meant to be.' Usually she basked in flattery. 'What have you been up to?'

Fisher considered, made her wait. In this large comfortable saloon car he could stretch his legs out to full length. Bridling, he determined to confess nothing. Immediately he rejected this; the woman had every right to question him, and deserved, at least, some sense in his answers. He laughed, laid a hand on her arm.

'I've never been married to anyone else,' he said, indicating objectivity by preciosity of diction, 'and so I can't say whether our home life was normal or not. But I'd had enough.'

'Did she not love you, Edwin?' He grinned at her voice, act one, scene two.

'She hated the sight of me. And vice versa.' Determined on flippancy. 'It was either the door or the poison-bottle for one or the other of us.'

Mrs Vernon did not move, or nod, settled massively in her seat, wearing a bright straw hat. Her legs, in immaculate tights, were large, but beautifully shaped, tapering to fine ankles, small feet. The ringed hands on her lap lay dead, motionless, white, unlined, delicate, plump.

'Disappointing,' she said, in the end, on an outgoing breath.

They talked, guardedly, for ten minutes, before she asked,

'Are you willing to give me your address?'

'Why?' Rude.

'David likes you.' She took no offence. 'He also hopes that this'll mend. He'll help if he can, and being able to track you down immediately might be of assistance.'

'Do you believe that?'

'That's what he said, Edwin. He's optimistic. More so than I am. He's also clever. And very experienced in this sort of affair. Not that that means much with Margaret.'

She talked on, equably, about her husband, as

if she were making discoveries. Sometimes Vernon described himself in the same sane, careful way, laying out the evidence before nailing the yet unreached conclusion. Small solicitor's office in Wrexham; University College, Aberystwyth, First Class Honours in Law; with Evans and Gough-Jones, Swansea, Law Society Prize in Finals. And then he described how these had meant working fifteen hours a day, killing religion, sex, drink and social grace to win these baubles he now thought nothing of. 'Maimed as a human being, ruined as an immortal soul,' he'd intone, his face bright with irony.

Fisher had enjoyed this performance more than once, and was not averse to comparing it with the gentility of an anglicised version. Finally, apologising to himself, he'd written down his address in Bealthorpe, and back home, before opening the door into the freshness of sunlit air. Mrs Vernon smiled at him, adjusting her white gloves, and drove off when he was a bare dozen steps from the car. He'd done wrong, he was sure, but it couldn't matter.

He walked inland into the dull fields and the poky houses, both solid and ramshackle, like originals of sketches in ink and wash by Rembrandt. He stood on the grass-thick platform of a disused railway station and peered over the hedges at the neat gardens of bijou bungalows. In one an old man picked beans, but broke off to describe the winter to Fisher until a shriek from indoors sent him hurrying back between the luxuriant rows. An engine-driver he claimed, who'd retired here and never felt so well in his life. 'I was brought up on steam, a skilled job, where it depended on you and your fireman whether the train ran or not. These diesels, now. A schoolkid could drive one.' He spat behind the canopy of bean-leaves and bright red dots of flower. 'Talkin' again,' the howl from the house. 'I think she's lonely,' the old boy said, but he paused only a moment for Fisher to admire the size of his produce before waddling off.

This was the place to see the sky, the great sweep of blue with its combed-out wisps of cloud. The land squatted, flattened, ironed out into, huddling into, bottom-low inches under the broad, eye-widening spaces of the sky. Man crawled like an insect; his houses seemed two dimensional, without height; trees brushed the ground, bowed. Fisher liked it best under piling cloud, but today the sky stretched like blue-glass breathed on, bright, hard on the eye, broadly impressive, but without the mountainous changes that he loved most.

Here he'd walked as a boy, escaping from the everlasting banalities of his father, and his mother's watchfulness; here, legging it, he'd hoped to meet those admired girls from the beach, those brown, bleached, long-legged young women who'd toppled his heart without ever noticing him. Now, today, without benefit of wife, he filled in his time walking the same roads, stopping at the same dusty clumps of hedge, the same sour stretch of dyke, thinking of something to do. His play, when he wrote it, would feature a man, half-way to age, sitting on a sand-dune calling out, like the young Tennysons at Mablethorpe, swooping lines of verse to the sea whose choppy wind would bundle the syllables back shattered and shredded. O, Beckett, Beckett.

The dullness of the walk, the final street lengths amongst Rose Garth, San Remo, Mon Abri, Seldumin, Sea Holly tired him so that he was glad to pull his shoes off, lie on the bed for half an hour before dinner.

That had been a good day.

He'd tried the sun, taken exercise, spoken to strangers and risked his privacy when he handed the address to his mother-in-law. He had satisfied himself in his own circumscribed way.

He debated casually what the Vernons would do. David would certainly act; no doubt about that, but how? At first they had no time for him as a son-in-law; however presentable he was a school-master without great prospects, because at best he'd end as a headmaster, or inspector, or in a chair of education, none of which was lucrative in Vernon's eyes. Of course, he'd private investments from his father, which improved matters, but not much. Moreover, they had just, after miracles of self-deception, accustomed themselves to this bearded, mincing, velvet-jacketed Malcolm from the training college, when Meg had ditched him and presented his successor, the slow-spoken, handsome usher from the high school.

He remembered Malcolm's dismissal.

On a Saturday afternoon, he'd turned down a game of cricket, he and Meg were sitting on a rustic seat in front of ribbon-built commuter houses outside a village. Lawn-mowers whined, and gloved ladies forked weeds before returning to coloured garden-chairs. The pair had walked since eleven, lunched in a pub, and Fisher still dizzy with beer needed to empty his bladder.

'Are you comfortable?' he asked. She did not reply.

'Are you sitting comfortably?'

Meg's face was turned towards a roof of emerald slates, staring wooden-jawed.

'I don't want to say anything,' she said, childishly.

'Let's walk, then.'

She stood, sluggishly and they moved beyond the houses, past a corn field, by a copse where he slipped away. When he returned she'd not waited as he'd expected, a few yards on but a hundred yards along the road seemed to be marching hard. Taken aback, he began to run, calling her name. She turned, and then herself ran, comically, knees together, but determined to make ground. Uncertain, he did not catch her up quickly, but trailed deliberately ten yards behind her. A short way up a hill, she stopped, swung round to face him.

'Caught you.' He put his hands to her shoulders.

Though her hair held tidy, he would have described her face as dishevelled. It was as if each small part had shifted out of place, lost its order, the sense of wholeness. Perhaps the defect was in his sight, his own shock. Her eyes had lengthened, cat-wise, and her mouth trembled after words.

'What's wrong?' he asked.

He put his arm through hers, she allowed it, and led her to a gate at the side of the road. Throwing his plastic mac on the grass verge, he made her sit down. She complied, again, wordlessly. He gawked over the gate, the field, to a line of trees, a house with breeze-block outbuildings, a distant hedged lane. When he turned to her, she sat quite composed, legs together, head on one side, twirling a large daisy between thumb and forefinger.

'Are you all right?' he asked.

'Yes.' Her voice cracked on the syllable, but she fished a a mirror from her handbag.

'What's the trouble, Meg?'

'Oh, shut up.'

Now she spoke steadily enough, but more quietly than was sensible, as though to herself. He leaned back, his elbows on the top bar of the gate, not taking his eyes from her, observing her back to sanity. They remained thus for five minutes. It seemed desperately longer, sheltered in the high hawthorn, interrupted by the frequent rush of cars both ways along the road.

When finally she looked at him, he smiled, put

his arms round her and lifted her so that they stood now precariously, his face against the coolness of hers, his hands gently on her back. She hung heavy on him.

They set off again, shambling, she brushing with closed fingers at the hair above her right eye. He neglected her for a little before he asked,

'What's wrong, Meg?'

Not a word.

'What is it?' A hand to her back. She began to cry, so that he took her arm as they stood under an oak tree in the hedge. 'Tell uncle about it.'

She gulped, like an inept child at a swimming bath.

'I've broken it off with Malcolm.'

'I see. Isn't that what you wanted?'

'It's not fair to him.' Indignation consorted curiously with tears.

'You don't want to talk about it?' he ventured.

'I don't mind.' Voice unblurred. He pulled his handkerchief out of his pocket. Thank God it was clean, unfolded from the ironing. She mopped her face. 'I told you. I wrote him a letter. And I saw him last night.'

'You agreed to meet him?'

'He asked me. And he came to the flat. The others were out. It wasn't too bad. I told him I wanted to break it off.' She bent to pick up a twig, which she snapped without theatrical effect. 'He asked me why and I said I'd met somebody else. He wanted to know who it was, and I told him.

He seemed to have forgotten about you at the Playhouse, or so he claimed. I don't believe that. Do you?'

Fisher shook his head. Eyes dry, much at ease, she spoke as if she were recalling something from long enough back.

'Then he asked, "How do you know this time it's for good and all?" and I told him I didn't. "You'll be throwing him over in six months?" I said it was possible. And he just sat down, as if he was taking a tutorial or something, rubbing his face. And then he pointed at me and said, "Well if you're sure." I said, "Sure of what, Malcolm?" and he shrugged. "Sure you love this Edwin or whatever his name is."'

'What did you . . . ?'

'I just told him that I was certain I didn't love him.'

'How did he take that, then?' Fisher felt that, somehow, she insulted him, and if not deliberately, then deeply, meaningfully.

'He was funny, really. He said in a dry sort of way, "Let's hear the advantages of Fisher over me, then." I told him straight off I wasn't there to discuss you and he said, "There are no obvious advantages, I see, or you wouldn't be making such a song and dance out of your excuses. It's just that he's new." We argued like this for a long time, and didn't get anywhere. He didn't shout, or threaten. He might have been handing me an essay back, because he said things like, "Rationality's

58

not your strong point, but this time you're less reasonable than usual." And he wanted to leave it at that.'

'Leave it?'

'Not break the engagement. Not irrevocably, he said. See how things work out. I was to go with you as much as I liked.'

'Until you got tired of me?' Fisher asked.

'I should think that was his idea.'

'And you said?'

'I gave him his ring. I told him it was over, that I was sorry it had ended like this, and that it was my fault. I took the blame, but I couldn't help my feelings changing. I liked him and admired him. I still do. It's true. He's full of ideas. And talented. He's a very good musician, for one thing. A pianist. But I didn't want him any more. That was the long and short of it.'

For the next hour they walked, or sat for short breaks, while she mulled over the subject, becoming gloomier from sentence to sentence. In the end she was openly crying, dabbing her face with his flying handkerchief.

'You think I'm a fool,' she said.

'Oh, I don't know. It's a shock. To a conservative like you. Or me. You change and you fear the dangers, or foresee them. I don't know. You're making a meal of it, I must say.'

That was the boldest statement he'd ever made; she might have thrown him over. His nature was compliant, longed for agreement, but he'd spoken out, against himself, as if to assent some ancient manly prerogative, the right perhaps to superior knowledge.

'I could kill you,' she said.

'Carry on.'

'You superior bastard.'

'I know all that.'

'You know nothing. In your Sunday suit on a Saturday afternoon. Why didn't you bring a cane to cut a dash with?'

'I might have used it on you.'

That stopped her. It could not be that she was afraid, or shocked. In retrospect he believed simply that she enjoyed the direct bullying, which no one but her father employed against her.

They moved on in silence for so long that he began to be afraid, so that when they reached a covered bus-shelter with a seat he pushed her aside, sat down himself. For the moment he thought she'd storm out. After some hesitation, she mopped her face, rather roughly, screwed the handkerchief into a ball, and plumped down at his side.

'Welcome home,' he said.

When they set out again, she was taciturn but cheerful, answering questions if initiating nothing. They found a cottage where they ate eggs, new bread and pippy raspberry jam while the lady of the place patted her silver hair under a poker-work board which read, 'Christ is the unseen guest, the unseen listener to every conversation.' When the proprietress went out, Meg said,

'That frightens me.'

'About Christ listening?'

'Yes. As if He judged every word. Weighed it.'

'And found it wanting,' he said. 'It seems a shame to waste His time.'

'I don't think,' she urged, 'they ought to hang things like that. If they thought about it, really imagined what it meant, they daren't.'

'If I were God,' Fisher said, 'I'd take a great deal of pleasure in hearing somebody say, "This egg's done just right"'.

'It's not often you say anything as innocent as that.'

'Come off it, now.' But he laughed. 'I love you. How about that? How's the Unseen Guest like that one, eh?'

She shuddered enormously, but answered immediately, in face of dread.

'I love you,' she said. 'Now he's heard both sides.'

They kissed, rapidly, but the landlady entered coughing, with hot water and a homily on tea-drinking. They acted politeness, began to feel it as if the woman were part of love.

'Who did that?' Meg asked, indicating the board.

'Oh, a soldier who was here in the war.'

'A religious soldier?' Meg giggled.

'Not that I noticed. He copied it off a bit of a card. Couldn't get it all on. I think I shall take it down. The letters aren't very good, are they?'

'It's made me think,' Meg said.

'I've had quite enough thinking to last me a year

61

or two,' the woman said, huffily, as though they'd offended her. 'Since my husband died, I've had plenty of time for that. Too much.'

They left in a hurry, in the end, sniggering, like schoolchildren from a crabby teacher. On their way to the bus stop, Meg had arranged for him to visit her parents, claiming with force, even with enjoyment, that it was useless becoming formally engaged until the elder Vernons had approved.

'They may not take to me.'

'They will,' she said. She seemed delighted, scoring off him, quite unlike the girl who cried for Malcolm's unhappiness. The Vernon family united to scoff at the pretensions of prospective suitors. He neither relished it, nor understood.

Now as he waited for the dinner-gong he wondered whether he should have read these early signs. Meg's behaviour was dependably unexpected. Now he saw her as a theatrical performer, acting against her father's reputation, ensuring that he did not outshine her.

She loved her father.

CHAPTER 5

On the stairs Fisher met the young couple accompanied by one child only, on their way down to dinner. Unlike him, all wore different clothes from those of breakfast or the beach.

'Had a good day?' he enquired.

They answered enthusiastically convincing themselves.

'Where's Number Two?' he asked, pointing at the boy.

'Tucked away in bed, fast asleep,' The mother smiled. 'I don't know if Colin 'll keep awake through the meal.'

'I shall,' the boy said, shouting, but shy.

'Colin.' His mother shook his arm, vigorously.

'Well, I shall.'

'We shall see,' his father said.

The child screwed his face into a scowl of hatred, so that Fisher remembered his own holidays here as will-combats between his father and himself. The old man loved punctuality, was always ten minutes early for an engagement. One could find no quicker way of driving him to fury than by dawdling when he needed to catch a bus or train.

On a late afternoon in this town Edwin Fisher, aged fourteen, had arrived, grubby, five minutes before the family procession towards high tea was due to start. The reception committee waited in the parents' bedroom; Mrs Fisher at the dressing-table fluttering at her face, Tina on a chair, with a book open but unread, wide-eyed for the explosion, Arthur by the window, white-faced with anger.

'Is that you, Edwin?' Mrs Fisher had called.

'Yes.'

'Come in here. Your father wants you.'

'We shall be late.'

'You'll come in when you're bid,' his father grated from the door. Edwin obeyed, The door was closed, and Arthur, hands behind back, stalked again to the window.

'What time is this?' he asked. Fisher consulted his watch.

'Three minutes to six.'

The impertinence was ignored.

'And where do you think you've been?'

'Out for a walk.'

'You're late.'

'I know. I ought to go and get washed.' He could not help pushing his father, though he saw the face mottle with anger.

'We've been home since five. I told you no later than half-past.'

'Where've you been, Eddie?' his mother interrupted.

'Just for a walk. I watched the afternoon pierrots, and then went along the beach.'

'Have you got a watch?'

He held his wrist forward; the father's eyes seemed to meet cruelly in his head as he slashed down at the outstretched hand. At the jar of bone on bone, the boy retreated a step.

'Can't you tell the time, yet?'

Now his father hit him, on the sleeve, with a flailing blow to each word. The pain was not great, but indignation and shame flared in him. He did not answer.

'Are you deaf now, then?'

Again the windmill of smacks, one of which caught a nerve end, or muscle, wrenching him with pain. He stood, stock still, eyes glaring before the ridiculous little creature.

They stood, man against man, shambling youth, pouter pigeon with moustache.

'Now get to your room, and stop there. If you can't come back when I say you'll do without your meal till tomorrow morning.'

He did not mind; he'd eaten chocolate. All he wanted was to clear his sight of this clown, but he needed to stay, only a moment, defy this goggle-eyed licorice stick. He did so, then walked out, bruising his shoulder on the door-post.

Inside that closet, his room, he stood in the yard-wide space between bed and wall before he took off his jacket and washed in the small sink. After changing his trousers and tie, he went on to the landing. From downstairs he could hear the clash of cutlery, crockery, the voices of the guests, the bray of his father's laughter.

He shut and locked the door, took a seat on the corner of the bed by the little window. The rooms in the houses over the road were blackly empty of visitors feeding below. He'd spent an hour at the pierrots', a wooden stage with a roped off enclosure of deck-chairs, at the back, one of the shifting six-deep idlers amongst whom one of the comedians in striped blazer at least twice flourished a straw-hat with matching band for a collection. Thank you, sir. To him. To a boy struck by a ludicrous, fierce-whiskery father.

The actors wore monocles, and sang hoarse songs: 'To Hell with Burgundy,' 'One alone to be my own', and told feeble jokes, smiling themselves as they apologised for the quality. But it was the girls he waited for; two blonde-haired charmers with whirling flared skirts who kicked high as they danced, flaunting their knickers. A man next to him had fastened fingers into Edwin's arm at the flash of white silk, sucking his breath in. Fisher would have been ashamed to show his feeling, blatantly, but he knew what that fellow meant. Beautiful girls in white shoes with flying hair showing themselves off to anybody on the sands, for a copper in the cady. Thank you, sir.

He read his library book, detective stories, about

a clever, g-droppin' surgeon, Mr Fortune, with a beautiful, beautiful wife.

Somebody rattled the door-knob, pushed. He ignored the signal.

'Eddie.' His mother. Sighing, like the man on the beach, he rose, turned the key. His mother carried paper napkins precariously. 'Your dad's wild.'

He held his shoulders stiff, not shrugging.

'I've brought you a thing or two up,' she said, unwrapping. A brown bread sandwich, a piece of fruit cake, a swiss tart, all unwholesome, handled. 'Your dad said you weren't very well, and Mrs Arrow told me to let you have these.'

'Generous,' he said. She looked at him in surprise.

'Well, you were late.'

'I was not.'

'Your dad says you were.'

He'd no idea what his mother thought, how she judged between him and his father. It probably never entered her head to adjudicate; they were as they were and nothing she could do would change them. Edwin acted the nuisance no more than four times a year with the expected result: an explosion of Arthur's bile. Thereafter, father behaved with exceptional politeness, even generosity. Elsie Fisher admired her husband because he made money; he might be an obsequious, penny-paring snivel of a shopkeeper, but his bank-account exceeded those of the car-owning, property-proud clients whose lounges he supplied with arm-chairs and studio-couches.

His mother sat uncomfortably, asked about his reading, and went away to the magazines downstairs.

Tomorrow his father'd greet him, man to man, shake his arm as he invited him boyishly out for a pre-breakfast trot along the front.

The godless boy called quietly on God, God, God.

In the dining-room this evening, silence blossomed once the families began to eat. Fisher enjoyed the activity, the tucking of bibs, the wiping of mouths, the tipping of plates for the last spoonful, the pause between courses where one put on a small show for the other tables or angled for the correct snippet of conversation which would set the rest to chatter or laughing. These people worked hard, holding their fingers correctly, not marking the tablecloths and this ceremony pleased him. In this room decorated with dolls and paper flowers it was proper to act the gentleman, ape the lady. When the standard was judged, by Monday evening at the latest, there'd be a relaxation, a few aitches would topple, salacious asides allowed, confidences would be exchanged, but at this the first dinner after a complete day's holiday matters were formal. That's where his father had failed; he'd played Tuesday's joker on Sunday. Odd, because the old man had never put a foot wrong in the shop. He licked every bugger's boots there.

Smiling, breaking his bread on to the plate, he wondered how the Vernons shaped in the Frankland. Too early for dinner yet, they'd be nattering each other gently to death, refusing to go downstairs for an apéritif, quite at home in comfortable warmth that did nothing for either.

He and Meg had spent a week-end at the Frankland soon after they were married. For two or three months he'd been applying for jobs, filling in wearisome forms, stamping envelopes, naming referees and then he landed the headship of a large humanities department in a London comprehensive. He'd not interviewed well, and was certain that the headmistress, a woman who knew what she wanted and how to get it, had taken a dislike to him, so that when he'd been called back and offered the post, he'd stood flabbergasted, but without too much obvious turmoil, as if considering, or perhaps they thought praying, head lowered, before he'd thanked them, said he'd do his best, accepted. And as he rode back to the school in the headmistress's car listening to her forthright comments on his rivals, the chairman of the education committee, his predecessor, he'd decided he'd take his wife out, do the heavy, be extravagant and that weekend whether she fancied it or not.

'Seaside,' Meg decided. 'Out of season. East coast. Bealthorpe. The Frankland Towers.' She rolled the words round her palate, father's daughter. He was surprised at her choice, expecting her to plump for

69

London, the theatres, concerts. Curiously he did not remember the Frankland from his holidays, though he'd stared often enough into the long lighted windows of the big hotels. This must have been built in the last year or two; who'd patronise it he did not know and said as much.

'You'll see,' she said, 'when you get amongst the chinless wonders.'

The service there matched the steep prices, and on both Friday and Saturday nights they went to bed in liquor. This surprised him, now, but he remembered that at the time it seemed sensible. To stagger along to the distant sea under the clusters of cloud-smudged stars or to sit comfortably in an armchair swigging whisky and water as he whispered verse to his wife:

> Perchaunce the lye wethered and old
> The Wynter nyghtes that are so cold,
> Playnyng in vain vnto the mone;
> Thy wisshes then dare not be told;
> Care then who lyst, for I have done,

seemed a perfection, as if he'd mastered life, or ambition, even death. He did not drink over wildly, since he was less used to it than she, but he smiled and quoted in a fine dizziness. Perhaps this was the end of his youth; from this time he began to be himself. He doubted that. He'd achieved something, though his wife was not impressed, and in this state of half inebriation could imagine that she celebrated with him. They made love languidly last thing at night, but she lay relaxed, pleased with him, delighted to be his love, his wife.

In the morning both were edgy with headache, fearing the size of the bill, but by lunch-time they'd walked, skimmed stones and were ready to make fun of the residents. Meg mimicked their voices, or rather fluffed them up out of her imagination. She growled comically military for a moustachioed man with oiled hair.

'Two yahs in the Grenadahs for you.' She pointed at her husband, who'd failed because of acne to do national service. 'Set you up, young fellah, sloppin' about like a stretch of four-by-two in a watah-closet.' Where she'd learnt that expression he'd no idea. One black-beaded old lady with round glasses and a pinched mouth she specially watched, and then, in the bedroom suddenly squeaked, so that Fisher knew immediately whom she mocked, head nodding, 'I would never allow my late husband, the bishop, to enjoy his conjugal rights unless there were an 'o' in the month.'

'Why, madam?' Fisher said, catching the spirit.

Meg pursed her lips.

'It is not for you, young man, to know the times and seasons.'

The old voice crackled, but he reflected uncomfortably that he seemed to be only a casually admitted spectator to her satirical self-entertainment. In her head he'd be bleating some banality, or worse some magnificence of poetry that would ring ridiculously pretentious as she imitated his voice or her walk.

Not that she gibed all day. She could laugh so that her beauty, which was statuesque, transformed itself into an adolescent helplessness. The green eyes flashed as she giggled; shoulders shook and she clutched him for support. He loved her, then.

This sense of unease, of peril about his marriage did not deeply disturb him. His life had been a series of obstacles, O and A, Scholarship, Schools, and though he shaped excellently as an examination candidate, he'd always been nervous, grew to live with it, be glad of it, use it to advantage. Thus he did not expect his new life to be anything but dangerous. As his first at Oxford proved its worth in jobs and attention, so the beauty of his wife. But neither was gained without sacrifice. One got nothing for tramtickets as his father told him. And yet he felt immature, unready for marriage, only satisfied when the pair of them managed to share something, a game, a drinking-bout, sex, mindlessly, never in the abstract. Perhaps that was usual.

He eyed his married friends, and made nothing of them. They behaved with such variety that he could draw no conclusion. He observed only their public life. One husband did the washing; another bathed the children; one plangently described his sexual performances; another claimed drily to envy adulterers.

Of course he was verbally adroit enough to give himself satisfactory answers. This lack of equilibrium, this uncertainty would disappear, so that he and Meg would settle to a workaday routine of children, promotion, househunting, retirement with honour. He neither wanted nor believed that. The snag could be bluntly put: though he desperately loved his wife, he was not convinced that she returned his love. She said so, often enough; muffled his fear with kisses, dragged him into bed, shrilled fiercely for him, even lay tenderly by him when she was satisfied, but then he remembered when he'd not done so well and she'd cried for what he could not give, and beaten him, in a curse of tears. On no more than chance, then, than chance, success depended.

Marriage, that oath, that sanctified state seemed nothing to her.

She'd talk about Malcolm, or her other boyfriends, until he flushed, jealous, near mad with anxiety. If she'd seen them, and they could serve her, then that service could be taken at her pleasure, without reference to vows and solemn declarations. She had, she lived with, her husband, expressed her pleasure at the condition, but declined to make it a matter of eternity. He'd no proof of her infidelity, did not believe that she'd been unfaithful, but was driven by her to understand she was undeterred, immorally irresponsible.

The small boy on the next table had finished

dinner and had been whisked away to bed by his father. Residents whispered congratulations to the wife, who queened it with her coffee, smiling openly at Fisher. Again he'd no idea why this was: perhaps she set her cap at him or perhaps her pleasure at being allowed ten minutes to herself in a beautiful dress with no dishes to wash left her so content that she demonstrated her pleasure to the nearest presentable male. Fisher returned the smile, but was surprised when she picked up her cup and came the three or four feet to sit at his table. The rest did not know how to take this, minded their own business openly.

Her conversation meant little.

She talked about a motor-boat trip they'd decided against, the number of ice-creams a child should be allowed, and finally she described her husband's behaviour in an amusement arcade. Now she pitched her voice low, not publicly, as she sketched the feverish thrusting of coins into the one-armed bandits, his bad temper when she'd remonstrated with him, his childishness. 'You allow him in there, and he goes berserk,' she whispered. 'Mad for money. He isn't at home. He's ever so generous. But there he'll change a pound note and glue himself to the machine until it's gone.' She questioned him, keeping her voice small, in intimacy. Under the light dress her skin burnt in hot gold, matching the heat of words.

Fisher answered stiffly.

To tell the truth he was frightened. Viewed from

a yard or two's distance on the beach or in the house she was attractive, the belle. Now she approached, she changed, coarsened into the typist-suburban housewife who talked inanities or ironed in semi-detached houses the country over. This tested him. Why should she malign her husband, invite him to join in?

Her husband returned, showed mild amusement at her change of position, but not at the lack of coffee. The girl, clearing away from other tables, rushed to supply him.

'Are they in bed?' she asked.

'Yes.' A slow monosyllable.

'Tony asleep?'

'Well away. Colin wants you to go up.'

She nodded, picked up her cup to drain the dregs, crooking her finger. She disassociated herself by that movement from demanding children, kitchen chores, but she soon left. The husband began to talk. A quantity surveyor he did not like holidays away from home, where he would have preferred straightening the garden, or working the lathe in his toolshed, but claimed he had to come away for his family's sake.

'Hard on a woman, y'know,' he said. 'This is the only relief she gets. A fortnight off once a year.'

Fisher sat impressed; the man observed, slaved for his wife, lived for his kids. Now, at this table, he apologised because he came home from work late, had to travel away, couldn't romp daily with the children. Fisher drew him out; he'd made built-in cupboards, done the brick-laying for the garage, added a conservatory, all inside four years, and yet felt guilty. Was he lying? Did he drudge at his property to dodge or exclude his wife so that now she complained of him. Here was no compulsive gambler, this honest man.

The wife returned, blond hair brushed again.

Fisher, back straight in his chair, asked them out for a drink. They ought not to leave the children who might wake. Fisher, superior, did not press, allowed them to decide on the pub at the street-corner once they were certain the youngsters were away.

While they waited this certainty, Fisher was summoned to the phone to speak to his father-in-law. Vernon invited him over. He refused at once, but gave his reason. Even as he explained, the whole thing sounded bogus and he imagined the exaggerated expression on his listener's face.

'Is there anything particular why you want me over?' he asked.

'Friendliness.'

'I see.'

'Oh, ye of little faith.' Vernon parroted a Welsh pulpit. 'No, we've not given you up. You're here. We know you; we'd like your company.'

'Thanks. I'm sorry, but I've promised.'

'That's all right Edwin. We thought you might be on your own.'

David Vernon threatened in this oblique manner. When one crossed him, he hung his head, murmured something polite and marked the incident indelibly down to be paid for at his leisure. He'd no time for sentimentalities.

In the pub the young wife, Sandra, chose cherry brandy while her husband and Fisher drank half-pints.

'We never go into a pub at home,' she said. 'Do we, Terry?'

'We don't often go out together.'

'I like this,' she said, flourishing the drink. 'I feel excited.' She did not sound so. Fisher disliked her common-place features, her redness of skin, the gentility of voice, of gesture. 'There's something about this.' It was, in fact, hot, noisy and crowded. 'Don't you think some pubs have atmosphere?'

'I suppose so.' Fisher.

'The landlord's a character. Or the clientele. We ought to go out more, Terry. Your mother would sit-in. But he's too tired. Do you like classical music, Mr Fisher?' They'd exchanged names.

Fisher now reeled off favourite orchestras, pianists, described his record collection, while Sandra, Mrs Smith, gushed and simpered as if she were tight already. Her husband manifested no offence, but smiled as if this animated silliness of his wife were commendable. She confessed she'd sung in the Harmonic Choral Society before she'd had the boys and was now considering rejoining them, claiming her voice had deepened, enriched itself. A contralto. He'd never have guessed that from her speaking voice. No, she'd not enjoyed Belshazzar's Feast, nor the War Requiem, but A Child of our Time wasn't too bad and the Berlioz Te Deum staggering. Fisher grinned; his highbrow colleagues might take exactly the same line without loss of face.

They drank again.

After her third cherry brandy, when he had told her that he lectured at the University on the philosophy of education, she screeched admiration, clutching his arm.

'I know you'll think me a fool,' another cackle, both hands on the crook of his elbow,' 'but I've not the remotest idea what that is.'

The piano struck up. Middle-aged faces brightened.

He tried to tell her, but diffidently. David Vernon, that bright day's adder, had poisoned him too often there.

'I can just see, Edwin, what the philosophy of education is. Only just.'

'Isn't there a formulation of principles behind law?' His father-in-law encouraged such circumlocutions.

'I'm sure of it. There must be books on it. Mind you, I've not read them.'

'Didn't they lecture on it at university?'

'I went only,' the sly voice whined, 'to a Welsh university, not to Oxford. And though they occupied us with branches of learning I now consider useless, I don't recollect any specific course on the philosophy of the subject. One or two, as I recall, tried perhaps to take us beyond the detailed instance, but I'd hardly have seen it as philosophy. History, perhaps, archaeology, sociology, economics, guess-work. Yes.'

'The concept of justice,' Fisher had snapped.

'The concept, yes. The concept.' Vernon smiled. 'I don't understand that. I steal your purse. At one time I am hanged for it; at another my hand is cut off; elsewhere you forgive me; nowadays I'm examined by a psychiatrist and put on probation. These are the forms of justice, are they? I don't know.'

'But as soon as you tackle that question you embark,' his jargon deteriorated, 'on philosophy. That's what it is; an enquiry to see what these actions have in common.'

'A desire to stop theft.'

'I don't know,' Fisher said. 'The religious men who . . .' Vernon waved delicate hands at him.

'If it is not, I've no further interest. If to wish to protect private property is philosophy then I philosophise.'

'It's the formulation in words that is philosophy.'

'Yes. I fear so.' Vernon gesticulated with a cigar. 'And a useless activity it is.'

'Oh, I'd agree if that were the only form of action. But for every single philosopher there are a hundred lawyers and a thousand teachers.'

'Who pay no attention to the one.'

'That doesn't matter. A purely utilitarian approach.'

And so they'd argue, Vernon murmuring, 'purely, purely,' and tracing, spoiling the cigar smoke with an ironical finger.

'How many philosophers of education, Edwin,' he'd ask, 'at present at work in this country have made any impact on the day schools? Or at long second hand on me, the interested general reader, so that I shall recall their names when you mention them?'

Fisher tried to argue pragmatically, to convince the other that it did prospective teachers good to struggle temporarily with these ideas, however dry or useless, or better, that his own approach, a close examination of the language in which these principles were couched was a preparation for life where words figured so largely. But Vernon had none of it. He voiced a low opinion of schoolmasters who were only that because they were incapable of anything else, lacking any special expertise, who preferred the privileged position in a school, dominating the young rather than competing with men in an adult world.

'It's obvious you've never been in front of a class.'

'It's obvious,' Vernon answered, 'Edwin, from your frowning and red face and threatening voice that you've barely been anywhere else.'

In fact Fisher rarely lost his temper in argument. He knew that Vernon's philosophy was materialistic; solicitors made money because they harboured no egalitarian heresies about themselves and because they worked as well as protected themselves.

'Go and ask your students,' Vernon pressed. 'I do. They'll condemn you out of their own mouths. Your course is a pleasant year's rest after finals. The Law Society's no such holiday home. Our exams may be boring rote-work so that one needs no brains to pass, but candidates fail in droves.'

'Because they get no proper tuition.'

'Perhaps, perhaps. But mainly because we have a philosophy of law. At least for these candidates. And it is that the lay-about and the half-prepared and the gas-bag will be found wanting and marked down. Unless an aspirant solicitor can write and figure, can give and take account of the laws of the land, he will not pass. Your students, and it was so even in my day at my nonconformist, puritan college, will be given a diploma whatever they know or don't know. And you cannot deny it.'

The voice splayed Welsh.

Fisher even as he returned to the argument suspected that his father-in-law envied him his niche. 'A doctor's cap presses my brow, and I walked gown'd.'

Even as he grappled with his father-in-law, Fisher wryly considered life which had presented him first with his own dad, an ignorant shop-keeper, and now this proxy, a graduate member of a learned profession, who both had envied him his status, his scholarship and poked round in reference books or flashy argument to prove themselves somewhere near equality with a son who'd make little claim himself to learning.

He explained, then, to Sandra Smith what he did, and she cooed softly as her husband smiled vaguely. They were acquiring experience which they'd retail to neighbours. 'Do you remember that university lecturer, Terry, in our digs? Talked about philosophy. Explained beautifully, didn't he?' 'Couldn't make a word out, myself.' 'Ooh, Terry.' And the neighbours' eyes would brighten at this high life as they countered with the man who offered them a ride in his Daimler.

Now the piano hammered 'Roses of Picardy' which the pierrots sang so that Fisher, head dizzy, hummed as voices joined in. He felt ashamed to do so, and when they left not long afterwards with Sandra between them, arm-in-arm with both, he embarrassed himself by breaking out again almost fervently into the song, as if it mattered.

'Are you a singer?' Sandra asked, hugging his arm tight.

'No.'

'What song is it?'

'The one they were playing in the pub.'

'I'd never heard it. Had you, Terry?' He had not. She wished, swaying, that she knew more about music, that she'd stuck at her piano lessons. Back in the house, he checked with them that the children were fast asleep, then considered inviting the husband out for more alcohol. But he had the sense to keep his mouth shut. He'd done them good, and they'd now sit downstairs smilingly trifling with the magazines or telly, and nipping, Terry at least, frequently into the lavatory. That sufficed.

He did not join them downstairs, but lay flat on his bed celebrating the shining roses of the song. Three pints. With those and a gin or two, he and Meg had lifted themselves into equanimity, into content, so that once she had sat down at the piano her grandfather had left her and played, wildly, a Brahms Waltz. It sounded rich through the house, with a brazen clatter, on this huge dark instrument which had stretched along one wall from a door to a door in the living-room in Wales, on that small-holding. He knew she could play, had heard her, or had he? But now, swaying slightly in their London box, he'd been overwhelmed by the great chords and the hesitating lilt of the piece, and thus desperate with love for the player and her mystery, he'd slipped his hands up her skirt as she giggled on the piano stool. 'Could I be drunk for ever, on liquor, love and fights?' Her hair grew so thickly, so magnificently auburn that she seemed inhuman, a golden goddess, as she loved him, sprawled on the floor where he could make out the worn, dim gold of the pedals of her piano.

Now he was alone.

He remembered that semi-detached in south London to which they'd moved when he'd taken

his second job, head of department in a comprehensive school. London he disliked, especially the
travelling and here again Meg acted oddly. She
had a job, as distant as his own, but claimed, with
all her father's perversity, that the time wasted on
trains was well spent, kept her out of mischief, in
form. Sometimes she visited two colleagues who
lived in a flat near the school and what with his
societies they never took their evening meal before
nine. He looked back to this as a period of
continual tiredness when they lay in bed till
midday both Saturday and Sunday. In the holidays they travelled, to Athens, Tunis, often to
France, once to the United States, returning burnt
brown, weary with talk of local wines or prices to
shoot at Meg's parents on the one-day visit allotted
to them. That became a game. 'Impress your
father.'

Vernon took his expected stance, that everything
worth knowing about the world could be found
in Cefn where he had grown up. All varieties of
humanity were there.

'But beauty, daddy. Pictures, architecture, even
weather.'

'If we wanted the exotic, we had the cinema.'

'Do you really think that seeing a film is the
same as visiting a place?'

'I do not. Often it is better, because it is done
with a more selective eye than one's own.'

'You speak for yourself,' Meg shouted.

'I do, my dear. And I exempt you from ordinary

mortality's limitations. But I could have the Parthenon or the Alhambra Palace in sunshine, the Taj Mahal by moonlight, and then compare them almost at once with our little Bethels or the public library in rain.'

'Who in his right mind would want to do anything so daft?'

'I would, dearest.'

'You wouldn't. You wouldn't. You go abroad yourself.'

'Of course. That's why I can make the claim. From experience.'

'He's pulling your leg, Margaret,' her mother interrupted. 'Don't encourage him.'

'I'm serious.' Vernon's head nodded aristocratically.

And on the way home, Meg would turn on her husband demanding why he didn't defend her. She drove; whirling through the traffic as if she had mounted knives on her wheels to hack her father's inane casuistries to shreds.

'He likes his little argument,' Fisher answered diplomatically.

'He wants to dominate me. And you. Especially you. And he does it when you sit there dumb as a baby without answering a word. Why don't you take him on?'

'I don't want to. I enjoy his whimsies.'

'At my expense.'

Then she'd be near tears, clashing the car into gear, braking with violence, stalling the engine.

He could not help thinking that he fought both wife and her father together.

Now he walked out again where it was cool, still light, with the sky pearly. In the gardens of their bungalows elderly couples stood, exchanging views with the neighbours. Young men revved up motor bikes and even the middle-aged walked hand in hand. At one raw house, Mon Bijou, he stopped to hear a piano thrilling at chords. The March from Tannhäuser. 'Hail, bright abode where song the heart rejoices.' When he'd first learnt that, at fifteen, he'd been sick with love for a parson's daughter. A serious matter, though he had mentioned his infatuation to nobody. Now as he heard the steady rhythm's solemnity, the turn, he knew that longing, or. Or. It could not be so. For a moment he was translated, but it was all over inside seconds. He listened as an adult who condemned both Wagner's banality and the tinny rattle of the piano. With relief, from himself, he pushed up the road.

Several passers-by wished him good evening. The world was full of people at leisure, doing him good. He replied in a loud voice.

'You sound so hearty,' Meg used to tell him. 'Like a milkman.'

'Shopkeeping's in my blood.'

'You're more like a back-door hawker.'

She meant nothing by it. Often he guessed she criticised him because it was her place to do so, had married him to purchase the privilege.

He made himself stop by a high, straight-trimmed privet hedge to ask himself if he wanted Meg back, or with him for an hour, this evening. On the verge of pity, he remembered these last weeks when she'd set out to annoy, to interrupt, crucify his work. These were not minor persecutions; her whole self concentrated, every minute of day and night, to molest him. She was not sane as she smashed glass to the floor, or woke him three, four times in the night, threw herself screaming fully clothed into the bath, burned the examination papers he was marking, announced to their neighbours, a well-to-do architect and his wife, that her husband had tried the evening before to murder her.

Nothing of game there. He had not laid a finger on her, though he could have killed her. And his love dropped away, dry as dust. Sexually she was as attractive to him as a pig or a skeleton. He wanted, against his desperate reason, to murder, but not with his hands. There would be something sensual, about fingers sweatily round her throat, squeezing away the rich life. He needed some science-fiction gadget to transmute that hated flesh into ashes, a half biscuit-box of dust. If he'd been stronger morally, he'd have struck her, slapped his conviction of guilt with his knuckles across her face, but he'd cringed, and put up, put off, so that he became an embodiment of frightened hate, sick to the soul with himself.

Now after a month's absence from her, he relented.

It could not be as he remembered. The struggle suppurated in his mind at the end of a tiring term and a wrangle with his professor. Walking past a field, littered with broken molehills, marked for building, he stopped himself, hand plucking at the wire strands of the new fence. One could not imagine the malicious lunacy of his wife; it existed, had forced him to newer, bitter knowledge. Meg hated him with her being; twisted every sinew to further that loathing.

One evening, less than six weeks ago, after a day's silence she had deliberately picked up a magazine and knocked his cup into his lap. She'd refused to speak, asked nothing, done nothing, sat at the tea-table clattering her cup, shifting her plate, tearing the thin bread and butter he'd prepared for her. Her face stretched pale with her eyes washed out, almost blue, tear-flushed, unintelligent. The day before she'd been to the hairdresser's so that her hair rose elaborately beautiful and she had, apparently, dressed with care.

Fisher had intended to stay at home, but her refusal to speak drove him out to his room at the university where he'd wasted time with books. He had announced his going, his absence for lunch, his expected return by four, but she, in dressing-gown paid no attention until he'd shouted, when she'd picked up the letters with which she was toying and went upstairs. On his homecoming he found the breakfast dishes still on the table and his 'Times' still where he'd dropped it. Mrs Roberts the cleaning-woman had not been in, or had been sent packing.

Quietly he cleared away, washed the pots, and prepared the tea. When all was ready, he marched upstairs, knocked sharply at his wife's door, announced the meal as she sat at the dressing-table. He poured out two cups and eating, began to read the evening paper. The dining room was large and polished, south facing, with heavy furniture on the light parquet floor where one white rug was laid in front of the dark marble of the fireplace. After ten minutes he walked out again into the hall, called upstairs, and receiving no answer knocked again on her door to make his announcements. She followed him.

'Your tea will be cold,' he said. 'I'll pour you another.'

This time, certainly, her eyes dropped towards the offending liquid. She screwed a small handkerchief in her fingers, stretched it. He took the cup to the kitchen, swilled it clean, dried it and returned to refill it. Then she looked up at him, briefly, noncommittally.

He returned to his newspaper but his appetite had deserted him. He chewed drily. When he glanced across, he saw her fiddle with her bread, pulling it apart. The eyes were hooded, pathetically; demure, she sat as if waiting for orders. Determined not to be angry, he said,

'Drink your tea, Meg, please.'

Perhaps she shuffled slightly. Outside the

brightness of roses splodged. He returned to the print. 'Newthorpe man's pool win. Official drought in Notts. M.P. warns miners.' By his plate he had laid a periodical still unopened from its folder. Meg shoved her chair back, half-stood, grabbed the journal and, flailing, back-handed his cup on to his 'Post' and his knee. Alarmed he jumped, feeling, not uncomfortably, the warmth on his thighs. Tea dripped from the sodden paper, so that he screwed it angrily into a bundle which he rushed out to the kitchen. When he came back, she had seated herself again to watch him, only half, a quarter, anxiously.

Shaking with rage, he failed to reach the table, but stood, incoherent, making sounds, a gibberish, before he turned upstairs. There he ripped his trousers off and flinging himself across the bed he pummelled it as breath failed. Then he lay, in a curse of fury, eyes closed, on fire, red: until he recovered sufficiently to walk to the basin and swill his face in cold water. Again, he sat, unbecoming. He forced himself to the bowl for a second wash, donned new trousers and combed his wet hair. He went downstairs where his slice, one mouthful taken, slopped in a plate brown with spilt tea. The table-cloth, stained, clung blackish to the wood. The carpet seemed barely marked, with a few dark spots. On the other side Meg sat, straight, her face harsh, hard, a parody of itself, hacked into a roughness of stupidity. It could not be her.

At this moment, he knew exactly what he should

do: fetch a tray, begin to clear the mess. But before that idol of a face, he was incapable of sense. It had no humanity in it and therefore no appeal for pity, help. It was botcher's work, sincere clumsy bungling. He had seen crude children's daubs, button eyes, streaks of nose and mouth which were livelier.

'I'd better clear up,' he said. His legs trembled; his voice staggered to a whimper. Meg did not open her mouth.

He moved from the room, began to work. The exercise did him good so that at the end of ten minutes he felt calmer, relieved, with the table dry and unharmed. During the operation she'd not shifted to help him, not backed an inch out of his way.

'That's that, then.' He rubbed his hands. She did not bother with him, not even pretending to ignore him. 'I'll wash up.'

He did not expect an answer, but her lack of any response suddenly riled him, rapped his body into anger.

His jaw worked in involuntary life, against all reason.

'You go upstairs, Meg.' There was no call for that, but he spoke it out of a desire to dominate, to impress that welled in nerves and skin, not in mind. She sat, hands locked now. 'D'you hear me?' he asked. 'I should go upstairs for a bit, if I were you. Have a lie-down on the bed.'

Nothing, nothing.

Now unreason flashed; he could not hold himself longer.

'Get out, and upstairs,' he shouted. 'Before I give you a bloody good hiding.'

The loudness took effect so that she swivelled her eyes at him and stared like an insipid doll. There seemed no intelligence, no attempt to understand, merely a limited response to the increase in power of a voice.

'Get out,' he shouted, now, thumping the table between them with both fists, 'get out when you're told. Get out. Get out.'

His anger shrivelled, in its own heat.

Fisher saw both, a wild man whacking the table, a zombie watching him. His hurt swelled in his throat while he leaned forward mopping himself, groaning, defeated. When, moments later, he quitted the room, the thought presented itself that she could not have cared, or shifted, it amounted to the same, if he had axed her head from her trunk.

He did not return to the dining room for an hour, and by that time she'd gone to report, he learnt later, to her parents, that he'd become violent. That was wrong. Not her misrepresentation, but the fact that she could put it, or anything else into words.

CHAPTER 6

When Fisher woke next morning, the weather was fair, as if the brightness of the sea reflected from the mirrors to the far wall. He disregarded a slight headache, crediting it not to the pint or two of ale, but to his puritanical conscience. He enjoyed his early walk in the deserted streets, and had managed to insert ten or so answers into 'The Times' crossword before breakfast. Sandra Smith, a different, light-blue outfit, smiled at him, managed her family quickly, won approval from the whole room.

Fisher sipped milky coffee, cup after cup, cautiously optimistic. The landlord made an unusual appearance; a dishevelled joviality signalled a secret.

'Gentleman to see you, Mr Fisher. Just arrived. In a very large Mercedes.' He gave that time to penetrate.

'A Mr Vernon?' Fisher said.

'Yes, sir. Do you want to see him?' Wheatley spoke truculence; new Mere or not, my guests are not troubled, unless. English independence.

'Yes. My father-in-law.'

'I see, sir.' Smiling now that the Mercedes man

could be treated with unction. 'Beautiful car, really beautiful.'

'Is it?' Fisher drained his cup, followed ungratefully into the lounge, where Vernon set his face to melancholy amongst the bric-a-brac.

'Guilty conscience. Can't sleep.' Vernon arose, face beaming. 'I'm interfering, Edwin, as usual'.

'At a quarter past nine.'

'Yes. My grapefruit doesn't occupy me long.' He slapped his midriff, blowing. 'I wanted to catch you before you went out.'

'And look at the . . .' Fisher indicated the furniture, the bunches of plastic flowers, the flounced dolls lining the television-top, the white mantelpiece with mother-of-pearl ashtrays, useless glass spheres, paper-knives in tartan sheaths.

'Yes. That.' Vernon's words sketched contempt. 'I've asked Meg to come across.'

'I see.'

'Would you be prepared to meet her if she came?'

Fisher thought, allowed the words into his head, did not find an answer, and sat scratching his knee. The elder Smith boy suddenly burst into the room, flinging the door back before pulling up silenced in front of the two seated, unspeaking men. His mother followed at once, like a torch of blue and white light, grabbed his arm and apologising ushered him willingly from the place. Her smile, her crisp dress made the interruption theatrical, or perhaps real compared with the sober silence of the two.

'No good would come of it.'

'I understand you. But it's been a month now. Both of you have had the chance to reconsider matters. In my experience it doesn't do to leave these things too long.'

'I don't think . . .'

'Just see her, Edwin,' The second use of his Christian name irrationally annoyed Fisher. Vernon never used the word any more than he addressed his daughter as Margaret; he acted here as a solicitor, soliciting.

'I don't want to be awkward. But in my view she doesn't need me; she needs medical attention.'

'Would it surprise you if I said she was of the same opinion about you?'

'No. They're all mad but me. Common symptom.'

Vernon stroked his chin, because this was the kind of situation in which he excelled. For the next ten minutes he and Fisher would argue, he suavely, the younger as he liked, and at the end agreement would be reached when his son-in-law capitulated. This morning, perhaps because of the early hour, the process took a little longer, so that it was nearly ten and the other guests had been heard to leave before they'd finished.

'Tomorrow, then. At lunch with us.'

'Will she be there?'

'That I don't know. I'm not making Meg out as a paragon of reason. You know that.'

'I'm sorry this has happened.'

95

Vernon blew his lips out.

'Phoh. Happening all the time, man. I get three a day.' A sly hand met Fisher's arm. 'And I've not got used to it yet.' Wry.

Vernon had gone, leaving Fisher vaguely distressed, uncertain. He had been driven by his wife to a state where he felt unlike himself, capable of criminal foolishness without compunction, and this had frightened him. Loss of temper or nerve merely bothered him, as annoying, lacking advantage, stranding one in an appearance of foolishness, but the conviction that he might knock his wife down, nail her dead, before the normal function of reason could operate, terrified in its novelty. Now he acted, or could do so, like a child, on impulse, without forethought or sight. His hand could murder before his senses could collect themselves to check the blow. Once he accepted this, had had it dinned into him, then he shrank, begged to retire, get out of life like a hermit for time to come to terms with his new self, this madman.

For the past month, he'd lived in a maze, careless, thankful to be rid of murderous fear. He had not considered going back to Meg, but the thought of a total break troubled him. It was an advantage to have a personable wife, and he had chosen exactly what he wanted. Meg, so handsome and yet wayward, dragooned his colleagues into admiration so that at departmental functions she'd be surrounded by men stretching their wits to win a glance or word of praise out of her. The prof's wife, a busy humdrum woman who should have been bustling behind a shop-counter, disliked it, said as much sourly.

'You'll have to watch that wife of yours, Mr Fisher.'

'I do nothing else.'

'She's fond of herself.'

'We're all that, aren't we?'

The old bitch is jealous because Meg snatches the men away from her, he thought, but there was something homely about Helen Walker, a likeable common sense, that made him careful about his judgement. He reported her remarks to Meg, who acted neither angrily nor distantly, but gave the appearance of thought, screwing her mouth, even sucking her finger, before she answered.

'I don't think I do anything out of the ordinary. Most of those men I don't like.' She laughed. 'No, not old Bogus.' The senior lecturer in child psychology. 'He doesn't know anything, you say, and he splutters, but he'd lend you up to fifty pence if you were pushed.'

'You talk just like your father,' Fisher said.

'I know. I do it to fluster you, darling.'

He could get no sense out of her in that mischievous frame of mind. Nevertheless, a wife looking and behaving publicly as Meg did was a social advantage. Moreover he was positive that if he left her, allowed her a divorce, it would not be long before she remarried, and this time made a success of it, with children, content, showing a settled face to the world. Even now in spite of his desperation, he could not bear that, because she belonged to him. He'd snatched her from rivals, and that was that; Mrs Fisher she was named.

She lived her life merely parallel to his.

Baffled, Fisher wondered if this were the case with others. At first, when she was teaching, she'd occasionally let drop some anecdote, but paid no more than perfunctory attention to his reciprocal pedagogic tidbits. To him it was odd that she never tried to derive common principles from his experience and hers; both did a job with similar grounds of interest but that was nothing to her.

When she became pregnant three years after their marriage, she seemed to withdraw more seriously or perhaps withhold herself from him. She'd talk about the child, or her relaxation clinics, or visits to the hospital, would laugh about the old wives' tales, but it all seemed a private business, between her and the baby. Pregnancy suited her; her pale skin shone healthily, her heavy hair took lively fire over the enormous swelling of her womb. But it concerned her alone.

'Edwin'll find his nose pushed out,' Meg's mother warned.

'It is already.'

'You're number three,' Vernon said. 'We had no more than one. I couldn't bear further relegation. I wouldn't even let 'em have a dog.'

'Or a goldfish.' Meg.

'My degradation was complete.'

'Your selfishness, you mean', his wife said.

'Irene Vernon.' He wagged a finger. 'When we married I warned you that my instinct for self-preservation was strong.'

'As if I didn't know.'

One evening the house seemed unbearably quiet so that Fisher became uneasy. He called out for Meg. No answer. This was soon after they have moved into their present home on his appointment to the university's education department, and neither was quite used yet to the spaciousness of either house or garden. Vernon had bought the place for them, arranged a private mortgage, so now, after their poky semi in London, they lived amongst the well-to-do. Fisher shouted again, not pleasantly; he'd been working all day on his research merely to discover that the last fortnight's drudgery had been a waste of time. He needed somebody to talk to, not about his failure perhaps, but somebody with whom he could exchange words to show him that the universe had not combined in enmity against him. He knew his exaggeration, but dog-tired, depressed, he needed his wife to sit with him while they complained together about the television programmes until he felt human again.

He went into the garden. There one did not shout. He tried the little summerhouse, the privet hedge hiding the vegetable gardens, the shrubbery among ash and lime trees at the far end. What he did, pushing among winter-dark rhododendrons and laurels he would have been nonplussed to explain; in fact, he told himself he was childishly acting out his own perplexities, peering under bushes for a wife he knew would not be there. Cold, dispirited, feeling he had missed some clue, he kicked his muddy boots off indoors and began a round of the house.

All stood neat.

No scissors or knitting or dropped newspaper, open book indicated her presence. The kitchen would have passed a barrack-inspection; in the lounge, dining and breakfast rooms every cushion was plumped, rounded. Only his study showed signs of occupation, the scattered dismal sheets of figures that spelt fourteen days of misused energy. He stumped upstairs.

The bedrooms were unoccupied.

He leaned for a moment with his hand violently clasping the rail of the cot they had bought second-hand in preparation. Angrily he shook the blue frame, and on the other side, the sliding panel clacked down, scaring him, puncturing his shoulder-blades with pain. He fastened the rail securely this time, glad of something to do, gaping at the transferred image of Donald Duck on the bed's head.

Perhaps Meg was having a bath.

No sounds of tanks refilled. The bathroom was cold, unsteamy; the porcelain innocent of a drop of water. From the lavatory along the passage, he heard his wife gulp, sob, a large, uninhibited whoop of distress.

He moved, there, called, stopped, spoke again. Inside, she held silence, not giving herself away.

'Meg, are you all right?'

Rattled the lock, gently, surprised at his shortage of breath, his fear.

'Are you all right, Meg'?

The door was bolted so that this time he knocked, foolishly, with his finger-nails, cat-scratching.

'Meg. Why don't you answer?' Exasperation retinted fear and embarrassment. Even in the seclusion of home, one did not appear at one's best, whispering through a privy door. She sobbed, one huge sniffing heave of breath.

'Open up, Meg.'

He waited, staring at the dulled sheen of the landing light on a leaded, stained-glass window.

'Open the door, Meg. There's a good girl.'

In the resultant silence, he felt daubed with foolishness. He had himself nothing to say, no opinion to offer as he stoodstaring downwards at the sea-green linoleum of the floor, so that when he heard the bolt move he floundered against the wall behind in relief. As his wife emerged, her hair pushed outwards, fingered into an expansion of untidiness, and her swollen belly seemed to account for the unsteadiness of her walk.

Fisher took her arm.

'What is it, Meg?'

She sniffed, allowed herself to be conducted into the bedroom where they sat together on the edge of the double-bed.

'What's wrong?'

He knew he must ask these questions, soothing, stroking her back to normality. It appeared not difficult in the dark room. Finally, almost solemnly like a precocious child, she answered his reiterations, but in a whisper.

'I feel so awful.'

'Physically, do you mean?'

'No. Not really. I just feel, feel, rotten.'

As soon as she'd outed the words, she began to cry, openly, without show. Her face rolled with tears, but she did not make a disturbance, though her body shuddered now and then as if she expelled a fighting devil. Fisher held her shoulder with his right hand, smoothing the upper arm, then gripping her into him, strong and weak by turns, support and comfort.

Her hand groped beggar-like, but he, suddenly acute, recognised the signal and thrust his handkerchief there. Still crying, she mopped her face.

He had no idea what to say, but held her to him, leg against leg. Her shape bundled uncouth, smock rucked, stockings laddered as she sat so that to him she might have been a poor stranger. If he had known then what to do, he was made. She seemed in need, willing to sit in his embrace, borrow his handkerchief or strength. He began to be useful, but only marginally. There must be some line of conduct that could break the barrier between them, deepen mutual trust, confess interdependence, but if it existed, he did not know where, could not even begin to find it, unless this, this proximity, the silent negativeness of action encouraged its life. It did not do for him. He waited, undecided, inadequate.

'What's up, then, Meg?' The colloquial approach masked uncertainty.

She shook her head, but it was a sign of revival.

'This won't do, y'know. Can't have his nibs upset.' He pointed at her womb.

Now she smiled, tentatively, with real bravery.

'Come on, then.' He put both arms around her, and her head, her wild hair, lay under his cheek. 'Let's hear all about it.'

'I felt so awful. So low. I thought I'd die.'

She offered this diffidently enough to be believed.

'I get so tired. And bored. I can't sit down for a minute without my legs, and arms jumping on me. Jim-jams. And I feel like iron, stiff and heavy as lead. It's all so long and so pointless. And I don't have anybody to talk to, and you're cooped up there with the work. Even at mealtimes, I can tell you're thinking about it.'

'I'm sorry.'

'Why should you be? It's my fault. I ought to go out more but I'm so tired. It's such a fag.'

'I've neglected you,' Fisher said. That seemed adequate.

'No.' A sharp word. 'It's silly to say that. You've got your work to do.' She patted her stomach. 'I've got mine.' She straightened herself. 'I feel better now. Honestly.'

She stood up, walked round the end of the bed, pulled the curtains to complete the darkness, tugged the light-cord above, behind him, and squared up to the mirror.

'I look a sight,' she said, touching the ends of her hair comically with her palms. Then she brushed, two-handedly furious until she was satisfied, when she turned, tugged her smock and with a cocksure air said, 'Let's go downstairs.'

He took her arm, and she allowed it.

'You must tell me what's wrong,' he said.

'Nothing, really.'

'Come on, now. Were you frightened? About the baby?'

'No, no. I wasn't.' She began to walk him towards the door. 'A bit edgy. Like anybody else, but nothing out of the way.' Her voice laughed now. 'I just get very tired, and it all seems too much. It's silly. I'll be glad when it's over.'

'And I neglect you.' He made the effort.

'I don't think so. You can't sit at home all day holding my hand.'

'I can talk to you at mealtimes. Go shopping with you.'

'Suppose you could.' She looked him over. 'Wouldn't be you, though.'

Now they stood at the top of the stairs, where

she disengaged herself, easily, charmingly from his grasp to walk down. He noticed she kept her hand, well-manicured, on the banister to help balance, but she had recovered, broken away from him, refortified herself with herself. He followed in frustration and relief. The status quo, unsatisfactory or not, could be put up with.

'I'll make you a cup of coffee,' he said, loudly assertive.

'No. I'd like lemon and barley, please.'

'It's cold, Meg. Haven't you noticed?'

'I've got my baby to keep me warm.'

'I shall have to improve on my performance,' he said, bringing the drinks in. 'I can't have you doing your nut.'

She smiled, held a hand out for him to hold, but said,

'Don't make a thing of it, there's a good boy.'

There, he blamed himself for his failure, though he knew she did not. He had done his bit, that exactly described it, but it did nothing to prevent him toying with the fairy story, juggling fictitious consequences into lively impossibility. Now, at the seaside, in a bright bedroom, having made his mind up which pair of shoes to pull on for the day's pleasure, he recalled his own wry decision at the time to do better even though better was not there to be done.

Perhaps he'd be in her company tomorrow.

Her father could not be sure; she could barely show certainty herself. Now he looked back to the time of her carrying of Donald as idyllic, darkened with apprehension perhaps, but shared between rational human beings, who could adjust and compromise as necessary. Angrily he snatched on his jacket, though he had the sense to move slowly downstairs, not drawing attention to himself.

Outside, the street shone, paint glaring in sunshine with even the monkey-puzzles polished smart. Dozens of brushes had been dipped, stroked earlier this year for this new-pin effect; blue, black, some green, odd reds, but mainly white to reflect the brightness of the sky. Suddenly Fisher felt heartened by the activity; the choice, the visit to hardware merchants, the blow-lamps' roaring, the humping about of ladders in order to make this street as fresh, as up-to-the-minute as the next. It merely attracted custom, he supposed, or preserved the property but this scurrying into a competition of cleanliness cheered him, so that he walked more jauntily and in his head shouted some favourite lines of his father's:

> And glory, glory dwelleth
> In Immanuel's land.

Striding out, shoulders back, he hummed the Victorian slop. A yucca stood in full ridiculous bloom. A child smiled at him from a garden gate. Dark, dark has been the midnight. A window-cleaner in boiler suit continued the process of cleansing, his mop thumping the glass. An electric bread-van hummed past and from over the houses he heard the clash and rattle of milk-bottles, a whistle. And glory, glory dwelleth.

As it was almost eleven, he turned in near the front for self-service coffee. The restaurant, a new flat-roofed place in one storey, was neat with plate glass and pebble-dash, and inside, though not yet crowded, already scarred with litter, screwed crisp-bags, balls of silver paper, spillings of salt and sugar.

Fisher stirred his boiling coffee. The man on the other side of the formica table claimed it was a fine day, in a cultured voice. A bald old man, with the hairless, severe face of Sibelius, a black askew crease between the eyes, who wore a striped shirt under a shallow white collar. Fisher had noticed all this as he had sat down and had immediately forgotten it in his euphoria.

'Ideal holiday weather,' he said.

The old man began in an authoritarian voice as if he wished the people on the tables round him to reap benefit from his observations. He had driven here, and he pointed across the road at a 3.5 litre Rover, for company.

'I walked this coast as a boy. I can still manage a mile or two. But the time is rapidly approaching when I shan't be able to drive a car. And you realise what that means, of course?'

His voice hectored the stirring Fisher, who lowered his head, murmured, unwilling to commit himself to an incorrect answer.

'I've a pleasant place, this side of Horncastle. But it's private, secluded. When one is energetic, able to travel, that is what one wants. As one get less mobile, privacy becomes imprisonment.' He wheezed militarily at his word play; not its first outing. It appeared he owned land, which he had cared for, but now his son had taken over the old man was relieved.

'Land needs bold decisions, these days,' he said. 'One has to be able to make one's mind up. You'd think you'd all the time in the world to decide when to cut some trees down. Not so. Investment's an easier game all told.'

Fisher, mildly interested, asked questions from his ignorance so that his companion began to answer at length. Sometimes, for he was slightly deaf, he misunderstood, and more often than not he meandered, once becoming angry, in a slow, mottled-faced way, at the politics of India and Pakistan where he'd served in the First War. He brusquely inquired about Fisher's job, and said he knew the University's Chancellor well and that he was acquainted with the Professor of Ancient History, who'd married a relative of his late wife. Was Fisher married?

The other's spouse had died six years ago, but had been something of an invalid all her life, though she'd borne him three sons. 'You any children?'

'No. My son died. He was two years old.'

The man paused, frowned at Fisher, deeply,

rolled uncomfortable in his chair, like a caricature Dr Johnson, and blubbered his lips. For a time his stiff-fingered right hand tapped the table, as if to call the company to order.

'Your wife not here with you, then?' he began.

'No.'

He did not seem to notice Fisher's reticence, but described his own sons, good boys in their way, who resented his longevity. 'I've handed my house over, the farms. I don't trouble them. Why should I? But they'd like nothing better than my money. I don't blame them. They're at an age when they'd use it merely for pleasure because they're all established. And that's the best way.'

Fisher mumbled about death duties.

'I've straightened that out. As far as one can.' But there followed no technical disquisition on the subject, and when Fisher said he must leave, the old man struggled up, brushing his tweeds, reaching for a black bowler on the hatstand. On his feet he seemed slower, more awkward, less monolithic, though Fisher did not offer assistance as he crab-crawled down the steps to the pavement.

'I'm eighty next,' he said, arriving, pulling car keys from his pocket. 'Feel it too, sometimes.' He glanced round the street. 'Do you ever think you've wasted your time?'

'Yes.'

'I didn't think it at your age. Certain amount of drink and cards. Nothing out of the ordinary. I'm not claiming that.'

'One must have recreation.'

'Eh? Eh? Oh. Recreation.? Depends what sort. Drink. I looked at women.' He spouted this to the whole street. 'Now all I want to do is sleep. Even when I remember things I'm confused. I never trained myself for old age. Never believed it would come. Nobody does.'

The old man tipped his hard hat, hobbled over the road to his car, and drove off without so much as a glance backwards. Fisher noted the number-plate, but knew that would have left his memory inside ten minutes. The meeting sobered him; he'd no desire to laugh at the fellow, landed gent's accent or not. It was as if he'd assembled a jig-saw only to find that key pieces were missing. By quizzing Arthur Mann, of the history department, he could probably get the fellow's name, and, if Arthur acted normally, half-a-dozen anecdotes, but that could only darken counsel. A wealthy man drove twenty miles to drink a cup of cheap coffee because that was, perhaps, one of the few ways he had left to amuse himself. As a sentence, that made sense, but was deeply unmeaning, fatuous. He struggled to put his dissatisfaction into words, but found he could not. His formulation lacked subtlety, perhaps, needed qualification, but his dismay sprang from an unpalatable event, not from his inability to describe it. Nobody should be left unprotected as that old man appeared; yet he was one of the lucky, with money, care, fair health.

Fisher sat on a low stone wall under a sandy bank.

'I never trained myself for old age.' That was the nub, the heart-cry. Not many people prepared themselves, but they did not confess it out loud in the street to strangers. How did he know that? Was it a statistical judgment? One person in a thousand made such a statement in such circumstances twice every three years? No. A man of good family, with property, financially comfortable, with the bossy voice of his class, the unshakeable appearance of superiority, had spat it out to upset his listener's prejudices and preoccupations. A bad omen. Someone about to meet his estranged wife walks warily away from ladders.

Chattering holiday-makers passed, repassed as he sat.

Terry Smith, with his two in tow, called out, 'Midmorning break. Ice-cream and a tiddle,' and moved on happily enough. Fisher occupied himself with mental accountancy, totting up the numbers of people he saw and did not know, and then listing the sea-side resorts where similar results obtained. The schema of tens of thousands of hurrying people, all unknown to him, appealed to his sense of what was right in the world, a huge complexity pursuing a simple unity. He knocked that on the head as useless.

Meg had taken him abroad, except for the one holiday when Donald was alive, and, as he remembered, her main complaint had been that

Athens or Florence were not exotic enough, had their quality adulterated by tourists.

'There's more English than Greek spoken here,' she complained.

'That's as well for us.'

'You know what I mean.'

'Yes. This is the Parthenon. A great monument of antiquity. The crowds come from America and England to see it. They speak English. So do we. If we condemn them, we damn ourselves.'

'You're never very funny when you try to be,' Meg said.

'I understand your argument well enough. It's too easy to come here on a package-tour. We should be the only ones, because we presumably are the only ones capable of benefiting. That's snobbery.'

'You're not talking to one of your pupils now.'

'I'm only pointing out that the Parthenon is either worth seeing or not. It's a worthwhile aesthetic experience whether it's easy to come by or hard.'

'Most people wouldn't agree.' she said.

'Most people are wrong, then.' He'd smiled. 'I'll admit, though, that no aesthetic experience is absolutely pure.'

She could not be mollified thus; both knew that.

'Why are you always boasting then of these little places you find in the back-streets where they have charcoal fires and rough wines?' she'd ask.

'Because, my love, when I talk to people, socially, I give them what they want.'

'That's not what you give me.'

'I would if I knew, or even if you knew.'

These arguments were rather formal, and, as he remembered then, sarcastically delivered on his part. He had, again as he recalled them, no difficulty in wiping the floor with her, but he was the one hurt. The more easily he scored, the sorer his lesions smarted. This caused his tartness, his sour pugnacity. He must beat her now and then because she had established a total superiority. This was no way to regard a wife, he was sure, and to be fair to himself, he did not hold this view consistently, but let her once advance a silly viewpoint, he was away, asserting himself at her expense.

Tomorrow he'd be penitent, look at his feet, attack nobody.

He quitted his wall, walked the long stretch of beach down to the sea. On the hard sand left by the receding tide two land yachts rolled in the sharp breeze, sails slapping, moving as yet clumsily. Children shouted, kicked, splashed in the bright flatness of the water. The girls in bikinis and their young men romped their energetic chase after admiration while a black labrador, stick in its mouth, shook himself vigorously. He was remote from all this; he'd nothing to say, and this had always been so. As a boy he'd been invited to join a game of cricket, but as he'd batted or bowled or caught, more seriously perhaps than the lark-about on the sands required, he'd been himself, not one of them, nobody's buddy, the outsider,

He'd bowled out one father, not a bad swash-buckling bat, with a fast swinging yorker and had marked the hostility among the chaps. Nobody's but his own. His dad never played cricket; he disapproved of dominoes. As a family they sat or made sand pies, nothing livelier.

Dissatisfied, he moved towards the queue for boats.

A straggle of visitors stood in the wind at the jetty's end, subdued, eyes narrowed as if preparing themselves for the sea-shine.

'One more. Just one more,' the boatman shouted.

The queue wavered as heads turned.

'Just the one. The other boat won't be ten minutes. Are you on your own, sir?'

Fisher realised he was addressed as the heads swung again in inspection.

'That's it, sir. Then we're full.'

They made way for him, though there was no need, to the wooden steps down to the boat. The single. The one. As the pierrots warbled, 'One alone, to be my own.' He climbed uncertainly into the swaying craft, and was directed to a vacant area of plank, 'between the ladies there.' He sat down as the boatmen administered comfort to those ashore, revved the stinking motor and headed them out to sea.

The boat lifted, dipped, lifted, but gently and the prevailing effects were brightness and cold. Fisher wedged between a middle-aged matron and a young married woman began to feel exhilaration; this summarised his adventurous spirit, half an hour on a calm North Sea on a summer noon. Children trailed their hands in the water while the boat made a heavy, quick progress, the iron roar of the engine strong all the time. Once, they without warning, crossed a wave so that a shiver of spray showered the passengers who squealed, burst into chatter.

'You'll wish you put them slacks on,' the woman called over Fisher to the other girl. 'It's parky.'

The girl looked steadily forward at the backs of heads, the horizon. The woman nudged Fisher, pushing the message through him, repeated, becking, 'You're goin' to be frozen there.'

Again the girl gave no indication she'd heard, but then shifted, very slightly, away from Fisher to mutter, 'Uh. Knickers,' through unopened lips. He could not be sure she'd spoken, but her companion shrugged, said aggressively,

'It's always cold, out here.'

'Aw, shut up, Lil,' the girl answered. 'Stop moanin', for Christ's sake.'

She was fair, with a pale face, handsomely trim as the wind pressed her light mac round her. Her nails were bitten dirty. Neither paid the slightest attention to Fisher who wondered why they'd allowed him to sit between them as they took their pleasures morosely.

In the back of the boat some passenger had asked their speed and the boatman had guessed twelve knots. This led to argument about the exact measurement of a knot which enabled the man who first raised the question to announce that a nautical mile, a term loosely translated by 'knot', was 6080 feet in Britain, but slightly more, 6082 feet 8 inches in the U.S.A. This he offered so glibly that Fisher wondered if he hadn't looked the information up first and then broached the subject to air his knowledge. There fell a small silence of admiration, and Fisher guessed that the girl on his right, though she made no sign, was impressed.

It reminded him of his father. That was the sort of snippet Arthur Fisher had stored away by the thousand, but he would have spoiled it all by some atrocious pun. 'They're not the knots we have in Notts.' He experienced an acute spasm of embarrassment at the word play he'd fathered so easily. When he'd recovered they were arguing in the back about water-speed records and whether one appeared to be travelling faster than was the case.

'It's obvious,' said the know-all passenger. 'When you're driving down the M1 your speed seems comparatively low because there are no near landmarks, hedges or palings or houses.' The voice whined on, not unlike his father's. Fisher resisted the temptation to turn round and check.

Conversation became desultory; the boatman laconic. The whole object of the trip was to enjoy the sea air, the movement of the boat, the sound of the water so that when they turned about and passengers pressed for information about the coast, grudgingly given, mildly argued about, this, Fisher thought, lacked propriety. He himself only, wedged between women, appreciated the solitariness, away from the hum of the flat shore, the sprawl or activity of bodies. Inland, the pubs were open, men considered themselves; out here, one rocked, a chilled nobody.

He was glad to step on to the jetty, stiff, none too warm. The woman next to him told the girl they'd 'have to find the others now.' She replied she knew, sulkily as ever, face mask-still. As he set off Fisher was joined by the know-all passenger, whom he recognised at once from the voice.

'Ah. Glad to use my limbs again.' Fifty perhaps, horn-rimmed glasses, bald patch.

'We didn't see much,' Fisher answered.

'Except the sea'. Was that a father-type word? Arthur would now have been humming to himself that he'd 'joined the Navy to see the sea, and what did he see, he saw the sea.' No. None of that. 'It's something. Quiet in its way, but satisfactory.'

'Yes. It is.' The man smiled agreeably at this support.

'I think it's what you make of it.' They were trudging in the loose sand in front of beach chalets. 'Take the town itself. I've seen changes here. I tell you one thing. There aren't so many visitors as there were seven or eight years back.'

'Really?' The man glanced up at the bourgeois question.

'No. It's the package tour. Stripped the coast,

y' know. Ibiza, Majorca, Costa Brava, Costa del Sol.'

'Is that good?'

'Depends on you. We had a holiday in Italy. I was there in the war. Always said I wanted to go back. We fly out. There in no time. Hotel, quite good. Meals not exactly what we'd choose, but well, it's what you'd expect. Weather. Sunshine every day, day in, day out. We have breakfast. Walk across the road, on to the beach. Had to pay for our spot. I'd go in the sea three or four times, that warm, like a bath. Back to the hotel. Eat. Beach again. And that was it.'

'Restful.'

'Real rest's very often doing something different, I think.' The father-tone again. Cue for hymn. 'Rest for the weary, rest for the sad.' We didn't show much initiative, I grant you. Have you been to that part of the world?'

'Yes.'

'Well, you'll know, then. There are plenty of trips. Hotel caters for you. Early breakfast, packed lunch, late dinner. Nothing too much trouble. But my wife suffers from arthritis,' he pronounced it arthur-itis to Fisher's grim amusement, 'and doesn't want to sit all day cramped up, nor traipse round buildings and galleries. That's why she's not with me now. So we didn't get out of it what we might.'

'You wouldn't go again?'

'I'm not saying that. And when I see all the glass

and glitter they've thrown up in this place. I can't help thinking . . . Mark you, it's what the public want. Bingo and beer-barrels. And if anything stops 'em going abroad it's all this stuff I hate.'

'How do you spend your time, then?'

'Certain amount in the deck-chairs, I tell you. I have a drink. Bit o' time off on the boat. Walk along if I feel like it. Meet new people. Get into conversation. Like us now. You won't believe it but I've known the wife go into the kitchen after dinner at night to help wipe up, just for the talk.'

'You'd think . . . ,' Fisher started.

'I understand it. She likes the landlady, known her for years, and they've got something to say. People, it's people who make holidays, in my view, not scenery.'

'Nature,' Fisher quoted, half-ironically, 'is fine, but human nature finer.'

'Ah.' The man seemed taken aback.

'Keats.'

'The poet. And yet there must be people here. Four-fifths of the holidaying population go to the coast, y' know. Common sense. These speculators don't build new palaces here for nothing. They'll get their money back.'

This led, as they stumbled through the sand, past bodies and castles, to an argument about the ways of capitalism, land prices, inflation, great skyscrapers of office blocks left unoccupied. Interested. Fisher found it impossible to concentrate as he watched his staggering feet.

'Ah, here we are,' know-all said.

As Fisher expected, nothing was missing. Against the windscreen, the plastic ground-sheet, the blankets, the baskets and bags, and presiding from a deck-chair, the wife, buttering biscuits, vacuum flask at the ready.

'Must be pushing,' Fisher said.

'Interesting, interesting,' the man replied. 'Ah, well.'

When Fisher looked back his companion had occupied the other deck chair, donned a panama, and was, against probability, smoking a cigarette. Goodbye, arthuritis.

Immediately after lunch, Fisher walked in the gardens, among the designs of house-leeks, the beds of Frensham and Peace, the nemesia and tagetes. A young man noisily mowed the lawns, while elderly groups sat, lined carefully, about the seats. 'Presented by Coun. C. W. Goddard.' 'In Memoriam Lt. H. W. A. Scott, Sherwood Foresters, 1922–45.' Though the motor-mower ripped the air, the place had the stillness of a waxworks. Sunshine on shrubs, on pale skins. A pretty housewife pushed her baby past in a bright orange pram, smiling, long legs tanned. A blackbird hopped, pecked, hopped.

Again, he knew nobody. Among these old faces not one he knew.

Then he must take pleasure in the exercise, march along these asphalt paths until he wanted nothing. No road had that length, so he made further along the promenade, in shallows of sifted sand to the amusement park.

Once inside, he was at a loose end in the casual afternoon. Amusements and stalls were not well patronised, and in spite of noise the place seemed languid. No life here, either. One or two men shouted across as he passed, inviting him to try his luck with a dart or rifle, but they cared as little as he. Whether it was merely the time of day he did not know, but the whole gave the appearance of running down, of being old-fashioned, unwanted. One-armed bandits, bingo halls with cups of tea and large, precise bonuses were here too, but they lacked the glitter, the faceless comfort of the newer palaces on the front. Human beings might walk in from time to time.

Fisher decided on the Big Dipper.

His father would never have allowed the family on this, invariably kept them out of the amuse-ment park. Though Fisher often had walked through on his own, he'd never dared defy Arthur by riding on that huge public railway ridiculously fearing perhaps that the old man at peace on the sands would cast his beady eye at the swooping cars and recognise his son. The boy had guiltily lost pennies on the machines, crept in on the tattooed lady and the Egyptian belly-dancer, but they were shows in the musty dark.

As he mounted to the pay-box, he felt fear. Would he be able to bear the whirling eviscerating dash? Behind his heavy safety bar he soon had his answer; a mild exhilaration, tense attention before the dip, and then a disappointment momentarily disappearing at each acceleration of the car. It needed a girl's arms round you and the carriage full of shrieking children. Hurled about alone, in middle-age. Thirty-two was not old. Guilt required; father's forbidding voice; his own rabid appetite for excitement. The sixteen year old had some advantage over the grown man. He eyed the distant sands, black figures unaffected by the blare of pop-music; he might be in the boat again, cut off from human endeavour, habitation. The drop in his stomach recalled the present.

Now he smiled as he walked away, in part ashamed not of trying the ride but of yielding to temptation.

He sat on a bench, stretched his legs and considered how he could tell his wife what he had done. In the running chaos of his mind, that surfaced as sensible, was dismissed, rose once more. When a man who has deserted his wife meets her again all he can find to say is, 'Do you know what I did yesterday? I went for a ride on the Big Dipper.' Immediately he began to justify himself. There was little else to offer except such snippets of social intention. It was better to announce that a man on the boat had made valuable informative statements about the British and American nautical miles, than to goad or strip so that in a few minutes they were back to former fighting, to cornered hatred. If he and that beautiful woman, he remembered her hair, were to attempt reconciliation they could do it only in humility, marginally at first, with sentences about fair-grounds and balding know-alls. He was slightly surprised that he could entertain the idea of, say, amnesty, olive-branches, without emotional perturbation. He switched his mind prudently elsewhere.

On a bank, sparsely covered with grass, three young men were lounging.

All wore long hair, beards, standard jeans; one, in round, gold-rimmed glasses strummed lazily at a guitar. Perhaps he even sang; it was impossible to tell. They sat as a group, idly watching, half-concentrated on the instrument, letting time pass so that when one pushed himself upright and strolled across, Fisher was mildly and pleasantly taken aback. The young man approached, took a casual position never looking the other in the eye square as he spoke.

'Could you give me a light, please?'

Clear this time or clearer. A non-smoker, Fisher carried a lighter in his pocket because Meg had occasionally needed a cigarette but never had matches with her. He fiddled, handed it over.

'Don't know if it works. Might be dry.'

The young man flicked, shook, flicked so that the Red Indian strips along his arm and the hem of his coat bounced, then inhaled satisfactorily.

'Thanks.'

Fisher pocketed it, waited for the boy to budge but he did not do so.

'I've seen you before.'

'Oh?'

'You gave a lecture at our place.' He named a technical college. 'Education and Prejudice.' He seemed pleased to recall the title.

'Are you a teacher in training, then?'

'No. I'm a lab technician. Went with a mate.'

The young man spoke barely moving his lips so that Fisher was reminded of film gangsters. This image was totally belied by the quietness of the voice, the mildness of the lad's appearance, the spinelessness, perhaps. It looked as if he might collapse, clothes and all, any minute, crumple to the ground.

'You made it quite interesting,' the boy said, stroking his pale cheek with the back of the hand in which he held his fag.

Fisher nodded, began polite questioning about holidays. The three young men had a tent over on the dunes, from where they bathed twice a day and slept when they came back from the discos. All this the boy delivered in driblets, not hurrying himself, giving the impression that he tried to make the recital as dull as he could. Fisher, half amused, looked for the language of the youth cult, the words he'd learnt from the Sunday papers, 'chick', 'pad', 'joint', 'turn on', even the daft 'psychedelic', but found nothing. If these were already out of date the speaker had not replaced them with immediately recognisable neologisms, but used the flat language of the factory floor, the supermarket, the soccer pitch. They were, a leer, on the lookout for girls, the birds, and had been moderately successful because there were some right scrubbers about here, he could tell you. They'd just do the week and hitch back if they could. If they couldn't? Have to be the bus, wouldn't it?

Fisher wanted to know why they didn't venture further, abroad, say.

'You need time for abroad. We want to be idle, and our own bosses for a week. And we might stay another if the weather keeps up. We're here, and we do as we like. We've got money, but we don't want to spend it in clubs, downing ale.'

'Do you not drink?'

'Sometimes. But eight or nine pints a night like some of 'em is stupid.'

Although Fisher guessed they were shorter of money than they let on, this jerky, undemonstrative account of a seaside idyll attracted him. Immediately he checked himself because he could pinpoint the boring fish-suppers, the interminable talk of women, the sitting about in unattractive dumps like this waiting for something to happen, and the weary drag on when it didn't. They weren't unlike him, making a little go a long way, because they'd neither the resources nor the energy to do anything more enterprising.

The lad took in a last lungful, dropped the cigarette to the gravel, didn't heel it in, made some sort of noise and left. When he sat down again, exchanged for a few moments a word or two with his companions, Fisher could not be sure that they were discussing him. Embarrassed, he strolled away, raising a hand to the group.

All three acknowledged, surprisingly. Two nods and a finger. Gave them something to do in a half-hearted way.

Middle-aged people ate silently at a whelk-stall; youngsters tore wrappers from ice-cream, dropped them to the sand. In the distance a young couple silhouetted with all the banality of a television ad. ran hand in hand so that they seemed immediately conspicuous by their directed energy, their aim. The rest tottered or splashed in a few yards of shallow sea; these two swooped, on their way, due to arrive.

Fisher bought a cup of abominable, strong tea, burnt his tongue as he sipped and exchanged words with the stallkeeper, in the slack of the afternoon. There he learnt that they still rolled mint-rock on the front, set out to find the booth, which was deserted, though its placards proclaimed, recently repainted, that the 'old firm' had won diplomas of merit in 1934/5, 1936/7, 1939. Had they lost their touch in the last thirty-odd years, or had kill-joy dentists won the day so that diplomas of skill and purity were no longer awarded?

Young men climbed the high diving board in the inland sea-water pool. He could see the top of the structure, which had not changed since his day, though he had neither lounged nor leapt up there, confining himself to breast or a few breathless strokes of crawl. In that place he had first seen a grown woman's nipple in a flash so that he hardly believed what he saw, when her shoulder strap slipped and he had blushed, tingled with desperate pleasurable embarrassment while others noticed nothing, got on with their own rowdy devices. The observer, the man on the side, the peeping-Tom.

A bus on the promenade disgorged its complement of old-age pensioners who creaked off the step to stand bemused on the pavement. One old man, face brown as a brick, hair-remnants ruffled, turned round on the pavement in his braces, mouth agape, looking for something.

'Won't you want your coat, Mr Wardle?' Female bossiness. The old chap mouthed sounds, turned obediently towards the bus. 'Don't you bother. I'll get it for you. It can be quite cool here.'

The leaders, middle-aged women in flowered dresses and cardigans, ushered their charges into a semblance of order, and one, hectoring, shouted,

'We shall walk down to a very nice little garden where we can sit. The flowers are beautiful. There are toilets there if you want to use them. It's not far to the sands from there, but I don't want you to go if you think you'll tire yourselves. You'll be able to see the sea, and it will be sunny and sheltered in the gardens. Now if you'll follow, Mrs Payne will show you the way down.'

Fisher watched the sad shuffle as they set off. The dictatorial woman took the arms of two bone-thin old ladies who were clearly delighted to be thus signalled out for honour.

'They've got some rum 'uns there,' the bus-driver said to Fisher. 'Some of 'em have no more sense than babies. One old fellow was going to have a pee in the middle of the bus. Had it out in front of all these women. But most of them are as lively as you and me.' The driver wiped his hands on his trousers back-side. 'The old fellow was weak in the head. Been inside a 'sylum, they said. Queer, in't it, how old-age takes you? Gi' me a nice, quick heart-attack any time. Over and done, then. Shock for them as is left, but I wouldn't like to be like some of these.'

'They won't want to die,' Fisher said.

'No more shall I when my time comes,' the driver answered. 'Well, I'd better lock this bus up or they'll have their handbags pinched. God bless 'em.' He paused, added, keys appearing in his hand as if by conjuring, 'The way some of these women get on to 'em. Worse than th'army. Stand up, sit down, polish your boots, wipe your arse. But I suppose if they weren't like that they'd never organize these trips, and these clubs, and these poor old souls'd never get a niff o' sea air. What a life.' He flourished his keys. 'Lovely, some o' these old dears. "Has the driver had a cup o' tea? Make sure the driver gets his dinner." Can't help liking 'em. I tell 'em, "Don't you worry your 'ead, my love." I say. "If they've flung every tea-leaf in the place into the North Sea, I'll get some'at to drink." And they look at you wi' round eyes, and cackle, and say, "Beer" like naughty school kids. "That's it," I tell 'em. "Pig's ear an' pickled onions. What us drivers lives on." And then some o'd biddy says, "I think the driver's drunk," and, by God, they're off. Ah, well.'

This time he went, locked up, slapped the back on his tour of inspection and made for the gardens after the procession, calling over his shoulder,

'Make the most of it, while you're young enough.'

'Where?'

The man spread his arms, flapped them comically as he retreated, kicking his heels up.

'Here. Here.'

Fisher walked faster up the promenade, less sure of himself, but gayer. A stout young woman, brown as a fisherman, slapped along with her children. One jumped, stumbled into Fisher who was passing, was jerked peremptorily upright.

'Look where you're going,' the mother called. 'Sorry.' She wore a short frock, rucked high up her legs from sitting.

'Quite all right,' Fisher said. 'Wish I'd that amount of energy.'

The mother locked her lips, but said nothing, plunging on again, the two lively at the end of her arms, like shifting seaweed on an anchor.

Now the place seemed crowded, as perhaps the

beaches emptied, and cars swished along the road, catching, flinging sunlight on their windscreens. But the life was tired, like the leaping flame as an old man put a match to his pipe in one of the sea-front shelters, a wild atom in surrounding enervation.

'They'll sleep tonight,' some grandma shouted, pointing at children upside down on the prom-rails.

'I know I shall,' their mother answered.

Meg had been a poor sleeper, prowling in the night, sipping glasses of water. If she took a sleeping-tablet she'd manage only two or three hours, and then wake to toss.

'Why don't you read?' he'd asked.

'And wake you?'

'I'd soon drop off again.'

He wondered if she woke like this to win time for herself. Even when she dropped with fatigue, so that she nodded off over a meal, when Donald needed night-feeds, she still became alert in the small hours.

'Are you worrying? Is there anything on your mind?'

'Not really.'

'What is it, then?'

'Just a bad habit.'

And she'd shrug him off, rationally, in what seemed to him a desperate appeal. He ought to settle her nerves, soothe or dominate her into sleep. Such fantasy nagged him. On holiday, at St Tropez or Tunis, when they were drugged with sun, satiated with sex so that every muscle of his body relaxed into a perfection of comfort, she'd be awake at two, creaking the wicker chair in the bedroom, staring out into the light darkness, towards the small trees, the pool of night-sounds.

'It's my nature, she said. 'I'm a nocturnal animal.'

Yet she loved the sunlight, hated the white strips of flesh round her breasts, buttocks, low belly.

'Ridiculous,' she drew his attention with her finger, unnecessarily. 'Look at that.'

And dizzy with the sun he'd tried with his fingers the change from sun brown to white until he lay exhausted inside her as she laughed and complimented him and tried without trying to reach for the bedside table a cigarette that was the symbol that she for once was sufficiently satisfied to demand a second gratification that was no concern of his, that did not spring from him.

CHAPTER 7

On the morning he was to lunch with the Vernons, Fisher sat on a towel on the beach.

The sky stretched hazier; the wind had dropped so that the day promised real heat. Children scuttled about as if to prepare themselves for pleasure, digging trenches and fortifications, jumping and shouting, delighted because their parents had, for once, got the weather they wanted. The elderly sat to respectful attention in deck-chairs biroing postcards, ready for the brightness, they remembered, every day of summer showed when they were young.

Fisher idly watched two young women who had settled near him.

Their preparations were priest-like; Pope approached truth in the 'Rape of the Lock.' First they laid the huge beach-towel, weighted its corners with their baskets and bags. This took time, circumambulation, calculation of the sun's position later in the day; both chattered with a kind of intensity, like a commentator into a hand-microphone, as if to ensure that their inanities arrived at the listener. He had been amused for a quarter of an hour before he realised that he was the target, he was the morning's eligible young man, mark one. They did not look at him much, but made certain that they had his attention, by constant movement, barbs of conversation.

Curiously, as he examined himself, he felt flattered.

They were pretty, stocky girls, blue-eyes with blond, fluffy, well brushed hair. Now they had whisked their frocks off, and in bikinis sat to oil themselves. At first this seemed haphazard, a dab at ankle or shin, but he found that they rubbed and smoothed with thorough care. He was, and he and they noticed, shamelessly staring at them. Their legs, strong-thighed, thick-ankled, were already tanned as their palms caressed, sliding over the youthful surface. One wore an engagement ring. After the arms, upper breasts, shoulders, belly had been leisurely treated, one lay flat for the other to deal with her back.

'Oh, I could do with this all day,' the patient said. There was something sexual in the whole performance as if they were inviting Fisher to join the ritual, the initiation. When the first girl sat up, she smiled at him, showing good teeth, patting her hair. After the second lubrication, one girl made a dart for the other who sat touching herself, to tickle; it seemed out of place, clownish compared with the hieratic slow ease so far, childish, a lout's trick. The second girl squeaked, thrashed over fast to dodge the assault, kneeing a zipped shopping carrier and a complement of sand on to Fisher's towel.

'Stop it, Tricia,' she squealed. 'You are daft.' She looked at Fisher. 'Oh, I am sorry.' She picked up the bag, began to brush sand ineffectually.

'That will do no harm.' he said.

She was deep-breasted, pretty, utterly humdrum.

'It gets into your food, it's so fine.'

'I shall go back for lunch,' he answered. 'I'm meeting somebody.'

'A lady.'

'Two. And a gentleman.' They were all laughing.

'In a restaurant?' the first girl, Tricia, asked.

'A hotel. Yes.'

'Do you think we could guess which?' she persisted.

'You could try.'

They preened themselves, brushing sand from their knees, for the game.

'The Frankland Towers,' the second girl said, eyebrows sarcastic.

'Yes.'

A small silence.

'Did she guess right first time?' Tricia asked.

'She did.'

'Good guessers never marry,' the first answered, fingering her engagement ring.

'I wonder what Philip would think about that.'

More laughter, while Fisher placed Philip as the girl's fiancé.

Soon they began to talk, not easily, and in their case with a modesty which he found old-fashioned. This suited them, as did their rather ample bikinis, in red and blue with polka dots; they wanted to chat to him because he looked sensible, dressed respectably, but now he'd proclaimed himself a patron of the Frankland, they were faintly suspicious, wondering what he was about, sitting alone on the beach. They were sisters, he learnt, and Carol, the elder, the engaged one, was a primary teacher. Patricia was secretary to a manager in a textile factory in Nelson.

He liked them, immediately, with their big healthy limbs, their common sense, their careful vocabulary delivered with a slightly northern voice. They were interested when he told them he used to be a teacher, questioned him about his schools, but did not press to know his present occupation, when he said nothing. They always took holidays together, were here this time because a fortnight's motoring in Ireland had fallen through at the last minute. In simplicity, he found them amusing talkers, sharp but charitable; both clearly had more intelligence than their superiors at work, but neither resented this, saw it perhaps as an order of nature. One evening a week they ran a uniformed group for small boys, and on another they attended together a class on oil painting.

'Do you bring your paints with you?' he asked.

'No,' Carol replied. 'We're both copiers.'

'We drive the teacher barmy, because we've no initiative.'

'I can't believe that.'

'It's true enough,' Carol answered. 'We go. We pick up tips. We turn out things our mother thinks are marvellous, but they're nothing to Aubrey.'

'Can he paint?' Fisher asked. They considered.

'I suppose so. He had plenty of daubs in the local exhibitions.'

'You sound guarded.' Fisher was enjoying himself.

'He's an excellent teacher. But very conservative, I should think, wouldn't you Tricia?'

'And trying to encourage us to splash out in the way he won't himself.'

'That's acute. I'm glad I don't teach you.'

'It's obvious,' Carol said, pleased with the comment.

The pair bent to pouring and oiling.

When later he went to fetch a pot of tea for the three of them, Tricia slipped on a short bath-robe to accompany him. They stepped over legs, rounded castles, laughing. She stood with him in the queue, chose the biscuits, chaffed the stall-keeper with the result that Fisher found the trip a source of pleasure. About these girls, he thought, there was an innocence, a goodness. If he had been asked to specify what this quality consisted of, he'd have been forced to mere picture-making. He could, for example, though they had made no mention of religion, imagine these two as members of a Harvest Festival choir, bearing a strong contralto, 'The Sceptre of Thy Kingdom is a Right Sceptre' maestoso by Sir A. Sullivan.

This pleased him, though he recognised it as fantasy. No such simplicities existed in real life. When these girls married, and they were the sort to become excellent housewives, their husbands would be plagued with their moods, and fears, and boredom, because this was universal; nobody was exempt. But at present he felt no qualms.

When he had first met Meg, that evening at the theatre, he remembered an element of guilt, of treachery. She'd called him over to spite her fiancé who was running at her pleasure. Fisher, attracted, had sensed danger, uncertainty. Meg's love was never more than half given, grudgingly displayed. These girls would open their fingers, clasp a man's hand in theirs, and mean it, whatever scarred or spoilt the future. Meg's whole self seemed devious.

Perhaps, he conceded, that he had fallen immediately in love with Meg and this had stirred the waters. He laughed out loud at his metaphor, in a mood to see his own faults while he was with these two. Very likely he needed a Meg, an indeterminacy, a treason to match or outpass his own.

'My, you've been long enough,' Carol said on their return.

'We had to queue.' Tricia.

'I thought you'd eloped.'

There'd been a little patch of awkward silence, then, but they were soon at ease with Carol pouring and bullying Tricia about her appetite for biscuits. At twelve Fisher made his excuses, spoke his pleasure.

'Shall we see you again?' Carol asked outright. Her ring gave her this privilege.

'Very likely. I'm here till Saturday.'

'We're usually round about this spot.'

He picked up the tray and teapot to return, arranging all neatly.

'You look really domesticated,' Carol said.

'I do my best.'

'Watch out at the Frankland,' she warned. Tricia said nothing, looking away from him except at the last moment when she waved, mouth slightly, attractively open from white teeth. At the stall, when he returned the crockery, took his deposit, it was as if he was selling off some valuable part of his life.

At the boarding house, which stood deserted, he changed shoes, suit and tie. He examined the handsome, respectable figure in clerical grey, eased himself breathlessly down on to his bed to waste five minutes.

The plate glass doors of the Frankland Towers stood open to the foyer, which with long windows, cunning neon-tubes seemed hugely filled with cool sunshine and banks of flowers. The surface of the reception counter was thick glass, the chairs modern, gay-bright, the spiked palms small and flourishing. Footsteps made no sound; no music, and even voices muted themselves in the high expanse.

Vernon was already by the reception-desk, at ease with the busy blonde.

'This way, this way,' he said, voice little, but suitable. 'I could guarantee you'd be on time. You're the only young man I know who is. The Tudor bar for you, I think.'

'Cymry am byth.'

'Ah, ah, No, not really. My wife is already there. Ensconced, shall we say?'

They moved along corridors into a stone room of darker, warmer light, low roof with black beams, mullioned windows, by one of which Irene Vernon sat. She had dressed herself for the occasion, with a toque, whorling upwards, a matching beige coat, both regimental yet flowing, block-heeled shoes; she ought, Fisher thought, to carry a white parasol, or a sword-stick.

She smiled, motioned Fisher alongside, brusquely demanded dry sherry, gently inquired how he was.

'Meg not here yet?' His voice was hoarse.

'She's due at one.' Irene made motions towards the clock, which indicated ten minutes' wait.

'Has she ever been on time?' her face asked. 'What's yours, Edwin?'

'Is she here, in Bealthorpe?' Fisher asked.

'That we don't know.' Vernon spoke back from the bar, where a man obsequiously, hands splayed, head forward, waited his order.

'David phoned her last night. At home,' Irene said, putting a gloved hand on Fisher's arm.

'She'll drive over.'

'I see.'

He thought of the phone in the hall, where she'd answer, by the Bellini madonna with its rubber-doll Christ across her knees. In the evening there'd be sufficient light for Meg's face to be reflected in the picture-glass, and he could see her fingers disarranging curls as she spoke. She would also, he was certain, leave too little time for the journey, if he knew her. He was not certain that he did. Shivering he looked about him.

They settled to their drinks, Vernon smiling, founder of the feast.

Fisher glanced round the other drinkers, who huddled over dark tables in conspiracy, never raising voices, bronzed as Indians.

'Your health,' Vernon proposed. They drank.

'Keep your eye on the clock,' Irene warned. 'It won't do to keep Meg hanging around.'

'Don't come between a man and his drink,' her husband answered, patting her knee.

A young man in a tail-coat approached, arm full of menu-cards.

'Are you ordering now, Mr Vernon?' he inquired. Already his father-in-law had made his name known.

'We're waiting for a fourth, John,' compliment returned, accepted. 'Shouldn't be too long.'

They now studied the menu, talked about food, though Irene clearly was on edge.

'It's one o'clock, David. Go and see.'

'I've spoken to Lilian there, and she'll ring through if Meg arrives.'

'And just at the moment she does, your Lilian'll be out at the back.'

The phone shrilled. The barman answered sotto voce taking care not to intrude on his guest's pleasure. The three waited, Fisher twirled his glass, stroking it with his thumb; they were not called over, and the instrument was replaced in its cradle.

'Go in, David.'

'You know what she's like.'

'Never mind. Go and look.'

Vernon mimed the unreasonableness of women, but obeyed. Fisher found himself watching Irene doodling with her little finger in the circle a glass had marked. She traced without pattern, from one side to the other, not crossing the line, holding her breath, four eyes on the bright-ringed hand. Fisher had finished his drink, had rearranged himself on his cushion five or six times, had hummed no tune to himself, had counted the escutcheons on the bar-canopy before Vernon returned.

'No sign,' he said.

'It's nearly ten past.'

'I went outside and had a word with the commissionaire. Her car is white, isn't it? A white mini? That's what I said.'

Fisher offered them a further round, nervously. Vernon jumped.

'No fear. You're not coming here at my invitation to spend your money on us.'

He gathered the glasses, made for the bar.

'Not for me, David,' his wife called.

He seemed white now, drawn about the mouth, bonhomie wiped off. When he returned, he put the drinks on the table despondently, apologetically.

They sat, in silence. Fisher, embarrassed by the discomfiture of his parents-in-law, stumbled through conversational openings in his head, but made none. The clock showed one eighteen; John appeared again but treated them only to a raising of brows, a nod of understanding; the phone lay idle.

Irene sucked the calligraphic little finger. Fisher tapped his foot to Mozart No. 40. Vernon licked handsome lips.

Now they were certain she would not come.

'I'll try again,' Vernon said, leaping straight. He, a fastidious man, graceful, knocked his stool over behind him. He seemed almost relieved to pick it up; it gave him occupation.

'Yes,' Irene said, sucked breath in. She sagged under her fine feathers, as if the powder would drop from her face like scurf. Fisher himself, chafed, reached out, took her hand which he held awkwardly for a moment. Vernon noticed before he left, and approved with a military nod. 'I don't know what's happened to her,' she murmured, when her husband had quitted the room. 'David was so sure she'd come.'

'You didn't think so, then?'

She started, as if affronted at his presumption.

'I don't think David understands.'

'He's had a lot of experience of this sort of thing in his office, hasn't he?'

'As a solicitor, explaining the law.'

She picked up her glass, still half full, and touched it with her lips, as at a last supper. Then she smiled, at him, shyly, like a child intervening among adults.

'Explanations,' she said, 'aren't much good to Margaret.'

'She may have run out of petrol, or collected a puncture. She might have lost her way, even.'

'She would be here on time if that's what she wanted.'

The mother spoke hopelessly, in a monotone of appalling certainty that approached grief. She fixed her eyes, which watered, ahead, on a hanging decorated shield. No more was said until the return of David. He shrugged, spread his hands.

'No sign of her.'

'You'd better ring her up, then.'

'I've done so, my dear.'

His contempt sounded, or his anxiety.

'We'll go in,' he said, miserably. 'I've ordered the soup and hors d'oeuvres. I hope you don't mind. Irene leaves that to me, usually.'

The meal was more cheerful than Fisher expected, as if all three were relieved by Meg's non-appearance. She was mentioned; Mrs Vernon grumbled though without malice; David started the meal with three or four anecdotes of the eccentric behaviour on the part of wives matrimonially aggrieved, but by the time the main course was served, he launched himself into descriptions of fellow-guests, and then, unusually for him, of the cars in the hotel's parks. They moved back to the Tudor for brandy, and there Irene invited him to spend the afternoon in their company.

'No, thank you,' he said.

'Are you doing something?'

'Not really.' He tried to show his concern. 'You've had enough of me for one day.'

The Vernons apologised, but he, sipping brandy, was anaesthetised against discomfort. He thought back to the beach, to the Lancashire girls in their innocent bikinis and knew he could not return to them his breath reeking of alcohol. They were symbols, he recognised, delightful pictures like these heraldic shields, ersatz comfort, with no connection with life. This saddened him; the whole world he saw in a dazed disproportion. He and those girls could make a go of it, he decided through the brandy-fumes, but while he drank, he could not approach them. The wry fantasy disappeared.

'I hope nothing's happened,' Irene said.

'She's decided not to come.' Vernon. 'Taken fright. Nothing we can do about it.'

When they left the bar, Irene ordered him to ring Meg again at her home. While he complied, the other two waited in the high light, amongst the sheets of bright glass, toeing the carpet.

144

'Nothing doing,' David said, in the end.

'Perhaps she set off.' Fisher tried, but the others did not respond. He shook hands, thanked his hosts fulsomely, made unsteadily for the door. Outside, it struck hot, the air rubbed his skin like sandpaper, after the silver moderation of the Frankland. At a bookstore, he bought a paperback complete with literary man's introduction and a publisher's note on the trial.

He removed jacket, tie and shoes, lay flat on his bed, read meaningful sentences sensibly, until he did not understand them, and dozed.

The curtains by the window hung frozen by the heat.

CHAPTER 8

Fisher fell deeply asleep, as though exhausted.

This surprised him, because he would claim to have left the Frankland almost unmoved, untouched by events. He was sorry for Irene, wished he could make up to her while he admired Vernon's masking of his anger. David hated to be crossed, and if Meg could not be punished, then the nearest would stop the kick. Fisher wanted to be out of the way.

Washing, scrubbing the morning's business off his hands, he wondered suspiciously if Vernon weren't up to monkey tricks, but could not see how this was possible. Irene had been genuinely, if genteelly, distressed; not that damage done there would hamper Vernon.

What troubled Fisher most was the feeling of having missed Meg; he wished to see her. This a week ago would have been impossible, but now, without pretensions to reconciliation, he wanted to meet, look at, touch hands with, her. Perhaps, then, this indicated they could make a go of it, with care; more likely, he needed a woman, and

146

his wife was supremely attractive to him. He tried to concentrate his attention, but could not. He lacked criteria, even the will to make decisions, and thus allowed his mind to rattle on its unending tumble of reflection, imaginative sillinesses pacing clumps of word-play.

He dressed carefully for dinner, spoke cordially to his fellow-guests, as if he owed the world something or feared retribution when he did not step vigilantly. Yet he felt genuinely pleased, a man who had done well, unlikely as that seemed. The Smiths invited him down to the pub, made a party up with the middle-aged couple; Sandra walked behind with him in a street that was still pleasantly warm.

Fisher ordered the first round while Sandra reserved him a place next to her.

They talked of children for a time, and education, showing Fisher deference, before they discussed violence. As they tilted glasses, they claimed they did not know what the world was coming to. The middle-aged man's wife sat like a mouse, not daring to touch her lager, with a little sweet smile thinning her lips from minute to minute. She took no part in the conversation, even when her husband broached marriage.

Terry Smith said he could not understand some people. His wife looked away.

'It's all a matter of give-and-take,' the middle-aged man, Mr Hollies, claimed. 'Once you've grasped that, half the problem's over and done with.'

Fisher found himself nodding, in the manner of pub-audiences when some wiseacre holds forth.

'Now,' said Hollies, 'I work at a printer's. We do fine work. It's a skilled trade.' Here followed technical details to which they listened avidly, it appeared. 'Now you couldn't choose of a steadier craft. And yet when I think of the way the younger fellows, all men who've served their time, treat their wives, I'm not surprised at the divorce rate. They'll meet for a drink or two, not a lot, these aren't wild by any means, sometimes after we've done, and it means, I tell myself, that there are dinners drying up in stoves and young women worrying. Needlessly.'

'Once their wives become used to the idea . . .' Fisher argued.

Hollies wagged a finger.

'They do not get used to it. Looking after children is an exacting occupation.' The words were a small, artistic triumph, delivered with panache. 'And they count the minutes to the time that back door's opened.'

'I long for Terry to come home, sometimes,' Sandra said, in simplicity.

'You've never told me that, before.'

Her scorn, his confusion were mildly noticeable.

'I like my pint,' Hollies continued. 'I don't deny it. But I am home every night exactly on time. If I wasn't, there'd be good reason. That's so, isn't it, Lena?'

His wife smiled, tinily, narrowing her eyes so that she sat like an old Chinese. She said nothing.

'That was our agreement. I clocked in to the minute. My dinner was ready for serving. It has always been so.'

'You know where you are,' Terry said.

'Exactly. You know where you are. And that makes the marriage.'

Further drinks were ordered, for there was hurry this evening when the landlady had agreed to keep an eye on the Smith children. Terry mouthed clichés, spoke loud agreement with every statement; his wife rubbed her leg surreptitiously against Fisher's under the table. Mrs Hollies sipped herself into inscrutable jade, while her husband spun a long-winded tale about a couple who'd made an agreement that each could live his, her, own life. Fisher, muddled, divined sense in this. The point was that such a pact, though mutually agreed, was incompatible with harmony. The young man took his old flames out drinking, but beat his wife when he found her in bed with the lodger.

Fisher did not see this classical situation of the smoking-room joke as at all comical.

'Do you know what happened?' Hollies seemed to deliver entirely to Sandra, as he leaned across the table, hand fanning oblique face. 'She threatened to leave him, packed her trunks, the lot. And then he gave the lodger a good hiding, and that seemed to settle it.'

149

'That showed her,' Terry said.

'What if the lodger had been a better fighter?' Fisher asked, bemused now.

'He wasn't.'

That stopped contention. Hollies sat back with the stiff pride of a man trying not to be sick.

'I take it you're not married, sir?' he said to Fisher.

At the question, there was a renewal of interest, a shuffling round of chairs, a straightening of mental furniture. Sandra's perfume became newly potent.

'I am,' he replied. 'But I am living temporarily apart from my wife.'

They murmured sympathy; Sandra's fingers momentarily fluttered on Fisher's

'Until', Fisher continued, 'we know where we are.'

'That's sensible,' Hollies claimed. 'If other people had the wit to do that, there'd be less trouble all round.' He sank half a pint.

'Sandra threatened to leave me once,' Terry said. 'We had a row about money. She said she'd run home.'

This he delivered without affection, with no mention of forgiveness, but as an interesting fact of life dredged from the bottom of his tankard. Sandra blushed, and her commonplace features hardened round indrawn lips so that her neat jumper and slacks seemed too well-laundered to match the coarsened face.

'It cleared itself up?' Hollies.

'In time.' Terry sounded reserved, now.

'Give and take. Give and take.'

Fisher provided further drinks so that Hollies spoke louder, his wife smiled more foxily and Terry Smith staggered to the lavatory. Sandra, lips parted, had recovered her poise. Now the conversation became a duet between Hollies and Terry on the subject of football, the vandalism of fans, the temperaments and skills of players. They blamed managers, financial temptation, the press, ignorant children; as far as Fisher could make out neither attended matches, merely followed games on television Saturday night and Sunday afternoon. Both were bold with their sentences of condemnation, fervent in support of the other, often contradicitng what had been said minutes before. A man from the next table joined in, as did the potman wiping tops and clearing empties. In the middle of this noisy enjoyment, Mrs Hollies said, out of character, squeaking,

'It's nine thirty, Jack. I shan't get my walk down to the sea.'

'You're right enough here.' Voice slurred.

'Have another drink,' Terry pressed.

'I am going,' the woman said. 'I shan't sleep otherwise.'

'I'll walk down with you.' Fisher, empty-headed.

'Let's all go.' Sandra. Terry looked disappointed.

'You ladies,' said Hollies, expansive chairman, 'take a turn down to the briny with Mr Fisher. Terry and I will sit here and set the world right.'

Smith looked shamefacedly at his wife.

'We'll manage,' she said. 'I could do with some fresh air.'

They downed drinks and the two husbands stood to usher the ladies out.

'Don't get lost, now.' Hollies beamed. 'We don't want you coming home with the milk.'

'We shall be back before you, I expect,' Sandra said tartly.

In the yard outside, it blew cooler and scuffs of cloud darkened the sky.

'I wouldn't be surprised if it rained,' Fisher said, walking in the middle. Sandra had immediately taken his arm leaning heavily on him. Mrs Hollies advanced with small brisk steps on his left side, unaffected by the drink. They laughed, began to quicken their pace, until still in step they ran together, charging the length of a treed street. Sandra stopped them, breathlessly, panting, shamelessly leaning on to Fisher who put his arm round the waists of both women.

'That's improved matters,' Fisher said.

Mrs Hollies hung on to him now as desperately as Sandra, her hat askew, her diminutive face on the cloth of his sleeve.

'Steady,' he called. 'You'll have me over.' He briefly fondled Sandra's small left breast, then straightened, before they set off with greater restraint.

'I bet they're still talking about football' Sandra ventured as they reached the promenade.

They climbed separately down the steps, but Sandra jumped the final three, landed on the sand, arms upthrust.

The march along the sands was slower, feet dragging. The cold chop of the wind buffeted faces and hair. They stood on the sea's edge where the waves were small, oily in dim light, in spite of the breeze.

'The weather's turned.' Fisher

Both women had arms about his waist.

'It's lovely here,' Sandra said.

'I don't know what those men can be thinking about wanting to stop in that stifling atmosphere.' Mrs Hollies, Lena. 'It's fresh.'

'Terry will be drunk when he comes home.' She put her head on Fisher's shoulder. He dropped an exploratory hand to her right buttock.

'As long as he's nice,' Lena said.

'Oh, tonight. It's tomorrow I'm thinking about.'

Fisher stroked; Sandra writhed minutely in appreciation.

'I know what my husband'll want,' Lena said.

'What's that?' Sandra whispering.

'A bit o' sex. He doesn't drink a lot usually, but when he gets in with somebody he likes, such as your husband, he'll have one or two above the odds. And then it's always the same.'

The woman spoke with the same timidity, and yet with perfect certainty as if she knew the exact effect of her words.

'He's fifty-six,' she said. 'Eleven years older than

me and he's still not lost his appetite for it. In strange bedrooms, you can be heard. Some of these walls are that thin. I keep telling him, but he won't be said.'

Fisher stood hot with excitement; the small voice at confession on his left, the strong delicacy of the girl's answering body on his right. He massaged; she moved with him. Nobody else about, they stood in the low swish of the sea, the darts of wind. Fisher, split with frustration, stared about, like a hare. If he could get rid of this Hollies woman – but she had tempted them, brought them out here, encouraged his groping with her sentences. He wished he could read Sandra's mind, or could swing her up in his arms, then flatten her stripped to the beach, cool his violence in her body, to the sound of sea-whispers.

'Let's have another race,' Sandra demanded.

'You young ones', Lena said. 'Not me.'

'You'd beat us both.'

'I'll say "Go." One, two, three, off.'

They set out in a diagonal towards the promenade first on the hard sand by the edge, soon on the softer, kicking up, filling shoes. Fisher allowed the girl to run ahead, trotting with no difficulty. After fifty, sixty yards, he could not judge easily, they swerved behind a beach hut and he put out a hand to her shoulder. She squealed, stopped, turned, put her mouth to his. They kissed hard so that he thought they'd tumble.

'Where's Lena?' she asked, in the end.

He stood now behind her, his hands under her short anorak. Her midriff was bare below the jumper.

'Can't see her,' he said, in shadow.

She stood breathless as he stroked her, thrust his hand down into the front of her slacks, along the belly, touching the pubic bush.

'Don't,' she said pathetically. 'I feel drunk.'

He withdrew his hand, but not at once, squeezed her hard, then allowed her to wheel, to kiss him again, her arms enthusiastically awkward round his neck.

'That's nice,' she said.

'She's coming.'

Sandra untwined, took his arm primly as they waited. Fisher bowed as Mrs Hollies pushed towards them, knocking on the hut's side with her fist.

'Ten o'clock,' she said. 'We'll make for home. Before you two do something as you shouldn't.'

She leaked her small laugh, slipped a hand into Fisher's and jerked.

'I bet it's still football,' Sandra said. She spoke coolly, recovered.

'No. Smut now,' Lena said. 'And boasting how many times a night they could do it. That's right, isn't it, Mr Fisher?'

'That's right.'

'Men. It's all they think about.'

As Sandra squeezed his hand, Fisher concentrated now on Mrs Hollies, who walked proudly,

swinging along. The timid animal of the pub had altered herself, not radically, but from a silent figure to a commentator. Her husband by no means had his own way. The three took the last streets pleased with themselves so that Fisher, breast clasping, kissed them both.

'Oh, if I were only a bit younger,' Lena said. 'I'd shake you.'

'Naughty, naughty.' Sandra.

'I'd be naughty all right.'

The men had not returned. Fisher, making from the lavatory, heard nothing from the other rooms. Despondent now, condemning himself for half-action, he undressed, lay reading on his bed. He heard the door downstairs, the ascent of the husbands who, subdued, oozed in whispers.

'Good night, Terry boy.'

'Goo' night.'

'Sleep tight.'

Again the small thud of doors, a mumur of conversation, the traipse for the toilet. Silence. Fisher dropped his book, walked to the window. Cars swept by; the pad of footsteps; in bedrooms lights sketched the drawn curtains; some man whistled his dog. Wednesday ended itself by the North Sea.

Fisher, Fisher.

CHAPTER 9

By his plate at breakfast was a picture post-card. Wollaton Hall.

Turning it, he read. 'I daren't. Sorry. Meg.'

He considered this, wondering how she knew his address; perhaps she's ferreted it out of her father; more probably he'd dictated it with an order to write an apology. She'd complied thus ironically. In green ink, untidy letters. Mr E A Fisher. Words level with the address, for the postman to read. His mother and father turned their messages at right-angles. He laughed when he considered the inanities they had confided to the cards. Weather. Distance from the sea. Meals. X marks our room. Hope Edna had a good time at Filey. Abbreviations. Hd. gd. time. 'Don't forget to take a pen out today, Arthur. We'll send the cards off. Wednesday at latest. Tuesday better so since they'll land before we're back.'

The Smiths arrived with vigour, the boys scrupul-ously scrubbed, their fair hair shining, little fists ready to bunch round cereal spoons. Terry, none the worse, waved; Sandra in short sun-frock concen-trated on the children and the exact position of their chairs, but she smiled, paused to inform Fisher that the transistor set had announced another sunny day.

Five minutes, last of the guests, the Hollies trundled in, Lena to the front. She wore a two-piece costume which emphasized her smallness, reduced her legs to matchsticks. The husband in a navy-blue suit looked more unbuttoned, as if he appeared in shirt-sleeves and braces. He'd plastered his hair flat with tap-water, and his broad face reeked with after-shave lotion. His greetings were effusive, but jovial so that Fisher grinned, delighted.

'We'll dispense with the preliminaries this morning,' he told the hovering waitress. 'Straight into the hard stuff. Bacon, egg, tomatoes, sausage, chips, spinach, the whole issue.'

'We haven't got any spinach,' the girl giggled.

'Where am I going to get my vitamins from, my lass?'

The pronunciation of lass, home counties, 'less', amused Fisher; northern phlegm, cockney spirit. The Smith boys paused from their leisurely eating to enjoy this loud performance. Sandra encouraged them back to their plates. Mrs Hollies did not speak, squinted down, not displeased, at her dish. Fisher decided he'd buy a card and reply to Meg. He began to compose his answer. 'Thank you for your card. Dared not what?' No, on this morning he could afford more generosity. 'I enjoyed seeing your writing again.' Better. He'd ring Vernon, and report communication.

He had a few minutes' conversation on the landing to Terry while Sandra supervised the final toilet-drill with the boys.

'Very pleasant, last evening.' Fisher's gambit. Had Sandra said anything? It was odd, he decided, that he could not trust her to keep her mouth shut. Just to rile her husband, or to pass the time, or compensate for a mild indigestion or a sleepless hour, she might have let slip some hint, or even a plain statement. That nice Mr Fisher groped me on the sands, while you were swilling beer.

'Yes, for a change. We don't go out much at night, you know. Can't with the boys.'

'Your wife enjoyed herself?'

'Yes.' Terry laughed. 'She said you had a run together. Reckoned that Mrs Hollies couldn't half get a move on.'

'She surprised me. Quite a talker, too. Never says a word while her husband's there.'

'Oh, there's plenty to her. I had a chat with her one day. Broad, y'know. Bit near the bone, I thought, some of it. Well, to somebody she hardly knew.' He frowned. 'Not that I mind. Can say what she likes.'

'Seemed such a mouse.'

'They're the sort to watch.'

'Didn't hear you come in.'

'Tried to be quiet. Didn't want to wake the boys. Sandra wasn't asleep.'

'You didn't get into hot water, then?'

'Oh, no. Far from it.' He wiped his mouth, like a man after a satisfying drink, appearing so naively, openly self-satisfied that Fisher envied him. Such simplicity ought not to exist. And Sandra? Excited by her husband's caresses, the rare breath of his drink, or the stranger on the shore? Or nothing of the kind. She emerged, chamber-pot in hand, ordered her husband without embarrassment to empty it, and asked Fisher what he'd arranged for the day.

'To tell you the truth I haven't decided. I ought to write the odd card.'

'I suppose we ought. I don't know though. Waste of money. You don't ever read them when you get them, do you?'

Fisher inquired her plans.

'Oh the usual. Down on the beach. Sand-pies and paddle.'

'And you like that?'

She wrinkled her nose as if she knew her attractions.

'On a fine day. I like sun bathing, so that people can see you've been on holiday. And they're not too bad, the boys, not too troublesome.'

'Your husband's very good with them.'

'Oh, Terry. Yes. He is.'

'Enjoy it last night?' he asked, looking her straight in the eye.

'Yes, I did.' She spoke with emphasis, defying him.

'We'll try it again, then.'

This time she turned, moved into her bedroom calling her family to order. Fisher knew a momentary qualm as he stood, but on her immediate reappearance she showed him her teeth in a full smile, reassuring him.

He allowed the Smiths a minute, then made off secretively for the nearest call-box, to ring Vernon. The connection was rapidly established. He reported the postcard.

'Thass a good sign, now, inn it?' Father-in-law's comedian from the valleys.

They talked desultorily until Fisher grew angry.

'Haven't you heard from her, then?' he demanded.

'Now, why should I?'

'She must have got my address from you, yesterday, so presumably you spoke to her.'

'I may just have telegraphed it.'

'Balls.'

'Or her mother talked to her on the 'phone.'

'She'd report it,' Fisher snapped.

'That doesn't mean I'd pass it on to you, though. No, Edwin, I'm thinking. It's a good sign that she's bothered. I phoned her; I left her your address. She actually started. Got as far as Grantham, and turned tail.'

'Why?'

'She's your wife. You should know better than I do. She's volatile, now.'

'Would she speak to me?'

'Last person in the world, I'm sorry to say. We've

finished breakfast. Walk over, if you will, and see us. I was most upset.'

Fisher heading for the Frankland Towers wondered what dramatic performance Meg had staged for her father. Usually at some trivial instance she whipped herself into histrionics; when her son had died she had been silent, pushing about small chores in the house as if concentration on these only could redeem her. Then he'd not got near her; unapprehended as the little corpse, she'd dusted and cooked with her pale mouth shut.

He remembered how one evening early in the marriage he'd come home late from his London comprehensive school. He'd forgotten to make a note of a parents' evening and thus had not told Meg. They had no 'phone, but he sent a message by a colleague who lived nearby. He, finding no one in, had torn the back off an envelope, had scribbled. 'Edwin has meeting. Home about ten,' shoved it through the door.

At ten-thirty, Fisher, fagged out, arrived to find his wife in dressing-gown waiting wild-eyed. For a moment he thought Preston had not delivered the message.

'You've come, then?' she asked.

He threw himself into a chair, began to unlace his shoes, then wrench his tie loose.

'They'd keep me gassing all night,' he grumbled.

'Have you been at school?' Flat.

'I sent a message with Adrian Preston.'

'I've not had it.'

He rummaged for his slippers, collapsed back into the chair. She stood exactly as before, taut, breathing fast.

'Shall I make a drink?' he'd asked.

'You think more of that bloody school than you think of me.'

'That's silly talk, Meg. Would you like a cup of coffee?'

He got up but when she refused him an answer he shrugged, turned for the kitchen. Just before he reached the door, a vase exploded on it. He jumped back, in surprise, shielding his face with an arm. A fragment hit his coat, gently, fell to the ground. He turned.

'And what's the idea?' He used the same steely tone to a fractious middle-school form.

'You arrogant bastard,' she said.

'Listen.'

'You listen, your fucking self,' she shouted.

He glared at her, blood pounding in his head, cheeks burning but stiff as ice, lips trembling. Her mouth opened and shut, not widely, wordlessly. Her fists were clenched dull white, her face drained, twisted unfamiliarly. Now his body shook, vibrated with anger, but it turned inwards, against itself, as if nerve revelled against wild nerve, sinew with sinew. He stared, not blindly, but into a landscape without perspective before he forced himself to turn his back on her, open the door and walk into the scullery. Even as he

163

did so, he felt his neck, his shoulders wince as at some missile, smashing through the closed door, felling him. He sat, confused, sickened, stomach weak with fright for some minutes before he filled the kettle.

He made his cup of instant coffee, but drank it there, slowly swilled and dried the crockery.

Usually he cleaned his shoes last thing at night, but he had left them by his chair in the dining-room. As he returned, he lacked all strength, limbs burdened, his gait unsteady. Still she stood, but he did not look at her, picked up his shoes, retreated. The exercise of polishing, Arthur had taught him that pride in this work, did him good so that as he packed the tin, the two brushes, the small velvet pad away, he knew he must speak to her. He considered the matter, then the words; made his mind up and rehearsed procedure.

Now he went in, stood back to the door.

'I'm sorry, Meg. I thought you knew.'

'Thought,' she said. 'Are you capable of thought?'

That did not displease him; a sarcastic question spelt some steadiness. In her case she now copied Father David.

'Not often,' he said, smiling sadly, conveniently.

'You're not fit to be a member of the human race.'

This sounded so ridiculously that he glanced up in the hope that she had now dissipated her resentment in this parody of anger.

'Probably.'

'Probably,' she mimicked. 'Probably. You stuck pig.'

'And all that. I'm going to bed. You can please yourself.'

'You dangling, ugly excresence.'

'Not very good,' he said. 'Bed'.

As he moved past her, she struck him, not hard, almost playfully on the upper arm. He grabbed the lapel of her gown, tugged her so that she staggered across him and landed stumbling over the table. Without haste, when he knew she was unhurt, he quitted the room.

Upstairs he sat without breath on his bed listening. Not a sound. Now he wound the two clocks, checked the alarm, and undressed. As causally as he could, for he knew he'd not sleep, he climbed into bed. Meg had squared these clothes, made sure the coverlet stretched creaseless, the pillow plumped comfortably.

From below, a shriek slewed.

He sat, straight in a strait-jacket of fear.

Now the house was thumped by heavy blows, as if someone beat a carpet violently but with lengthy rests between the thuds. He could not understand what she did, but imagined her standing with a broom thwacking the leather back of the new settee. The whole bloody neighbourhood would hear the performance; at eleven at night; through these thin walls their semi-detached privacy was small. Out of bed, dragging on his dressing-gown, he hesitated, agitating himself round the floor, not daring to go down.

She was quiet; the cannonade had done.

Cold, he wished he smoked, he made ungainly but without noise for the stairs. He opened the dining-room door.

The light burnt still, but the air smelt thick with dust. The settee and the two arm-chairs were overturned, as was the table. She'd snatched some books from one of the chimney shelves and hurled them about the floor. A mere dozen, a score, bright wrappers intact, they made a pitiful scatter. The television, the radio were untouched, as were the tradescantia in its basket, the ugly Renoir reproduction 'La Loge', the china cabinet, the photograph of her father and mother.

The scullery door gaped.

Meg leaned over the sink. For the minute he thought she vomited, but she did not stir.

'Come on to bed, love,' he'd called. She did not answer; he expected nothing, but he took her by the arm. Now, the violent wrench, the obscene abuse, the pummelling of her fists. Nothing. With docility she allowed him to lead her out into the wrecked room where she made a large, weary gesture which he understood easily.

'When I've got you in bed, I'll square it up,' he promised.

They had difficulty mounting the narrow stairs together, but they made allowances, stumbled generously. She crept into bed, did not speak, or cry or cover her face, but lay down, easily, when he ordered it, pulled the sheets up to her face like a pampered child. He bent, kissed her, received no response and tiptoed downstairs.

The cleaning took longer than he anticipated, but he enjoyed the work, took care to sweep with the Ewbank, to dust flat surfaces. He expiated thus a guilt he ought not to feel, but when he returned purged, she was asleep, neither shifted nor sighed as he entered the bed.

Awake, untidy in his mind, he did not touch her.

Mid-morning performance at the Frankland at half-eleven. A young man on the desk phoned the Vernons' room, asked Fisher to sit, and on appraisal of his suit mentioned the adequacy of the holiday weather.

Vernon joined his son-in-law on the out-of-the-way sofa he'd chosen. The older man had not shaved, nor brushed his hair into any shape of tidiness. He soured his mouth, glumly creased his expensive jacket. No inquiries were made about coffee or drinks.

'What did she say?' Fisher began.

'Precious little.'

'Do you mind my hearing that then?'

'She made a start. Got as far as Grantham. Felt afraid. Turned back. Was at home sitting about, all of a shake, when I rang at four. Had had no lunch.'

'Why,' Fisher pressed, 'was she so scared?'

'I don't know. I don't know if her story's true.

She may well have realised that she'd gone further than she intended when she agreed to meet us.'

'Why would that be?'

'You're just as capable as I am of guessing the answer, answers to that.'

'Do you honestly think she set out?' Fisher asked.

'She said so.'

'That's not what I asked.'

'How can I be sure?'

They traversed this ground once or twice more until each felt sorry for the other. No enlightenment; that became obvious. Fisher concentrated on his father-in-law who had been cheerful earlier on the phone, and now spoke sullenly, shifted about in discomfort.

'May I ask you something?'

Vernon looked up with a grin, a touch of devil, then, courtly, waved Fisher on.

'Why are you so uncertain now, David?'

He rarely called the older man by his Christian name although he'd been invited often enough to do so.

'Am I?' He didn't want information; he spoke like a convict recaptured.

'Has,' Fisher pointed up, 'Mama been on to you?'

'Not really. She wants to rush back. She has her little weep. No, it's the other one I'm upset about.'

'To the extent of not shaving?'

'Oh, I see. You think I've been so busy administering sal volatile and soft soap to Irene that I've not had the time for this.' He rasped his bristles. 'No. Part of the holiday.'

'I like Irene,' Fisher said, off target, deliberately oblique.

'Good, good. No, Meg sounded dull but sensible enough. That's what I didn't like. She had the sense to turn round.'

'I don't get you.'

'No. I don't know myself. You see, I thought we might meet and speak. Nothing miraculous, but the talk would be beginning.'

'She sent this card. It's an apology.'

He passed it across. Vernon spent more time on the picture than on the few words.

'She'd realise you'd be shaken. She's not without imagination, would you say?'

'I never knew.'

'No. One doesn't. One doesn't She could play the bastard, I expect. But I see her as a child, still. It's not so long ago to me since we wheeled her out in that war-time pram. On my leaves. I can remember her as quite dependent.'

'She needed a dozen husbands,' Fisher said.

'Sexually?'

'No. Not there. That's one place where we were matched. Bed. No. They all say that, I suppose. Nobody admits inadequacy there.'

'You'd be surprised.'

'Oh.'

'She was sane enough, do you think?'

'Why do you ask that?' Fisher was unquiet.

'Don't know, don't know. You ought . . . Oh, God, Edwin. She's a monster.' He laughed, then, as if at some recondite allusion.

'Come on, then. What d'you suggest?'

'If I knew that I'd tell you.'

'Shall I ring her?'

'Do you want to?'

'Not particularly. I'm the sort to let it drift.'

'But willing to stir the mud from time to time?' Now Vernon was expansive.

'Well, yes.'

Vernon reached inside his collar, scratching his hairy neck.

'We're not getting anywhere, Edwin, while we talk like this. We need Meg here, herself, irrational as she likes. At least she'd see us, that we haven't smoke coming out of our ears. She lives in unreality, that girl.'

'I don't think so,' Fisher said.

'Let's hear.' Fisher's yawn concealed no boredom.

'She's had it rough. Nothing's come up to standard. And then, to top it, Donald dies. God knows she was unsteady enough before that. Now she must be twisted.'

'It's over a year. Nearly eighteen months. That's time for recovery.'

'Depends what form recovery takes. Hers perhaps included ditching Donnie's father.'

'Won't do. Won't do. Makes no sense. It's as if you said she left you because she didn't like the wallpaper in your dining-room. I don't believe it. It fits with nothing.'

'You don't want to . . .'

'Don't, won't, in, out. I don't know, Edwin, but that one doesn't satisfy.'

They sat, moving their hands, extracting handkerchiefs, feeling money, adjusting dress.

'What's Irene say?' Fisher began.

'Seems on your side, if anything. Thinks Meg's obstinate. But she doesn't consider a wife should leave her husband.'

'Even with provocation?'

Vernon nodded, deeply, as at profound truth.

'Will she talk with Meg?' Fisher started again.

Vernon's head moved largely sideways.

'She's never been up to her, you know. When Meg was small she'd beat her mother. Irene has one or two ideas or preconceptions or prejudices to suit every situation. And she's not to be moved from them. She can be angry, or hurt, but not convinced.' He sighed, whistling loud, and slapped his fleshy ribs. 'That's a bloody daft thing to say. As if a sentence can sum a woman up. Even one's own wife.'

'I know what you mean.'

'More than I do.' He acted out a coughing fit. 'Meg once stole two pounds out of her mother's purse. Did you . . . ?'

Fisher shook his head.

'She'd be fifteen, fourteen. I don't know. She

needed money for shopping, but there was nobody about, so she helped herself. She'd only to ask, mind you, but there was nobody in the house. And Irene's like some little old-age pensioner with her purse. Weighed to a farthing. So she accuses our bright young lady, who's come back in a paddy because she could not get what she wanted and she denies it.' He coughed again. Drily, this time, near choking. 'Classical situation.'

'What happened?'

'It was like that poem of Wordsworth's about the weathercock, weathervane. Taught her to lie. They were flying at each other's throats in no time. Meg slams out, locks herself in her bedroom, and when I get back home Irene's broken down, near hysterics.' Vernon took a handkerchief, shook it loose, mopped his face, blew his noise violently. 'She screamed at me, ordered me to go upstairs and sort Meg out. Oh, I sat her down. Got the details. Then we had a cup of tea. You never heard such a ta-ta.'

'And you were calm, man of the law?' Fisher asked facetiously.

'Of course. All this stuff about the cleaning woman being suspected didn't mean anything. Nor did two pounds. She was frightened that it would be five pounds next time, then ten, then forging cheques. You see? And lying. Flat denials. Never be able to believe the girl again.'

'What did Meg say?'

'That she hadn't taken anything.'

'Did you believe her?' Fisher asked, objectively, as if he did not know the protagonists.

'No.'

'So what happened?'

'I told Meg I believed her. That did nothing. She'd buttoned herself up by then. I told Irene I'd done my best and that Meg denied it and I'd no option but to believe her. She wasn't pleased, but she was over it in a day or two.'

'And what's the moral?'

'Don't plead guilty unless proof's overwhelming.' Vernon grinned, pulled his face about, rasped his chin along his collar. 'I think Irene flew off the handle and frightened Meg, who's obstinate. That was that. The child was bursting, I guarantee, to hand that money over. She's very generous. I'd bet she'd give it Oxfam or the missionary society or some charity.'

'But?' Fisher appeared portentous.

'She wasn't to be shown up by her mother. That's why I don't put much faith in Irene in this matter. Let's say the relation is coloured.'

'By this?'

'Of course. And similar . . .'

'This is fifteen years ago.' Fisher sounded incredulous.

'None the less.'

'She was only a child.'

'She won't forget, Edwin, I can tell you that.'

'You mean you won't. You've not forgotten it.'

'Your word, Edwin, your opinion against mine.

But if it comes to some really serious matter I don't think Irene and Margaret are capable of sorting it out between them.'

'On account of one row? All that time back? Not possible?'

'All things start. In a small way.' Vernon spelt it out. He sounded like a parent reciting a nursery rhyme to a baby without language.

'Well,' Fisher chided. 'And how did you come out of the fracas? It made no difference to your relationship with the girl?'

'I'm sure it did. At that stage kids don't see straight. She might have thought me a fool for believing her. Or an idiot for not seeing through her denials. But either way I was sympathetic. And that's what counts.'

'At the expense of her mother?'

'Look. Irene set this up. She made the fuss in the first place.'

'She may have been right. These things start in a small way. You said so yourself.'

'She may well. But she made too much fuss. That's all I'm claiming. I'm not saying that she shouldn't have checked Meg, chided her, told her to be careful. She'd have my support in that. But to blow her top, put the child's back up, have the whole house in hysteria seems not very sensible.' Vernon brushed his neck along the back of his collar. 'I don't need to tell you that your-lady-wife needs some handling. You think I spoilt her, don't you?'

'She likes her own way, granted.'

'It's damn' difficult for me to see this in perspective. She could be maddening, but she was generous, and helpful.'

'And wilful.'

'Could you trust her?' Vernon's accusatory finger hovered.

'I wouldn't know how to begin to answer that. When we were first married she had a job at which she was good. Then she was at home with Donnie. Sometimes she'd say she'd do some chore. 'I'll clean that spare room up today.' You know. But it didn't get done. I think that was a kind of suggestion. 'Would it be a good idea to clean etc. etc?' She wasn't idle. She was always doing things. Often surprising . . .'

'She annoyed you?'

'Let's say I could have been consulted. She rubbed a beautiful mahogany sideboard down and then painted it baby blue. I could have murdered her.'

'But,' Vernon frowned his interest, 'did she realise how furious you'd be?'

'That puzzled me. I thought anyone with a shred of taste would have been horrified by what she'd done. But to her, the shape of the thing was ungainly, its mirror a bit fly-blown and these defects made it worthless. The polish, the grain, the lustre of the wood meant nothing. I think now that my reaction horrified her as much as her action did me.'

'But you were wrong?'

'I suppose I was.'

'You raved on at her?'

'I suppose my few sarcasms could . . .'

'It still annoys you, Edwin?'

'Not about a piece of furniture. The fact that I was so stupid about how she felt.'

'Like me, you should have given in?'

Fisher nodded so that the two sat miserably on their settee watching the constant movement of guests like princely fishes in the high glass foyer. All shone, washed in brightness; no one approached them because there was a plenitude of room. So they kept up their puzzled grief together, added to it by words which no eavesdropper inhibited.

'Something I'd like to ask,' Vernon said, brusquely, rubbing his hands. It was then, Fisher thought, he seemed most hypocritical. He did not wait for permission. 'Who left whom?'

'Technically, I walked out. But for weeks now we've both been threatening the other. Or inviting. It's pretty childish, when you come to look at it.'

'I expect you'd got on one another's nerves. That's serious.'

'That's so. But our behaviour.' Fisher, launched, wondered at the wisdom of his confession. 'We were snarling and scratching for the slightest verbal advantage. I feel ashamed. But if I went back it wouldn't be long before we were at it again.'

'The marriage is finished, you think?'

'I don't know what to think. After a rest we might

patch it up. Have another child. I've nothing to compare it with. Did we quarrel more often than other couples who stay together? Or more violently? Or efficiently? I haven't got those answers.'

'Do you love Meg, Edwin?'

'God knows.'

They embarked on further rounds of questions. Who did, who was, who could have? Both knew the uselessness of the exchange but at least they mentioned Meg's name freely and this comforted Fisher.

'I think,' he said.

'Well?'

'Doesn't matter.'

'Come on. Out with it man.'

'I think you should invite her again. See what happens.'

'No'. Vernon shook his head, deepened his wrinkles. 'No. You're going back on Saturday. And we'll let things ride. Let her stew.'

'She may need help.'

'I'll see her next week.'

Fisher considered, jinking money in his pocket. 'I'll reply to her card.'

'Yes, do that. But be careful what you say.'

Fisher nodded. Vernon stood, held out his hand. 'Thank you Edwin. I can't say how sorry I am about all this. It makes me feel, somehow, that I'm at fault. But many, many thanks for coming.' They shook. 'Now, I'll go to get rid of these whiskers.'

At the door, the commissionaire saluted, perhaps because no Rolls was arriving that minute. Fisher felt cheered, considered stepping back in for lunch, but made rapidly for the town centre.

The beach seemed noisier, more crowded than before, brighter with bathrobes and wind-breaks. Balls were flung and kicked; families played cricket, shouting and cheating; the shallow sea was blackly dotted with people. He passed Carol and Tricia, in bathrobes, eating ice cream in the company of two young men. Though both girls smiled and spoke, they did not seem pleased to see him. Their beaux, in briefs, were flabby, hairy, on the way to paunches and thin hair. Fisher, half annoyed, wondered why he felt saddened. Mr and Mrs Hollies both jumped from their chairs to wave, to shout.

'Going places?' Hollies asked.

'I've just come from the Frankland Towers,'

'They say it's lovely there,' Lena said. 'I've never been in.'

'The booze tastes the same. It's the price as is different.' Hollies.

They invited him to sit down, but he refused, though he did not immediately move on.

'Are you going in for a swim?' Lena asked.

'Could be. Are you?'

'That'll be the day.' Her husband laughed.

'I don't know. Your wife showed Mrs Smith and myself up last night. She can run.'

'Can she, by God?' Hollies said. 'She'll be running

away from me.' He amused himself, nobody else, with a wry face. 'I could go a drink. How about it?'

Fisher declined.

'Tell you what, then,' Hollies spoke expansively, doing the world a favour. 'You keep my seat warm here with Lena while I go. Shan't be half an hour.'

'Perhaps your wife would . . .'

'You don't know her. That's obvious. She'd as soon go in a church as in a pub at dinner time. You sit down. Keep her company.'

Fisher did so, not pleased. Hollies pulled his jacket on, checked his pockets and stumped off.

'Wouldn't he have gone if I hadn't arrived?'

'Might.'

'He enjoys himself.'

'I'll say this for him. He'll stop only the half hour. But he'll pour beer into himself. And he'll spend the whole afternoon trailing back and forward, back and forward to the urinals.'

She passed Fisher a bag of fruit, from which he chose an apple.

'He's a man who knows his mind, I'd say. Sociable with it.'

'More so now. When I first knew him, he was a devil for pushing his nose into an argument.'

'You didn't like that?'

'No, I didn't. But he was well-built. So he didn't get into trouble. Now, at the weekends they have a stripper, and they all sit staring.'

'They don't invite the ladies?'

'No. Though some'd go.'

You don't like the idea?'

'I wouldn't do it myself, if that's what you mean. But he does. All men's the same. You would, I expect.'

'I expect so.'

She laughed, screwing up her eyes.

'Have you never been to a strip-joint, then?'

'No.'

Slightly worried, she adjusted the hem of her dress.

'How do you like that Mrs Smith, then? Sandra?'

'Very much'.

'She was setting her cap at you, you know. Last night.'

'Do you think so?'

Mrs Hollies nodded, largely uglifying her face.

'I bet she leads her husband a ta-ta.'

'He seems a nice chap.'

'Wet. Useful with the boys, which is more than you can say of my old man. But he's got no go about him, no life. No nothing. I like a man who is a man. I'm not saying shouting and yelling his head off, but who lets you know he's there.'

'He's too self-effacing?' Fisher asked. 'I hadn't noticed.'

'You hadn't time to notice much with milady playing you on.'

'Really?'

'Really.' She mocked him exactly. 'You want to watch her Mr Fisher.'

By this time Mrs Hollies had completed a

complicated operation involving starch-free biscuits, cheese-slices and tomatoes. Now she began to eat, carefully catching the crumbs in a paper serviette, edged with dim roses.

'I'll be careful,' he said maliciously. She did not answer, but ate steadily, rather noisily, tongue licking lips clean.

'I'm not blaming you,' she said, dusting her hands, 'it's her. I known her sort. Different's better. You're married, aren't you? Or have been?' He nodded. 'Your wife's not here?' Shook. 'You know all about it. But I've seen her sort.'

'Why don't you like her?'

The woman looked up, sharply, almost, he thought, ironically at the naive question, barely disguising a sneer, but not immediately answering.

'I know her sort.'

'You mean,' said Fisher, 'that you're not judging her for anything she's actually said or done, but that she reminds you of some people whom you consider disreputable, and you therefore think she's something of that nature.'

Mrs Hollies considered. She'd understood the question and grinned wickedly at Fisher's impudent formality.

'Was she nuzzling up to you behind that hut? On the sands? Rubbing her titties on your arm?'

'Were you?' he asked, sharp.

She blushed, suddenly, redly, so that he felt ashamed, degraded.

'I'd had one or two, but I didn't go that far

181

wrong,' she said. Her voice was humorous, but he could not forget the little hot face. Malice with modesty. 'I'm not saying I didn't enjoy walking along clinging to a handsome young fellow.'

'You flatter me.'

'No, fair's fair. And I could give you a better time than that little bit. But I know what you'd fancy. I don't blame you.'

'What would you say if I told you, Mrs Hollies, you surprised me?'

'Not a word.'

She held the fruit bag out again, and neatly took the core from his fingers to drop into a litter-box. Now she sat quite composed, enjoying herself.

'You don't mind my talking to you like this, do you?'

'No.'

'Come on, then.' She laughed, richly in her throat.

'I thought you were a quiet little woman, under your husband's thumb, so that you did surprise me last night.'

Mrs Hollies returned to her eating as if she needed time and mastication to deal with his statements. She finished another elaborate biscuit sandwich.

'I like you, Mr Fisher. Not only in that way. There's something about you I don't always get. I'd give you a pound to a penny on what my Jack'd say or do at any time. But not you. What are you laughing at?'

'Something you said last night.'

'What?'

'Nothing'.

'About Jack?' She fiddled again in a receptacle for a knife and a fruit tart. 'I said he'd want his sex, didn't I? And you wonder if we had it. That's what you want to know, isn't it?'

'No. As a matter of fact . . .'

'Well, we did. I don't mind telling you. It's a natural thing, and I don't see why I should keep it secret. We enjoyed it.'

'I see.' Fisher looked away. Nearly naked sunbathers trotted or sprawled round him.

'You think I'm dirty to tell you. You wouldn't let on to me, would you?'

'No. I don't think I would.'

'Not with your wife, even? I don't mean that Sandra.'

'No.'

'Well,' she said, blowing sugar-grains from her lips, 'we're all made different. Wouldn't do if we were all alike would it?' Her voice had changed; she had read his warning signal and prepared for generalities. She chatted about her home, its value, its deficiencies; she recalled the terrace in Woolwich where she'd been brought up; she sketched her father's skill, her mother's compulsion to work.

Interesting as he found this, he guessed that she talked to win back favour, to excuse a moral lapse. He examined her. A few years back she'd have been pretty, but now she was thin, thinly

183

lined, her bosom too large for the small, lively body. Her slender legs were well shaped, hairless, lightly tanned, those of a young woman. He could have stroked them. She recalled a rabbit she'd kept in a back-garden hutch, and a cat. Her neck stretched stringy, a tense bundle of nerves. Her fingers scraped skin off the air.

Humming, nodding, he encouraged her reminiscence.

When her husband returned, exactly on time, she became, quiet, immersed in preparation of his meal. Embarrassed Fisher excused himself, wasted time in an expensive fish restaurant where the silver knives and forks were heavy and the waitresses skipped in black frocks and lace caps. Free again, he sat on a bench in the street, picking up scraps of conversation.

Thursday, now he strolled towards the Methodist Church, where the iron gates were padlocked, and posters of scragribbed refugees faded in the sunshine. Thursday.

When he was on holiday as a boy the first three days had passed slowly, but by Thursday time flew. Friday flashed a nothing. One brought presents; one ventured into the sea, but home, wash-day, errands reestablished themselves in the mind.

Thursday, of a week at Bealthorpe, on the North Sea. Thursday on the German Ocean.

Ye cannot serve God and Mammon (Matt. 6,24). He served neither. A time-server. A person of no consequence.

He remembered Meg shouting at him, 'Don't you believe anything?' Round them the Yorkshire valleys and a crisscross of fields, small mills on the rivers, the ruins of railway tracks and beyond the bald mountains, hunched and ugly, scowling in the summer sun, the moors. The two of them sat, he remembered, under a fantastic pile of rocks, like pillars of grey toffee, curiously smooth amongst the grass, the tall willow-herb, the sycamore bushes that would soon be trees, tired, angry with each other because they'd clambered up a steep road, and kicked about a disused quarry and now at midday were miles from a drink. They'd sat, eating dry sandwiches, swatting at flies, searching for a subject to quarrel over. Money. They were not paying enough for their keep, she claimed.

'I wouldn't put you up for that. Clean linen – Dinner. You kicking your muddy feet round the carpets.'

'Mrs Knight looks well on it.'

'That's all you think about.'

'No. Their small holding will provide a living. This will spread the jam.'

They argued prices. Supermarkets charged here no less than those in London. Tourists flashed their loose coin and spread inflation, Meg argued. Fisher knew she didn't care. Just as she'd please Mrs Knight by a townswoman's expected raptures over the cade lamb, she'd get her own back on a husband who'd forgotten the map, who'd delivered her to this dust-dry hill top.

'Why don't you enjoy your holiday,' he asked, 'and forget other people?'

'It hits you in the face.'

'It hits you.'

He moodily lobbed three stones at the rock tower, hating the clang, the ricochet or the failure to reach target. Nobody else had climbed; they seemed alone in a dry stream-bed, chewing unpalatable bread and foreign apples.

'You're probably right,' he said pacifically.

'I don't like to see people cheated.'

'My impression is that Mrs Knight's got her head screwed on. She knows what people will pay, what will fetch 'em in.'

'We're exploiting her.'

So she blurted away at him, accusing him of hypocrisy, a Britisher living at the expense of sweated labour, short life-expectancy, misery, plague. As he lay back in the brightness of the sky, springy grass under the hands clasped behind his head, he could barely believe she was serious. Yet she seemed so. Before long he feared she'd throw her scone at him, but he became drowsy, immune to the attack, not answering.

In the end, he'd reached out, touched her bare knee, expecting a repulse. He pushed, stroking up the smooth warmth of her thigh as she opened to him.

'That's all you believe in,' she said.

'Better than nothing.

She answered his love there on the quiet top

of the world, powerfully submissive under him, and then sat wide-eyed, sun-drunk, fulfilled, her head against his pack.

'It hot,' she hummed.

'Don't blame me for that.'

'I shan't argue.'

She laid herself flat, primly, her skirt smoothed down now, blouse fastened, fell asleep, quiet, beautiful, no harshness, no plangency, naturally in the grass. She had discovered one belief he thought. That claim was shameful, but her temper, her principles had withered, flowered themselves out of existence.

Grass-stalk between teeth, he watched the birds swoop about the rocks, and the hints of mist smudge the far surface of the valley, and his wife asleep, red-bright hair heavy over her hand.

CHAPTER 10

He posted his card to Meg, then fetched his car out for the first time this week.

It was four o'clock now and he'd little joy as he ran out of the town into the flat countryside along a road that seemed composed of sandy dust. Why he bothered he did not know. He stopped by a house, built out on its own, surrounded by sheds, hen-coops, while in the untended square of ground in front a broken boat lay, massive, but holed, paintwork grubbily overlaid with pale dirt. Nobody moved in the place; no dog barked, cat slunk. He wound the window down to brood on this dump.

The house which might have been lifted from an industrial town had at one time been daubed white, but now the paint peeled from the bricks as from the woodwork of the sashwindows, the dull green doors, the drainpipes.

Still nobody moved, as the sun's brightness emphasised the shabby exterior, the litter, the trodden grass, the ruts. Fisher leaned out for relief, patted the hot metal of his car. On this Thursday he did not feel depression, merely inertia, a lack of determination. He had decided, in a rush, to spend a week at the seaside, the kind of holiday he'd not known since he was a boy, and here he lounged, bored, staring at a pile of old wood, slightly distracted by a buzzing by his head. That was all he could expect; he'd deserved it.

He pulled himself up short.

A week or two back he had walked out on his wife. After a series of nightly quarrels, none serious taken singly, but indulged in by both with an energy that now seemed mad, he'd said, steadying his voice,

'The best thing I can do is leave you to it.'

He wondered now in what sense he'd meant that. The words were clearly enunciated, in a moderate tone, demanding and deploying reason, and yet he had not designed them seriously, to be answered. The sentence merely attacked his wife from a new direction, suggesting that he, unlike her, was willing to discuss their dilemma, act with an eye to the advantage of both. Thus, put in her place, her shouts and insults, her flounces and swearing, tantrums, gestures were shown for what they were, the infantile behaviour of an unbalanced woman.

'You go, then.'

'I'm serious, Meg.'

'What the bloody hell d'you think I am?'

He'd sat down, furious but determined to speak coldly. He'd considered the pattern in the carpet by his shoes, crossed his legs, intertwined his fingers round his knees before looking at her.

'I mean what I say, Meg.'

'Do it, then.'

'You realise just what this will mean, don't you?'

As he'd spoken, he knew immediately that he'd not a notion of the significance of this.

'What's it matter?' she'd asked.

'Do you want me to leave you?'

'You know best. You always do.'

He'd noticed that her voice was as controlled as his, as cool, though her mouth seemed tightly held, almost frozen.

'I'm asking you a question', he'd said. 'Do you want me to clear out?'

'Make your own mind up.'

The quarrel appeared to be petering out but as he'd sat a fiercer anger had flared, perhaps at his own ineptitude, perhaps at Meg's casual disregard as she touched her nose in front of a mirror.

'Tomorrow,' he'd said. The word barely lobbed out.

'What?' She continued her beauty treatment.

'I'm going.' His breath was constricted as if his chest had suddenly shrunk. The whole centre of his being seemed concentrated above his mouth, behind his nose, in a thick snot of ignorance.

'Good riddance,' she'd said. Childishly. And sat down.

He'd jumped, leapt from the room, slamming the door shut. He slept in the guest room, drove at nine o'clock across to the university where he'd found Bill Price-Jones already in his lab, and demanded room in his flat. Price-Jones, pulling faces stroking his beard, asked Fisher if he was doing right.

'How in bloody hell do I know?'

'I can provide you with a bunk and a sitting room. Does it make sense, though? Meg's your wife. I'm not married.'

Bill's thin voice, disconnected sentences, hurt.

'I want to come,' he'd said.

'Please yourself.'

Price-Jones sighed, returned to his page of mathematics, pushing his spectacles up. Fisher, deserted, sidled from the room, stood in the corridor before the heavy door of the laboratory, under the neat gold lettering, Dr W. A. C. Price-Jones, before pushing off to fidget in the library over a book he could not bring himself to understand. Now he was committed, had announced his decision, if Bill had not already forgotten it under a welter of integral scrolls.

Now here, today, in front of this hutch of a house he reported progress to himself. In spite of the sun, mist seemed to seep from the land so that distant objects over the flat earth were blurred. He had the apartment to himself, for Bill was away at a scientific congress in Austria, but he had not stayed there, had come out on instinct to this razmataz of a place. But when, against likelihood, he'd run up against David Vernon on the first Sunday, he'd seen luck turn his way, his matrimonial problems settle. Then suspiciously he'd

191

dismissed coincidence; Vernon had ferreted him out, had followed. He dismissed that summarily; whatever Vernon's arts he'd not hypnotised his son-in-law into the pub. Fisher, in his car, tapping the door panel, enjoyed the notion. Thought-transference. Vernon, veins in forehead knotted with concentration, sweat dripping in, squeezing out the order over the resistant air, into the reluctant brain telepathically compelling him to go in.

A young man had come from the back of the house to stare suspiciously. Fisher raised a hand, so that the other, screwing his eyes, dawdled over.

'You all right?'

Fisher thanked him.

'Not broken down, nor nothing?'

Greasy hair, not long, but combed back into swathes. Overalls, with three cheap biros in the breast-pocket. A heavy pair of unpolished army boots.

Fisher, at ease, began to question the man, who, with only a token of unwillingness, seemed glad of the company. Well, no, he didn't live here; it was his dad's house. No, not his own, rented. His dad had worked on the roads and the county council had provided him with the place, allowing him to keep it on his retirement. No, the road menders worked in gangs, nowadays, bounced out from the towns in lorries. Nobody would want to live in a dead-and-alive hole like this, would they? He was redundant, a month ago, but had another job laid on, starting next week, because his dad had had him apprenticed. He lived in Leicester, and he'd go back on Sat'day.

Fisher remarked on the quietness.

'My dad don't hardly speak since me mam died. Not half a dozen words from morning till night. Healthy, apart from rheumatism; can look after himself; strong as a horse at sixty-six, but surely, says nowt, don't shave, lets the clothes rot on his back bit by bit.

'Does he get bread deliveries, meat, and the like? Groceries?'

'No. Not exactly. He shops once a week. There's a bus as comes past. You'd be surprised what he puts up with. He can eat bread as stale and as hard as stones.'

'Not much of a life.'

'None at all, if y'ask me.'

'He's independent, I suppose.'

'Independent my bollocks. What good's that? I'd sooner enjoy myself, get a bit of pleasure, cock my leg over a bit o'th'other any day than have y'r independence, or owt like it. He's a silly old man, obstinate, that's all. There's an old people's flat for him, for the asking, in the town.'

The man eyed Fisher's car professionally, nodding approval.

Above the sky stretched misty blue in the sun, faded, dusted with faint fog like the distant ground.

Fisher, sky-dazed head back, looked at the individual stockily at his side. Here, at it again, he'd met, questioned, made friendly contact with a stranger when he ought to have been at home on his knees to his wife.

'The trouble is,' the young man said, 'that people like my dad get used to this sort of hole, and think they like it. It's damp, it's miles from anywhere; I'd as sooner live in the middle of a turnip field. But he thinks it's what he wants.'

'As long as he's satisfied.'

'Ay, but it won't be long before he's a nuisance. Ill all winter. Heart attacks. Prostate. I've seen 'em. Then they have to haul 'em out, lug 'em into hospitals. Social workers running hither and thither wasting petrol.'

'What should happen?'

'At seventy, seventy-five they should put the lot together in homes, where they can be looked after. And then they could let places like this rot and crumble away.'

'Would you like it to happen to you?'

'At that age, I wouldn't mind.'

'You won't be popular.'

The young man wiped his chin hard with the palm of his left hand as if deciding whether or not Fisher was worth arguing with.

'I've seen old 'uns. They crack up. And in my dad's case it won't be long, I reckon. He was getting on when I was born. In his forties. And when he does get ill, I shall be expected to run up here and slave for him in every spare weekend I have.'

'Who'll expect it?'

'He will, for one.'

'And you?'

'I don't want to, I can tell you that.' He ran his fingers back through his hair, leaving it in different, no tidier hunks. 'I want a bit of pleasure out of my life. I work hard, and I'm entitled to it.'

'What's your pleasure?'

'Same as yours. Drink, woman, bit o' time on my back. I earn them.'

'Because your father apprenticed you to a good trade.'

'I'm not saying he's not a decent man. He is. But as soon as he starts, or his body starts to pack in, he should be looked after.'

'He's a human being.'

'What am I, then?'

'We'll all be old,' Fisher said.

'All the more reason for 'aving a fling while we can.'

A thumping on the window at the front of the house preceded pulling open of the plank door.

'Who it is, Kevin?' No one appeared yet at the first wide crack. 'Who is it?'

'A gentleman.'

'What gentleman?'

'One who's just passin'.' The young man mimed humorous exasperation. The door was pulled wider, with squeaking obstinacy.

'Shall I light a fire?'

The old man appeared, powerfully built, dirty

in ragged pullover. He'd been a somebody in his time, thrown his weight about, probably terrorised his lad. Now he stood, lines darkly deep into his face, a shy toothless grin like a beggar who knows his rights but expects no alms.

'Please yersen.'

'What d'you think?'

'Wouldn't bother, if it was just for me.'

The father flapped his arms, shrugged indoors, squealed the protesting door shut.

'You wouldn't think a fire'd be necessary on a hot day like this,' Kevin said, answering Fisher's unasked query. 'But in that hole, at night, it's as wet as if the sea came oozing up.'

The two talked on about builders, houses, damp-courses and inevitably motor cars. The younger seemed glad of company, unwilling to let Fisher free.

'Are you on holiday at Bealthorpe?' he asked in the end. 'I thought so. That's a sewer for you, now. Shops and stalls. They'd have the clothes off your back to pay for a fivepenny orange.'

'This is your holiday?' Fisher asked.

'It'll have to be. And I'll be glad to start work, I can tell you.'

'You're not fond of your father?'

The man stuck a finger noisily into his ear, poked roughly round, as if purging himself of Fisher's impertinence.

'How could you be?'

'He was a bully?'

'Ah. Bossed me about and my mother. Give us both a good hiding and think nothing of it.'

'You don't hold it against him?'

'Why should I? That was his way, and he followed it. When I was big enough, I got out, went off to Leicester.'

'But you came back?'

'He's my father, when all's said and done. He gets on my tits, and I've nothing to say to him. But we see each other. I buy him the odd thing or two and he provides me with a bed. Fair exchange. Suits us both. But I tell you, mister, I wouldn't chase over here, nor lose an hour's work, if I knew he was dying. We may be father and son, but they're names.' He looked at Fisher. 'You don't think that's right, do you?'

'Well.'

'It's what most folks do, given the chance, I'll tell you.'

'Would mean more on my tax bill.'

'You can afford that if you can afford this.' He punched the car affectionately. Fisher asked if he'd like a lift anywhere.

'No. I s'll go back in there. Smoking like chimneys, the two of us. Few cups of tea. Telly. Bloody life, in't it? He'll be making the fire, now he's asked. Roasting the legs off us trousers, and backs damp as fishes. And next Tuesday, I start again.'

'Tuesday?'

'Monday's a holiday. I've got a car round the back.'

'I see.'

Fisher drove off, disconsolate, down in the mouth. As the road turned to cross a dyke, he looked back at the house, a cube of blackness in a sunshine that looked rough as india-rubbings on a child's drawing. He was in no mind to fault the young man, who spoke out of his own depression perhaps, talked thus sullenly against a society that promised, proffered him nothing. Half an hour later as he repassed the place on his way to Bealthorpe, he noticed a twist of smoke from the chimney, and the door fast shut. The kettle would boil in the fag smoke, and they'd hack hunks of bread and margarine, and hump there, in dislike if not hate, each man of himself if not the other. Fisher slowed, resentfully, the world on his back.

The young man spoke without hesitation, because he'd thought it all out, put it into words, and now did not object to trying it out on a stranger. Everybody judges from the point of view of his own inadequacy. Now, warned by unemployment, Kevin did not want a blazing revenge on his father, did not show much resentment even, but merely wished to be rid of the responsibility and, unusually, was honest enough to say so. Perhaps the father stood formidably yet in his age and weakness, a giant in complaint.

A dog scuttered across the road so that Fisher realised he was paying little attention to his driving. A brand-new bus forced him into the side while windowsful of children waved, jeered, cheered.

He ought to go back to Meg. A prodigal.

Immediately, with a lump of joy, he remembered a talk his father had delivered at the Sunday bible-class. This had been unusual for though Arthur Fisher was only too willing to hand round his opinions or snippets of knowledge, he never spoke formally at meetings. Perhaps he was not asked. On this occasion he had been invited to give five minutes on the parable of the prodigal son. This worried the old man: he tried to talk to Edwin, to his wife, even to Tina about it, but they brushed him off. The children made it clear that they did homework without assistance, so should he. So Arthur thumbed the concordances, trudged to the library, gave a strict account to his family of the way of scholarship. Elsie, much occupied, wished out loud three times a day, double-measure Sunday, that he'd never embarked on the project.

Fisher went to hear the result.

The old man spoke nervously, with a kind of special delivery which led to the occasional dropped h or grammatical indiscretion. Secondly, there was no attempt to make the topic palatable; all was delivered without fervour in a choked voice. But what impressed the boy was his father's line. Arthur missed much that was obvious, misread once or twice, but stressed the clause, 'But when he was yet a great way off.' The father must have been waiting, on the look-out. Fisher had not thought of that himself, hadn't noticed. What commentary or sermon Arthur had picked it from he did not know, for he was not willing to ascribe originality to the old chap, but he was shaken.

'How did your dad get on?' Elsie had asked.

'Not too bad. He made a very good point.'

'Only one?'

'That I hadn't thought of.' The young Fisher had expounded.

'And he didn't make a fool of himself?'

Elsie must have passed the comment on, for in midweek, Arthur had given his son half-a-crown 'to go the to pictures.' Both knew what it meant, though neither put it into words.

The memory whirled like the dust from the car wheels, settling gently after a time. He could not deceive himself with the sentimental notion that Meg was on the watch, in love, for his return, because he did not believe it. But she had sent a card. He'd certainly visit her as soon as he was back.

That brought no comfort, only a further memory and its small dust storm.

Once, before Donald was born, while they still lived in London, Meg had forgotten to call in at the post-office for stamps so that he could catch the evening's post with important applications for jobs. Fisher had to chase round the neighbours interrupting tea and television. Moreover, when he'd returned, successfully, he found she'd burnt the meat; it was not exactly uneatable, but he found no pleasure in the black strips.

They sat to it.

Furious, he determined to say nothing. When she was angry or disturbed, she sniffed, strongly, unbecomingly, like a snuff-taker, goading him. He hacked at the blackened steak, rereading the same short item in 'The Times', not, understanding a word, stabbing the lines with his eyes. He could not eat, and pushed a large half of the course with unnecessary clatter to the side of his plate. Meg, sniffing, finished hers, cleared the dishes.

'I haven't made a pudding,' she said. 'I thought you might like an apple. Or I could open a tin of fruit.'

She spoke apologetically.

'Don't bother,' he said, waving, crackling his newspaper about.

'Will you have an apple? Or a banana?'

'In time.'

She cleared the table round him without his help, moved to the kitchen and began washing up. When he joined, her, she seemed relaxed, sniffing no longer, making less fuss about the chore than usual. He took the tea-towel. She spoke.

'I'm thinking of joining an evening class.'

Immersed in his angry broth-boil of thoughts he did not hear.

'I beg your pardon.' Superior.

'I'm thinking of joining an evening class.'

'Oh, yes. In cookery?'

He continued placidly drying the knives and forks. Very deliberately, Meg took her hands from the bowl, shook them free of surplus drops, and picked a dinner-plate from the drying rack. This she held between her palms as she turned to face him. He forced himself not to look. She smashed the plate to the tiled floor where it exploded; she waited a moment, then walked from the room. Shaking with rage, but pleased to have wrung this tantrum from her, he took the brush and dustpan, cleared the floor, finished the dishes, tidied around. Satisfied he retired to the living-room. No wife. He began to read.

For perhaps half an hour he struggled with an article on 'Junior Drama in a Rural Comprehensive School', when he began to see sense. Meg taught part-time now and had done a morning's work in the classroom, shopped, forgotten his stamps, done the washing before he'd arrived with his bellyaching. He forgot things; it did not matter a tinker's damn whether or not he dispatched his applications tonight, she snuffed air into her nose because she couldn't bring herself to confide in him; burnt or not, her meal was preferable to committee stew.

Where was she now?

Mild irritation spilt with the question. He made himself smile as he walked upstairs. She had switched off all the lights.

Meg lay in bed, the sheets pulled up to her face, only a small patch of bright hair splashed on the pillow. Her clothes, as usual, were nearly folded or hung in the wardrobe.

He, in the light from the passage outside, put a hand to her shoulder.

'Would you like a cup of coffee, Meg?'

She stirred.

'A delicious cup of coffee.'

She opened her eyes so that he thought she would smile. Suddenly she buried her face under the clothes she dragged upwards. Watching, weighing prospects he tried again. Very gently he smoothed the sheets above her.

'I'm very sorry, Meg,' he said. 'I've acted like a boor.'

As he said it, he wasn't convinced he pronounced the word properly, but he waited for some re-action. When she did not move, he laid his hand more heavily on her shoulder and said.

'I'm very sorry, Meg. I really am. I shouldn't have behaved like that.'

Her father had taken him aside just before the wedding to tell him, 'Never sleep on a quarrel, Edwin. Apologise, even if you think you're in the right. That's good advice now.' Fisher had been surprised at the approach. For all Vernon's clever-ness, and he did not question that, there was about the man a kind of naiveté, a touch of parson's flatulence, a belief that life could be summarised, and helpfully, in Christmas cracker apophthegms. Perhaps it could, or at least perhaps these bits of old wifery did no more harm than most advice. If Fisher warred with Meg, and that was almost inevitable, then he'd withdraw when it suited him, not tie himself to this rule-of-thumb simplicity.

Nothing.

He stared down, shifted his feet.

'Would you let me get you a cup of coffee, love? It'll do you good. To show you I'm sorry. Would you drink it for me?' He should have made the bloody thing and stirred it by her ear. 'Please.'

Not a movement. It was marvellous she could keep so still.

He would not be irritated. Again he placed his hand on her, stroking her back.

'I'm sorry, Meg. I am.'

He wasted his time. Again he straightened the edge of the sheet, and left her. It took three days for the quarrel to heal. At breakfast next morning, she'd ignored him in bed, she did not speak, but when he returned for the evening meal she'd become monosyllabic. By the weekend, they spoke normally, enjoyed a theatre visit, grum and gruff Ibsen once more, made love. Meg had never mentioned the incident again, but he felt the breach, feared it. If they had to row, he preferred her tongue lashing, or her fists.

That had not been the only incidence of such behaviour, and he wondered if the withdrawal was her only way to sanity; she punished him by leaving herself fallow. The explanation made no sense, but neither did her conduct. He could never tell when a remark of his would provoke turmoil, or start laughter.

Oddly, he thought as he drove, he'd never concluded that she was in any way deeply disturbed, insane. These were the kicks of a free woman, a selfish woman, at marriage. Shackled.

Then why had she married him?

On the rebound from Malcolm and her father she'd chosen him because he was both cleverer and livelier, yet did not make limiting demands on her. He seemed to want her for herself, not for some different person she could with care be shaped into. On artistic matters he had ideas, could be explicit about them, but he approved her, daily living, wildness and all, for what she was. Whether that had been a suitable beginning to a successful marriage he now doubted, but he realised the attraction to Meg at the time.

She had not been a virgin, but was close about her boyfriends. He never, for that matter, knew whether she'd had sex with Malcolm; certainly she had begged Fisher to leave her untouched until they were married. He'd argue, in a desperate way with her, out of jealousy, perhaps, so that she'd collapse into tears, accuse him of not loving her. On his part he was guiltily ending an affair with a woman nearly ten years older than himself, a widow who expected to become his wife, though she claimed she'd refuse him. He did not give her the chance, ignored her letters, phone-calls, prosaic heartbroken shrieks he did not understand. Three months after his wedding to Meg, Thelma had married again, a suitably rich man of her own age, had moved from her poky flat into a magnificent Old Rectory in a village ten miles out and had given birth to two sons. He had no dealings with her, but saw her occasionally at concerts where she seemed unchanged, as energetic and bogus as when she tiptoed stark naked about her flat gesturing, posturing, hands like a ballet-dancer, sallow and athletic. Now she smiled sadly at him and said, 'Good evening,' but did not introduce her husband. She'd not been without brains, but felt she must convey herself through her body, think with breasts and vulva.

He'd acted badly, and considered that the ditching of this decent *puppenfee* was no real foundation for a marriage. When he'd confessed to Meg, she shrank, as if frightened at the confession, or perhaps dreading that she needed to reciprocate, but ended by saying brusquely,

'Don't boast, Eddie. It doesn't suit your style.'

An answer learnt from father.

'I'm sorry.'

'And don't stand there so miserably. It's nothing to be ashamed of. I don't mind.'

'I wish you did.'

'That's stupid. What you were up to before I knew you is your own affair.'

'I'm jealous when I think about you with other men.'

'Why?' Her word was no stronger than a mere question; perhaps she saw advantage for herself.

'I hate to think how well they knew you, and of all the things you did together that I can't share.'

'It means nothing. I never think about them.'

He did not believe that, because he remembered his first girl at the university and how they'd walked hand in hand, slid in winter across the frozen ice of the pond. Probably if he met her now he'd find nothing of interest, but she was embedded into his memory, an imposing monument, casting a huge shadow, still.

Meg would smile, finger her lips, and say,

'One must be grown-up about this, darling.'

'I'm not, if grown-up means pushing it all out of my system.'

'I know that.'

'But, Meg,' he said, 'when we've been married ten years, will you want to forget the first?'

'Very likely. We shan't need it?'

'I shall.'

'We shall be leading a pretty poor life, dearest, if we need to remember all that fumbling and stupidity.'

'They were great times,' he said. She screwed up her eyes, as in pain, nodded, nodded.

He dawdled so long on his return journey, stopping twice without consulting his watch just to sit in the idleness of late afternoon, that when he returned the other guests were already in the dining room and the clash of china, pot, spoons told they had begun. As angry as his father at himself, he rinsed hands, raced downstairs and sat downcast over his soup-plate. The rest seemed excessively noisy, boasting of silly exploits. He could not understand this rage, which almost prevented his chewing, cut short his smile at the verse Tony Smith sang for them all in tune, each word clear, between main course and pudding.

At the end of the meal, Hollies leaned across.

'Shall we have the pleasure of your company this evening, Mr Fisher?'

He waited so long in reply that the answer appeared an insult.

'Where are you going?'

'Well, squire?' Hollies bawled across at Terry Smith. 'What's the venue?'

'I don't know.' Smith blushed, looked for help to his wife.

'He asks, you see,' Lena Hollies said. 'He consults Sandra first.'

Now Sandra blushed; it embarrassed Fisher to see the fair skins flush as the children smiled and wriggled good naturedly.

'Tell you later,' Smith muttered.

Fisher completed his meal, rushed upstairs, threw off his jacket and lay on the bed. Outside in the street, the noisy family next door performed antics round their car. Though they talked nineteen to the dozen, Fisher could not make out what their evening's destination was. It seemed to matter.

A tap on his door interrupted the exercise. Fisher stood, straightened the coverlet, resumed his jacket. Sandra. He invited her in.

'What a lovely room,' she said.

He pointed her to a chair, where she sat, knees together, hands clasped, evening sun from behind throwing up a halo of light round her fair head.

'Are you going with them, tonight?' she asked. 'The Hollies?'

'Yes. He drinks such a lot. Terry's been off all day today, running to the lavatory. He doesn't usually have . . . Well, you know.' She smiled up, in innocence.

'What do you suggest?' he asked.

'I wouldn't mind going for a drink, but we'll have to come out early, I mean.'

'We did so. Last night.'

Again the fair skin reddened, deeply; her eyes watered.

'Terry, I mean.'

'You can always say that an hour's long enough, that you've got to get back to the children.'

'Yes. That's what I told him.' Grateful. He would have liked to have walked across, touched her, stroked, say, along her collar-bone easily, without guilt.

'He thinks that's not manly?' he said.

'You know what men are.'

'I know what I am.' She flushed again. 'When I've had enough, I come out.' She nodded, miserably. 'I'll leave with you. I've got letters to write.'

'Will you?'

She stood so that her hands seemed to flutter towards him. He took one and it struck chill, while the hard nails, dug into his palm. They stood thus for a time, as it were, in secret with the door closed between them and the rest of the world. She made no move towards him, did not lean on him, merely kept her place with her hands coldly in his and an expression of frozen pleasure on her face.

'I like this,' he said, nodding towards her hand. She did not answer. 'Very beautiful.'

Still she did not speak. Two people, intent on the sound of breathing. From the street outside a clatter, then a shriek. 'They're enjoying themselves. Let's look.'

Still holding her, he moved to the window.

A young man and his wife laughed as an old lady edged herself heavily into the back seat of the car.

'Grandma's in,' Fisher said.

'They're funny. They've three cars, but they all go off together in one of them every day.'

'How many are there?'

'The old lady, that married couple, another young man, and a girl, and then a child.'

'All related?'

'I don't know.' They stood, hand in hand, behind the lace curtains. On the other side of the road he noticed the fair girls Carol and Tricia strolling, rather heavy in frocks, thumping the pavements. He'd not seen them before in the vicinity.

'All the world's out for a constitutional.' He let go of her, saddened and sat down. She edged the lace curtain into neatness before she arranged a time of meeting, left to help Terry get the boys to sleep.

They spent an hour and a quarter noisily at the pub and when the Smiths rose with Fisher, Mrs Hollies joined them.

'I've had enough,' she said. 'Jack can look after himself.'

'I can,' Hollies shouted 'Why, it's not dark-hour yet.'

The Smiths went to their room, Lena Hollies to the television lounge, and Fisher to his letters. He slipped on a light mac, set out to post them. Immediately after he'd closed the front door, it was opened, and Mrs Hollies asked if she could join him.

'Only going to the end of the road.'

'I'll get my coat.'

She came out in a short, smart coat of red wool, and a tam o'-shanter. He posted his letters, asked,

'Do you want to go any further?'

'I like a walk.'

'Which way, then?'

'Not down to the sea. I've had enough.'

'I'm not ambitious', he said. 'Not initiative. Never tried the other way.'

They walked the length of three streets, crossed a main road, and branched off past a children's play park, locked now, through a hedge and into flat sandy fields. The place lay uninviting, with the sprawl of the town behind and the useless, scrubby grass in front.

'Not very attractive,' he said.

'Somewhere to walk. That's the idea, isn't it?'

They paced half a mile, chanced a sandy footpath which led them back to within a hundred yards of their digs.

'That was luck,' Lena enthused.

'One could hardly go wrong.'

'Yes, but not so near. Might have been made for us.'

When they entered, they could hear television from the lounge. Fisher said he'd turn in. Lena, quiet fiddling with the scarlet coat followed him upstairs.

'You've got a nice, flat little bottom,' she said.

'Thanks.'

'I've too much round there.' She smoothed her frock tight round her buttocks. 'Too much beer and bacon.' She laughed, unattractively. 'Is it ten o'clock yet?'

'Quarter to.'

'He won't be back for an hour. I hope he's quiet, for the sake of those children.'

'I didn't hear a sound last night.'

'Good job.' She stood looking at him, red coat swinging on her arm, eyes black in the corridor's half darkness. 'You don't like me, do you?'

Fisher considered.

'Yes,' he said. 'I do, as a matter of fact.'

She screwed her mouth into a sour grimace so that he suspected she was about to parody his voice, but when she spoke again, she'd recovered.

'Are you enjoying your holiday?' she asked.

'I think so. Aren't you?'

Now she scratched her belly loudly through her frock, unaware of the action, caught up in some spasm, convulsion of thought which demanded her whole attention, rounded her mouth to a whistle.

'It'll soon be over,' she said. 'Either way.'

She folded her coat more neatly over her arm, moved towards her bedroom door, and wished him goodnight, near tears, he guessed. If he could have touched her without committing himself he would have pulled her into his arms, but again she was unattractive. Advantage rarely comes of it.

He took a book downstairs to the television set.

CHAPTER 11

On Friday, the last full day, Fisher decided to go inland to Lincoln.

The weather was slightly less settled, with cloud about and the glass dropping. He did not hurry himself, started late, and made for the south side of the town, where he parked by the Brayford Pool, and standing on a railway bridge tried to recall pictures of the cathedral he'd seen, sketched from here when the town was rural, reedy and the swans white. De Wint had lived here, he thought, had doubtless painted that massive confection of a cathedral on its hill, in its sky, over the flat town when the flatness was pretty and white and noiseless. He watched a dredger clearing the pool, its grab leaping from the water with a few rusty lengths of dripping iron. A group of three children dodged back each time from the heavy sprinkle of filthy water as the crane swung towards its accompanying, flat-bottomed barge. They squealed at the driver in his cabin, but he took no notice, could not hear them perhaps.

Past traffic lights, a chapel, shops with television sets or castles of cornflake packets he moved to

Steep Hill, the Norman house, climbing steadily in shafts of sunlight. He smelt the second-hand books in the windows and eyed copper kettles and an early Victorian desk. Other tourists moved round him, mostly young people with enough wind to laugh or chide as they mounted the slope. An elderly couple stood to catch their breath, the man wiping his brow with a large handkerchief, his wife perfectly composed her arm through his. He smiled at Fisher, blew a comical sigh, said,

> And labour up the heavenly hill
> With weary feet and slow.

Fisher knew joy then, a minute prod of delight so that he strode vigorously away from the pair, not to spoil the pleasure. Ramming his feet down he made forty or fifty yards in a burst, and when he turned the old people had still not moved, stood there like rocks as a tide of children, in cheerful chaos, swilled round them. Fisher waved, but they took no notice. That was right.

At the hill-top he watched a small procession of slow cars before moving through the gate into the grounds. The pottering vehicles, with anxious drivers, passengers' eyes glazing for space to park, seemed medieval to him, reduced to handcart speed but full of dirty energy, ill-temper, rough words. He dismissed the conceit, turned his back on what seemed now an unbroken line at a standstill. Ulcers and vacuum flasks, know-all wives, bored children; he turned his back on them all, faced God's house.

Here all teemed lively with visitors.

Bright frocks and voices in the sunshine under the heaviness of the building which from below seemed to float but now oppressed the hill with its weight. The stone was yellow, a clay-daub colour, where it was not black, unpalatable. He stepped round, among the crowd, and through the door, from gothic to classical in a step as the thick wood swung balanced shut. Into the nave, and there he stopped, neck bent, under the height which dwarfed the clacking figures below. He nodded to himself, satisfied, in a aisle, and eyed the colours of stained-glass splashed onto stonework, dark reds, Victorian purples, pompous and self-admiringly religious. But the pillars stood deeply coloured, not with a thickness of enamel but as if the darkened sunlight had penetrated them to the heart.

Fisher admired two boys and their mother on their knees at brass-rubbing, the whole attention engaged as they fitted one square to the next, unspeaking, workmanlike. He indulged in his usual brief fantasy; he and a pseudo-Donald at such a job, replacing a pane, clearing the garden of rubbish, painting the garage. Together. Father and son. It meant nothing now, was a mere habit of thought, did not even smart. The poor little devil lived a miserable two years, three times in hospital; these lads here were sturdy, could throw off a buffet or two. But Donny sometimes opened his eyes, green as Meg's, wide with intelligence, to look you over, you thought, get you taped. Fisher wished he knew what prayer was, so that he could shove a word or two up towards God in this huge place. What would he pray for? Another son? Donald's immortal safety? Meg back? His own concerns? God knows, that is, doesn't know. The great bands of vulgar colour, cream-thick, lavish purple, washed the nave, humanised the godly height, the austere majesty of wall and pillar. 'God bless Meg.' Fisher said, aloud, in a small voice. Nobody noticed; children looked up and tripped round as parents nosed the guide-book. St Hugh. Bishop Grosseteste. Solemn men in black kept an eye as Fisher purchased a guide book in the Great Transept. God bless Meg, whoever she is. He looked at a bishop's statue, a learned, holy man, in a fantasy of clothes and vows and postures. Thou also art that. Margaret Adeline Savile Vernon, now Fisher, soon, soon like the glass, without pattern, flung into a glory of haphazard light. Slowly he worked round towards the choir, his eye narrowing at the little tablet to Lincoln's most gifted son, William Byrd. He rated a few square inches of space and a bloody marvel he got that. Jesus wept.

A young woman rattled a push-chair and baby the step or two down from the choir, at home in her anorak, frowning, worried, un-impressed. Now Fisher stood back to the high altar, facing the organ, among the seats of dark wood. Suddenly he knew depression at his own inadequacy; this forest of carving, of man's inventive craft should have lifted him, inspirited his morning, but instead he felt like a dog in an auctioneers' store-room. Piles of furniture, black ugly wood, towering above him, black as burnt toast, crowded him, lost its delicate outline, its balance, its subtlety of work. He, myopic, dyspeptic, stared down the building, turned, escaped, glad to get back to light, to the width of the altar, the bright morning. Church dignitaries would flaunt themselves on those chairs, prelates, voting to award Byrd's genius its tiny lozenge of commemoration. He shied away now from some wooden sculptures.

Meg had never had time for places like this.

Her eye remarked neither the beauty nor the power. In Winchester she'd stood, whispered mulishly, goading him,

'This is built to God who doesn't exist.'

'It's beautiful.'

'It's a foolish waste.'

'But would men have planned it and built it without the idea of God?'

'More fools they.'

She'd flounced off, in a velvet, wine-red cloak, he remembered, and taunting, denying Jehovah in His tabernacle. He'd loved her for that, even though he suspected that her objections sprang from temporary discomfort or disappointment rather then deeply-held principle. He'd followed her, as she brandished her guide-book in scorn.

'It's a pleasure to get back into the open air,' she'd announced.

'Don't be mean.' He had to stand up to her. 'That's a great achievement of mankind.'

She nodded.

'I suppose it is. And a waste.'

'"Tax not the royal saint with vain expense,"' Fisher quoted.

'Shut up.' She gulped as if she were insulted, revolted by the building. That in itself was a kind of compliment. She did not hate by halves.

He'd never been certain of Meg's reaction; cat-like, she pleased herself, arrogantly without exertion. If she were here now, she might clip round the place in ten minutes, dismissing it all, while at another time she'd spend an hour over some detail of carving, borrowing a biro and torn envelope from his jacket-pocket to make an ungainly sketch. She could not draw; she knew it, but claimed that the exercise served to deepen her memory.

Fisher, half-comforted now, casting his eye at random as he made up his mind whether to sit when he reached the west end, and then work round the building again, shuffled to the tomb of Little St Hugh. He stood at the back of half-a-dozen others, whose shoulders, necks, heads conveyed nothing to him except for a scent of toilet soap. When they moved on, he read the notice which apologised to the Jews for abominable progroms. It surprised him. Sucking his fingernail, he wondered what anti-Semites had built this cathedral? A negro with a white stiff collar joined him to read, unmoved.

> She went up to the Jew's wife's door,
> And knocked at the ring.

He remembered the death of Donald.

Half-distracted he'd taken a tutorial group that afternoon in which one young man had argued against all restriction in schools. Two more had disagreed so that by the end of the hour the three had been near violence. He seemed cut off, ignoring the wide-open eyes of the girls, incapable of protracted thought, waiting for 3.50 when he'd close his doors and drive headlong for the hospital where Meg had been all day. The flurry of words, the spilling of text-book jargon, the spattering of non-supporting circumstance, even the clenched fists and the raised voices made no impact. It is true he spoke; perhaps his usual sceptical approach to their dubious or misread evidence could be seen, but in reality he concentrated, was concentrated, on a sentence his wife had 'phoned him at one-thirty. 'There's no hope. He'll die in a few hours.'

It was impossible that she had spoken that so flatly. Immediately he'd said he'd drive down, but she'd prevented it. He must take his class, and then he could please himself.

'Did they say . . . say . . . ?' He'd gabbled.

'What?'

'When?'

'Did they say when he'd die?' The calm voice, clear as unruffled water, spoke his mind.

'Yes. Any time. Any time?'

'Shall I come, Meg? I can easily . . .'

'No.'

It was as if she must suffer this for herself. When a fortnight ago, Donald had first been ill, with a cold it seemed, she'd been angry, flustered, flying round, bullying, energetic. She'd reprimanded the doctor who'd left them until last on his round because he lived close; she'd cancelled a visit to the film-society saying she could not leave the child. Fisher had argued. Donny had caught another chill; that was all. Now, with hindsight, she'd acted correctly, set about this last fight early, judged its seriousness with exactitude. She'd rushed, hysterically about, cried easily, been red with temper, neglecting everything but the boy with his snuffling nose, bubbling lungs, rising six, ten, a dozen times in the night to peer anxiously into the cot. Eyes down, hair neglected, she'd rushed, routed, at a desperate double, cruel, quarrelsome, making the world ache for what she suffered. For a boy with a cold, she martyred herself.

She had been right.

The child grew worse, was rushed into hospital where antibiotics failed to save him. At first the doctors had been sanguine; boys were tough, could stand any amount of battering, but for the last three days, they spoke modestly as if they knew they'd lost that life. They did not give up; they hoped still, but they had failed. Later Fisher learnt that this was mere subjective impression; until the last day there had been slight improvements, minor gains so that the final relapse had come to the physicians with a shock of disappointment.

Fisher drove to the hospital, found no difficulty in parking, but prevented himself from running down the street, with its eighteenth century, early Victorian houses, now the consulting rooms of physicians and surgeons. He signalled to the man on duty in the office, who raised a finger, allowed him through.

As he pushed up the stairs his breath pumped short.

The heat of the place, the bareness, the pipes about the walls oppressed him, suggesting a science which could offer only bogus hope to him.

At the end of the ward where the child lay he saw Meg in the corridor, quite still, face firm, hand in hand with the sister. Then he knew Donald was dead. Meg nodded, nodded, nodded, answering his unspoken question, so that it was the nurse who spoke.

'He's gone, Mr Fisher.'

'When?'

'Half-an-hour ago.' She checked on a tiny wristwatch, holding it higher between thumb and middle finger. 'We came out to wait for you. Your wife said you'd be here any minute.'

'Can I see him?'

Now she nodded, gravely, a plump young woman in this odd, hard uniform. She turned Meg, held her by the arm as they two led him into the first partitioned sector of the ward. The other beds stood empty; Donald's was curtained, over by the window, large in light.

The sister scraped the curtain along, ushered them forward, lined up with them in the part-darkened space. The child lay straight, in a white gown, his fair hair brushed neatly flat, his small lips pursed tight, taut as if he were about to resist some demand; death, perhaps. The little face had about it a kind of obstinancy, or purpose, that should have been accompanied by a puckering of the brows, but the forehead was clear, unmarked, perfect. One could see. Look there, look there.

Fisher was most aware of the other two with him, their stiffness, their silence. In their ordeal, they did not want anything from him, nor observe him, only waited on the little face, the carefully combed and parted hair, knowing nothing but that small beauty, the delicacy of nostril. Then the father wished, suddenly, without reason, that he could see the hands. On the child's first day of life Fisher had put his finger into that small palm and the answering fingers had closed, as if from choice. As he wished, his throat tightened, and tears scalding his eyes spattered. The women stock-still towered, supremely, superbly by him. Edging a step forward, he lifted the sheet, from the hands. Tears splashed the nightgown.

He kissed his boy, the coldness of a nose by his upper lip, replaced the sheet and returned into line. At this the sister took his arm, while he dredged in his mac pocket for a handkerchief.

Meg did not move.

His lips trembled, shook in a painful spasm which thrilled in the stiff mask of his face.

'He looks nice,' the nurse said. It comforted, that silly unexpected sentence, delivered as if Donald lived, had prepared himself for the inspection. 'Poor little man.' She allowed them a minute or two longer, then led them outside, to a cup of tea and efficient sympathy. All the staff seemed to know as they looked in, stood a moment, until Fisher in his maze of grief imagined the whole hospital, surgeons, administrators, physicians, nurses, technicians, porters, cleaners, therapists, orderlies, cooks, queueing in their places to add weight of fellow-feeling.

'I should go home, if I were you,' Sister said, 'and get something to eat.'

'Where is . . . he, he, now?' Meg asked. Fisher wanted the answer.

'He'll have gone over to the mortuary.'

Over. So easy.

Meg, stiff as a guardee, shook hands and muttered thanks. As Fisher copied her, his eyes gushed tears again, but his wife paid no attention.

She allowed him to drive, ordered him to leave the car in the street. As soon as they were indoors, he put on the kettle, cut bread and butter while she 'phoned her parents. He listened to her sober announcement, learnt one or two of the day's facts as Meg, voice clear, very steady, instructed her mother. Without panic she spoke or listened and once, when he moved near the hall door, he saw her right hand fiddling with, shifting the memopad about the polished surface of the table.

He in the scullery was shaken with gusts of sorrow, physical heaving that doubled across his body. When he'd last used this teapot, Donald was alive, breathing; no fingers had touched these cups since that time when he had, if barely, a son, a boy. Now that child was dead, on a slab, a little area of corruption, though beautiful still.

Meg returning announced that her father would make all arrangements for them. Fisher bit on bread that had been baked while Donald lived, choked, tears drowning the slaver from his sagging mouth. She sat, eating nothing, supping at the tea, staring above him. When he offered to refill her cup, she nodded, smiled briefly at him, locked her fingers together.

In the next days he never saw her composure broken. Now and then, as she stood at the sink, or in the garden, or finally bowing in the crematorium chapel, a tear, a single drop hung silverly on her cheek, marking her, rain on marble. She did not forget her husband, but cared for him as one feeds caged animals in a zoo, by habit, by numbers. She read the many letters, replied; spoke to visiting neighbours; submitted to his gestures of love, but deadly, without spark, perfect and adequate and killing.

Fisher wished her to go away, even if only to stay with her parents, but she refused, pressed on with her daily business until he was better, could see the child's bedroom without pang, forget his grief for an hour's length. At first he'd been stunned, but recovering found himself trying to understand her calm, wanted it otherwise. His Meg lived wild, in tempest, in flurries of tears, angry exchanges, china smashed; this woman bore the death with a stoicism that he feared because it presaged the end of their marriage. She had borne him a son who had not survived. Her quiescence condemned him.

When, in ordeal, he'd spoken about this to David Vernon, his father-in-law had shrugged away from him, with the same indifference Meg showed.

'It's no use,' he said, 'fretting. Affects one one way, another another . . .' Leaving the sentence unfinished, he'd appear to pass from Fisher's life, discarding him, erasing their relationship.

In the cathedral, before little Sir Hugh, Fisher indulged in a pleasure of melancholy, under high arches, coloured space. No longing for the child cut him, no personal grief, but a sense of delectable sadness.

Perhaps in this neglected spot is laid
Some heart once pregnant with celestial fire;
Hands that the rod of empire might have
    swayed
Or moved to ecstasy the living lyre.

One could not claim that had nothing to do with death, but the rattle in the throat, the gnawing consumption, the blood clot, the cancer were moved aside for generality; death was embalmed, pickled, in sonorous beauty. These pillars, these arches that leapt and spread had done so when Bach grasped that Art of Fugue or Mozart thought K 488 or 595. For all he knew Gray had visited this place, perhaps even Shakespeare. Certainly the young, spring-hungry Lawrence had come here with his mother. Another couple were down on their knees on a brass lathering into their paper. The crowds talked loudly, not dwarfed now, unawed, enjoying the large elbowroom, laughing, demanding the imp, congratulating themselves on their cultural initiative. Fisher walked round again, listening to conversation, astute and ready, a sonless man, warmed into content.

He walked the perimeter, gave Tennyson short attention and then queued for apple-pie and cream. People crammed thick; in the castle-dungeons, coolly dark even now, children hallooed and scampered, scuttering in nuisance, earning clips in the ear, threats. In the prison wild voices echoed about the wooden pews so high that only the preacher could be seen. This house of God stood soulless, so that Fisher, on the hard wood of the back row where the condemned, brought in last, were preached at before they met their Maker at the rope's end, shuddered, hurried from a world that seemed mechanical, drawn to a puritan scale, cruel even now when these children played their foot-thumping hide-and-seek. He escaped, admired the repaired stone-work, climbed the steps, stood, one among many, and returned to walk downhill towards the shops, the factories, the car-parks, and bingo-halls where men lived dirtily. He exchanged words with the attendant by the Brayford Pool and set off for the coast.

He seemed, as he drove, to have learned something or become some other man. Now he expected nothing from Meg, and recognised the sense of that conclusion. He'd enjoy the dinner his landlady had prepared, plaice and chips, with lemon, for sure, and pay his bill and know the week, this silly dart-throw of a holiday, sand and cackling, pubs and ice-cream, was as good as over. His father would have drawn some conclusion: 'We're down in the mouth now, but in a fortnight we'll feel the benefit, so let's all go for a last evening's leg along the prom.' Everything was an investment to Arthur Fisher. Pity his dividends accrued so tardily. Spinning along, Fisher did not award his father any palm; the old man was a hymn-singing till-opener, who'd worked hard, made a bit which he'd no idea how to spend and had died before he'd had chance to retire, dragging, it seemed, his wife with him. They'd produced and reared a university lecturer, a man of straw, and a doctor, a hard-headed woman who'd feel pride if she skilfully diagnosed a fatal disease in her husband. The world a better place? Unfair. Time worked efficiently and that brought its reward.

'Ring Mr Vernon, Frankland Towers.'

He did so, was invited to dinner. Refusing, he explained his own meal was almost served. David had been twice on the 'phone to Meg, long talks, and though she had declined to come over, she wanted her husband to call in on her Saturday evening on his return. Vernon was dry, admonitory; his son-in-law must realise what had been achieved. This had been worked for.

'How did Meg seem?' Fisher asked.

'Reluctant.'

'What does that mean?'

'She wasn't keen to talk to me; she didn't want to see you.'

'Why should she, then?' David had annoyed him.

'We can't let things go by default. This girl has to be told bluntly. You know that. If your marriage is worth saving, then an effort must be made. And if you won't, I will.'

'I see.'

Fisher rang off, Vernon fuming.

As he washed, stood, smart in a brand-new shirt,

wide tie, he pondered his reminiscences. He and his wife had grown apart since Donald died; they had quarrelled with petty violence of late, but before that had stretched a period where they had nothing to say to each other, where every conversational urge had disappeared in boredom, where inertia had prevented all contact but the habitual. He had taken her a cup of tea in bed, but often without a word. If they rolled together in sex, it was joyless, masturbatory, a spurt of pleasure for him, a dull reminder of sense to her. So that their more recent quarrels had blown up like a civil war, against the flat place, the indifference, the despicable existence in the same house of himself and this young unknown woman, who had made no demands, or sacrifices, and to whom he owed, he considered, some debt of love she would, could not claim. Her flung plates, her moody outbursts relieved him, because now he knew what she felt, or imagined so, and could direct his behaviour accordingly. He would be polite; no result. Against his volition, he lost his temper, and she raged back. They did not make up. They shouted, fisted the table, kicked furniture in bitterness, frustration, mere tantrum, but they had no profit from it. Today's quarrel done, where's tomorrow's gall?

Meg must have been wearied into agreement; she could argue, but briefly, and without either belief in or desire for a conclusion. He'd see her; they'd look at each other, and he'd tell himself that he scrutinised his wife. Where her thoughts flew, or rising anger, or her boredom he would not fathom; she'd sit through the bit of desultory chat they managed, apparently as puzzled as he, and at the end they'd shake hands or take a drink together and part. He'd admire her, even if her eyes were dark and her hair unkempt, but he would not be shaken by either the fierceness of possession or the passion of belief in one marriage that could make him forsake all, cleave only to her at that minute. He cared for her, would do her good, wished to help if he knew how, but he was incapable of stretching his arms out, begging her to resume wifehood. It was not that he was frightened of a rebuff, or that he feared the cat and dog life they'd resume; the appeal was not worth, no, wrong. His present self had not the energy to make it.

He looked well, in wide-striped shirt, light tweed, hair curling over his forehead, sideburns bushy.

At the gong he took his place.

This evening noise swelled; they bandied sentences, witticisms between the tables, because tomorrow they'd return sun-bronzed, and after Sunday's flatness they'd start work, while new guests blinked at the prospect of expensive idleness. Both Smith boys were in bed, dog-tired. Sandra wore a silver maxi-dress that made her taller, less sturdy. Terry had oiled his hair. Lena Hollies in lemon, had visited the hairdresser, so that her coiffure stood brilliantly from her head, but suiting her, marking

231

the good cheekbones with a new air of subtle defiance. She'd shadowed her eyes in green, hung thick cubic beads and had heavily ringed both hands. Beside this mild brilliance, her husband wore sober blue, and had reshaved, so that he seemed substantial, a man of, not wealth, but integrity, community interest, widely respected. His shouted banalities belied the appearance, while his wife, for all her sartorial sparkle, said little, acted politely. Beyond them the other guests at the two tables by the bow-windows acted hilariously, batting a balloon up, and donning, then passing on, a red paper helmet.

The landlady, the girls splashed smiles as they served. One of them, Lisa, had a date with an Italian boy and received advice all through the meal from Hollies and a paterfamilias by the radiator.

'These Mediterranean types . . .'

'They're passionate . . . Oooough!'

'You take my advice and stand by the fire extinguisher if you can; he'll need it.'

'So will she, as you ask me. Every time she puts a jelly on my plate, the steam comes out of her ears.'

'Oh, our dad. Behave yourself.'

''s not me. 's 'er. Look at her now.'

The girl juggled with dishes, red, but not put out. Tips would make up.

'I'd give her a kiss myself if there was nobody else about.'

'Go on, Mr Hollies.'

'Would you kiss us, love? I've dabbled me after-shave behind my ears.'

'She daren't, you see. Give him one, Lisa. Get a bit of practice in.'

In the end Hollies rose, took her into his arms, kissed her in cheers, as the landlady acted out suicide by carving knife.

'How's that?' Hollies shouted. 'How about you and me tonight, then?'

'What about old Eyetie?'

'What will Mrs Hollies say, ne'er mind him?' the landlady asked. Mrs Hollies said nothing, but eyed Fisher under the confection of her hair.

'How about this girl?' the other men shouted. 'Our Sally.' She was sallow, perhaps fifteen, wearing glasses, daughter of the house. 'She'll be a one, won't you, my lass?'

The child smiled, only just, mouth thin.

'Who's she meeting tonight, then?'

'The washing-up machine,' Sally answered.

'Ay,' said father. 'That's what my wife calls me.'

Noise swelled; grown men acted like children, and children watched, cautiously, the antics of those who tomorrow would be handing out smacks or threats. Fisher enjoyed himself, remembering, without embarrassment, his own father. There'd have been no sexual innuendo with Arthur, but he'd have matched these in coarse noise, in neighing laughter. And yet he'd not be jovial as a rule at his own table; his sociability he expended in public, at the shop, on passers-by, in holiday parlours. Fisher fingered the buff envelope containing his bill, and upstairs wrote the cheque immediately. Money well spent. Nobody to confide in. On the corridor downstairs he could hear continued merriment, the almost fierce chatter of voices, the roars, the explanatory material that always followed a well-received joke. At that he smiled; who was he to be anybody? What claims had he to put himself above these? He did not envy; he did nothing. The guests trooped upwards, breathless with laughing, paused on his landing to extend time of fellowship. In the clatter of talk, of voice-slinging, Fisher caught one sentence which seemed to come from the father of the family by the window, Hollies's rival in bawdry. He must have been close by the door, and his words pitched through, deep, in clarity.

'Lovely piece of mahogany, that. Beautiful.' He commended the banister. Full of the pleasure of the hour, he extended his joy to an inanimate object. No answer was given; doors banged; people climbed higher. God bless Meg.

He packed his case, cleaned this evening's shoes and the pair he'd wear tomorrow before he settled to a book. He did not enjoy himself, glanced out of the window but the street was noiseless, deserted, as if on this last night the visitors made long, special efforts of clearing and cleaning before the last round.

Knocked door.

He looked up in surprise, called an invitation to enter. Mr and Mrs Hollies edged in, wife first, were asked to sit down. Lena murmured words on the size and lightness of the room. Her husband hummed, made an awkward little excursion into politeness saying how much they had enjoyed Fisher's company. Touched, Fisher returned the expected clichès. Hollies enlarged on his views, still not altogether at ease, but determined, bursting through words like brushwood. Man of parts, some sense in observations, not arguments without backing, pleasure to be had in hearing the language put to that sort of use, not often had the opportunity, the privilege. Mrs Hollies seemed brighter-faced as if this effusion from her husband suited her, expressed her opinion; it in no way embarrassed her, as it did Fisher.

Hollies, paused, hoisted his trouser-legs, waited, self-satisfied.

Fisher nodded, cheesed. No gracious lady could better that.

Well, then. Hollies started. He was, he'd make no bones, going down to the pub now. There followed a long, lucid explanation why he could not drink long hours at home and why this was such a treat, a necessity. Made the holiday. Lena didn't want it. She enjoyed a drink, but in moderation. He did not blame her. This was the crux; would Mr Fisher like to walk along a little later, and perhaps Lena could accompany him. The young Smiths weren't coming. Bed early for them; they'd need to start early. Hollies dropped no sexual hint; the broad tongue of the dining room he'd discarded for a politer approach. Didn't take his drink too well, Terry Smith. Thinking too often what his wife would say. This statement showed no mark of malice; truth must be spoken. But he'd be glad if Mr Fisher agreed, would walk along with Lena, join them in a last pot, because he, for one, would not forget this acquaintanceship.

The man could use words. And about him was solidity; he was strong, would frighten if one crossed him, wasn't without intelligence. If Fisher's father had gone round to the next bedroom with a similar invitation, not that he would have visited a public house, his son would have squirmed at the pretension. Delivered in his father's squeaky counter-genteel the identical sentiments would have stood condemned; in this deep voice, from this square frame, they flattered, became acceptable.

Fisher said yes to the proposal, if Mrs Hollies were agreeable.

Mutual beckings concluded the agreement, so that Hollies rose, announced that he did not want to waste good drinking time and that it would be very near eight before he supped his first mouthful, armed his wife out.

Pleased beyond reason, Fisher settled again to his book.

Once, returning from work, he'd gone out of his way to call in at a little shop where the man baked his own bread. Back at home, he found that Meg had been out all afternoon and that the roundsman had not called. He produced his offering, swathed in tissue-paper.

Meg had kissed him, at once, and the bread had tasted delicious, crusty. They chewed and praised, delighted with each other. In the evening, they'd taken a walk round the streets, arm in arm, a man and woman in love, saying so, showing it. Meg had never seemed so uncomplicated, and he'd attributed the day's victory to his lucky call in a shop which he remembered as smelling delicious. At about that time Donald had been conceived.

Now he felt something of the same simplicity of triumph.

These people wanted his company, came to ask for it. He lay on the bed, watching the light on the ceiling, hearing the purposeful steps or voices from the street. Half an hour later, he'd changed shoes, washed again, and in his shirt sleeves was filing his nails when Mrs Hollies tapped.

'Are you ready?' he asked.

'I'm in no hurry.'

He invited her to sit down. She seemed small, and the lemon frock, well cut, with a wide hem, brightened her. Ten years back she would have been pretty, with a pertness, a vivacity of expression that was only part obliterated now. As she sat, hands in lap, she promised more than modesty, or diffidence; it was not a flaunting, but more of a statement, an affirmation that she was a character, a lively woman who for her own purposes hid her light. He wondered, amused, what that light was.

'I see no sense in mere swilling,' she said.

'No.'

He had not yet donned his jacket.

'This is the best room in the house,' she stated.

'I'm lucky. I just phoned three days before I arrived.'

'There'd be a cancellation.'

That conclusion pleased.

'I'll tell you what,' he said. 'We'll have a drink here. Before we walk down the road.' He undid his portmanteau, pulled out his half-bottle of gin, and a couple of bottles of tonic water. He poured into plastic mugs.

'Your health,' he said.

She stood, looked comically round, stiff as a toy soldier; held the glass aloft, took a hefty sip.

'I like gin,' she said.

'Why do you?'

'Relaxes me.' She tasted again, with all the zest of her husband.

'Damn braces, bless relaxes,' he said.

'And the same to you.'

He grinned, closed the book lying open, sipped with his back to her, though he watched her plain features through the mirror. Head lowered, she did not move, like a child in disgrace, until she straightened suddenly, shying mare, snatched at her gin, drank.

'Happy?' he asked.

She caught his eye, reflected, waved her glass round, downed more.

'I like this,' she said. He poured again. 'You'll have me drunk before I start.'

He described his visit to Lincoln, and she the round of shopping for presents. These bargains moved her; earning a reduction here, a better buy there she delighted herself. On Sunday afternoon next she'd be at the eldest daughter's distributing largesse, while Jack, replete, dozed in or bawled from an armchair. She talked about her husband for a time, not without affection, but sharply, knowing his weaknesses. He had a good job at a colour printers, looked after her, but needed to be told when to change his shirt or socks. 'I pick his clothes for him; he don't care. He'd go out dressed like a scare-crow if I didn't get on at him. And yet he's as neat as a pin. When he's finished at 'The Plough' tonight, he'll be tipsy, but there'll be not one drop of beer spilt down his suit. You see.'

'He's a good husband, then,' Fisher said.

'Yes. He is.' She hesitated.

'Here's to him, then.' Fisher picked the mug from the dressing-table. 'And his lady wife.' That delighted her, but he recognised the stilted phraseology of his father. She stood to acknowledge the toast, took a step or two, claimed she was dizzy, sat on his bed.

'What will you think of me, Mr Fisher?'

'You're on holiday.'

'That's one thing about Jack. I don't have to go down to the pub if I don't want to.' She looked small, pathetic on the counterpane, moistening her lips. 'Did your wife drink gin, Mr Fisher?' He noted the tense.

'Now and then.'

'I'll drink her health.' She stood, drank, waved, plumped down. Tight already. 'What was she like?'

'She's still around,' he answered.

'You don't want to talk about her, do you?' A sentimental smirk disfigured her face as she swilled the gin round her cup.

As accurately as he could, as though at a grammatical exercise, he described Meg, her appearance, her hair, the bright clothes, the way she walked, her voice. He took his time, making it matter. When he'd finished, Lena Hollies, head on one side, a look of quizzical sympathy in the bright eye, said,

'I think you love, her, Mr Fisher. Don't you, now?'

'I was married to her.'

'That's a different thing. The way you put it, why it was like a book.'

'I'm used,' he said, in untruth, 'to talk in that fashion.'

'Our Jack isn't.' She tilted the cup. 'He can talk if he wants to. You've heard him. But not to me. "Get on that bed, Lena." That's all he can say. That's all his love.'

'Perhaps that's as good.'

'I'd like somebody to tell me things. Like you've done with your wife. He speaks about work, or unions, or jokes, and filth.'

'You're not happy, then?'

'I don't know about that. I don't know who is.'

She spoke in a parody of his earlier precision, probing some philosophical difficulty. 'But now and then I wished things was different.' She wiped her face, briskly. 'That's nothing, I dare say.'

'You've never thought of leaving him.'

'Why should I?' She smiled. 'And to tell you the truth, it never crossed my mind until just recently. Now the children are grown up. Not that I bear him ill-will. He's as he is, and never makes out otherwise. He's strong still, but he's not so quick as he was.' She spoke now in autumnal mood, musing. 'I married him at seventeen. Nearly thirty years. He was a sergeant in the army. I don't like them Smiths,' she said suddenly.

'Why's that?'

'She looks down on her husband. She'd leave him if there was half a chance of anybody better.'

'Wouldn't you?'

'We're getting to that stage,' she spoke slowly again, 'where he'll begin to need me. It's a funny thing to say, I reckon, but he will. He's never been poorly, strong as a horse. But he had a tooth out not long before we come on holiday and it took him days to get over it. I had to nag at him. "It's a tooth you've had out," I said, "not a leg amputated." But it floored him. It did really.'

'He seems full of life.'

'Here? And he is. He enjoys every minute. Mind you, sitting in a pub swilling and chewing about football isn't much of a way.'

'Better than bingo.'

'Who told you I played that?'

'Nobody. Don't you?'

'I've more sense. I go out doing a bit of char-ring three mornings a week.'

'Does he mind?'

'Why should he? Nice class of people. Like yourself. A solicitor, and teachers. Both out at work. And it makes a change for me.'

Fisher felt out of it, put in his place, an absentee employer.

'More gin.'

'No, thank you. I want to walk down to that pub. I don't know; I don't know.' She keened, swaying slightly.

'I shan't be sorry to go home,' he said. 'Back.'

'Promise me,' she moved towards him, 'promise me you'll go and see her again.' She stood over him, quite steady. 'Make it up with her.' She sketched reconciliation vaguely in the air with her mug. 'Will you? Will you?' He lifted the gin-bottle.

'I'll visit her.'

She drank again, then surprisingly, catching him out, sat on his knee, but primly, like a maiden aunt on a piano-stool. She perched lightly, feet above the floor, laughing at the reflections in the mirror.

'You don't like it, do you?' she asked.

'Oh, yes.' She laughed more shrilly.

'You're very nice. I could fall for you,' she said. 'All the people I like want somebody else. Oh, don't pull that sour face. It's not the end of the world.'

'You'd be unfaithful to your husband?'

'I didn't say anything about that, did I, now?' She blew breath out, got up, straightened her dress. 'We're on holiday. It's a temptation for some. I caught him at it once. With a woman. Touching her up.' She spoke without emphasis, now, almost without interest as if she'd started on a topic politeness only demanded she should complete.

'You didn't mind?'

'Hard to say. Now. I could see he was frightened that he'd done something he'd regret. The woman, well, seemed quite educated, well-spoken. Husband there. Big, bald chap.'

'Were they drunk?'

She flicked her hand mildly at his genitals.

'Why should they be that? They liked a change. Jack's the sort who'd get it. Wasn't the first time. Won't be the last. Not worth making a song about it.'

'And you?'

'I just fancy men quietly, say nothing. In my mind. That's better.' She put her mug on the sink. 'Come on,' she said. 'Let's go if we're going. And don't forget what I tell you.'

'I'll see her.'

She made him race to the pub, her arms swinging, as if she wanted to get off the streets.

Hollies was crushed into the corner with the Smiths, who shouted explanations of their presence. A piano banged; Jack procured seats; at the next table an old man, thin white hair neat, hummed and conducted 'The Rose of Tralee'. In spite of the bustle, the noise, the emphatic gestures and demands, drinks appeared only slowly, were shuffled through the crowd.

Sandra twittered how the landlady had persuaded them. 'This is your last chance, love. You make the most of it. I'll see to the boys.' Beautifully laundered blouse, pink mini-skirt; hair that seemed young and alive compared with Lena's elaborations of curls as Mrs Hollies' wary face watched, took it all in, muttered approval, but kept her counsel.

Fisher drank slowly, listened in to conversations round him, marvelled at the shifting facial expressions about what he could not guess. Though the place was crowded, thick with movement, he for the moment sat listlessly, but as if at a concert, eyeing the orchestral players as they drifted in and knowing that excitement was close at hand. At the next table a man and his wife described in contradictory duet how a fight had broken out that afternoon on the beach between two well-dressed West Indians and how some woman had intervened, ordered them to clear off. Racist talk flowed; a street fight in which somebody had cracked his skull open on the edge of the kerb was argued over until the words flew like knuckly fists. Nearer home, Hollies, chest expanded, very slowly spelt out to Sandra what he understood by a good holiday, and why he was more likely to find it here than abroad. The pint in his hand stood supreme, that and the food. 'When I want to grease my tripes, I'll walk down to the chemist's an' buy a bottle of olive oil and drink it. And not before. I happen to know what sort of lubrication suits me.' Sandra smiled, lips parted slightly from her white teeth, intent on his every syllable. He did not speak loudly, almost fastidiously quiet in this mêlée, but hypnotically, with authority. Terry, face brick red and burning, twitched at his open collar envying the older man.

Now Fisher grew detached, immersed in his own thoughts.

Slightly dizzy he considered his play. That was the way to think a non-existent work of art into being, in a happy tipsiness, that paid no attention to decision, or alternatives, or the bore of writing, the chore of flogging oneself to get down on paper ideas that expand grandly while they're vague.

As he sipped, he considered his conception, his great drama of a family. They were as yet innominate, but started back with the Luddites, where one young father was taken and hanged, a strong figure with the voice of righteousness in his clenched fist. Then his children, the Victorians, washed with the blood of Jesus, but running the bawbees up so that one of the grandsons killed in the trenches left a tidy fortune. Now his children lived richly in London, with grandchildren, awkward as the first ancestor under the veneer of public school and Anglican agnosticism.

How this would be crammed on stage he did not know. Brechtian scenes with lines of verse, shouts of song, revolutionary coarseness at the end against the polite southern voices. Impossible as King Lear, but in the daze and rumpus of a public house the design unfolded into symphonic proportions. He must catch and stop up time. That was the right, true end of a swaying man in a bar: to make his peculiar scratch on the flying scud of years. The green leaf and the twig, oh. Anticipation was all. Her husband smiled as Sandra rubbed her left breast on Fisher's upper arm. Nothing could be held. All flew, evaporated, shredded into fine mist and from this tenuous stuff the poets wove their solidity of memory. Christmas Day, damp and dark, but the whisky bottles stood ready on sideboards, and the television, and the nut crackers, to spoil another landmark until words stiffened the banality, made something of nothing, scarred that initial on the expanding universe. The broken knife and the boy's end.

The two women either side pressed into him, became part of the pleasure. Hollies described the strip show at his club on Sunday lunch time to Terry Smith, who smirked stupidly, character wiped from his face by beer and fellowship. A vigorous guffaw rewarded a story two tables away and the ancedotalist sat back, justified. Sandra's scent, the tang of lacquer on Lena Hollies's hair. A group round the piano wailed in chorus; Fisher neither recognised the tune nor the words.

'Better than pop,' Hollies said. 'On in the clubs now.'

'You switch the telly on,' Terry started, slurred, sagged back.

'I know, If you want a decent act you've got to sit through hours of shouting and bawling by these long-hairs. All bloody deaf.'

'I like it,' said Lena.

'You don't. You're always telling me to turn it down.'

'Some of it's good,' Sandra ventured, close to Fisher.

'Entertainers have got to cater for a large young public. They're the majority. They're the piper-payers.' Fisher said. 'They call the tune.'

'Peter Piper,' Mrs Hollies giggled.

'I don't call it tune at all,' Hollies said, laughed. 'Bloody noise.'

Meg liked pop, because she felt it, she claimed, in her muscles. 'You move to it; it's dance,' and it was true that he'd find her jigging between the stereo speakers to the incomprehensible thump and squeal of a group. 'This isn't intellectual. It's bicep music. Bone jigging. Vaginal. Testicle.' He'd wondered at the truth of this. To him it had the rough sublety of the old fairground cake-walks, a bang up and down against which you imposed a counterpoint of steps that risked throwing you. Meg believed, cut herself off from him. His up-bringing, education had blocked him from this pleasure. Yet she loved Mozart, played with an unaccustomed steadiness some early piano sonatas she'd learnt in her youth. But she'd shuffle away to this barbarism; wrong word, this boredom of noise. 'Of course it's mainly rubbish,' she'd argue reasonably. 'I know that. But it's new rubbish.' There, in her father's courtroom manner, she mocked him. 'Ninety per cent of human cultural production is worthless,' he'd pontificated. She'd remembered and in the amplified bumble she'd danced and scorned him.

'That chap as plays the piano can't read a note o' music.' A leaning neighbour.

'By ear.'

'Ah. Learnt himself.'

'He can tickle 'em,' Hollies said.

'What would he have been like if he'd had music lessons?' Fisher asked. Why that question reared, was spoken, he'd no notion.

'Might h' spoilt him,' Hollies said.

'Been playin' Bach opuses to nob'dy but himself.' The neighbour.

'That would have been bad?' Fisher pursued his point.

'He gi's pleasure. To hundreds. Night after night.'

'And swells the proceeds.' Terry, joining the rush.

'Swills.' Hollies, cheerfully rough.

'If he'd 'a been taught,' Lena said slowly, 'there'd still be dozens as wasn't. You'd not go short in the pubs.'

'Thank God,' Hollies said.

'And our lack of educational opportunity.' Fisher.

This led then to schools, and all were talkative. Sandra, pert and assertive, argued that education was the means to social mobility; she wanted her boys in a grammar school so they'd become qualified, get on. The rest approved, but felt that this was a course for a favoured few, with brains, with aptitude. They did not argue this strictly, but hobbled through anecdotes about fortunes made by people thick as two short planks. Fisher, mildly, pressed for a culture which offered a fuller life. Hollies checked him magisterially.

'You schoolmasters are all the same,' he said.

'He's a lecturer,' Sandra interrupted, a personage now.

'Same kidney and fry. You don't know what it's like to do a hard day's work. At the end of that you don't want Beethoven and Rachmaninoff's concerto, what you want's an arm chair and entertainment. I've done both. I know.'

'Have you taught all day?'

'No. Nine till four. Two hours' breaks. Forty weeks a year. You don't know you're born.'

They could not be serious. Eccentric teachers having a drag behind raised desk-lids. Navvies leaning on shovels, brewing tea. Straps and canes whistling. The difficulty of getting the simplest repair done. Voices shouted up in enjoyment of pessimism, and Fisher, king-happy, mused again, ruefully accusing himself of delayed adolescence. Tomorrow he'd see Meg, just as his Luddite ancestor met the hangman.

Over the far side of the room a man raised his hands above his head, then stood to demonstrate in no space a step or two from the hokey-cokey. A clap, a cough, cheer, punch and he sat, face into beer-mug. That symbolized all life; a gesture, on account of circumstances not properly completed, representing something beyond and equally trivial, for a short time, then over, done with, done for. His play would carry symbols, top-heavy as Ibsen. Gibbets and candle-sticks, fetters and table-napkins, a word in the cold dark, repartee over wine, and all life shone there. He sipped his beer for want of better occupation, moved, emotional over nothing, faculties softened by alcohol. Expansive he put a hand on Lena Hollies' thigh; she wore suspenders; he felt the aphrodisiac rubber button.

He refused another drink as Terry fought up to his feet. A young man fell sideways from his stool, was replaced.

The neighbour, leaning across, frowning, half-pint held round the glass, began on industrial relations, was ordered by Hollies to shut up because they were on holiday.

'Don't let him boss you about,' Lena said.

'It's all right, missus.'

'You say what you like.'

'No. We are on 'oliday, though.'

She gave up, but without disgust, asking Fisher

to read a cartoon advertisement on the far side of the room. Smoke drifted. Terry issued new drinks as Hollies returned to the urinal. 'Straight back to the brewery.' Circles of moisture interlinked like weals on the red table top.

Near closing-time the piano seemed silent, though Fisher could not be sure that he had erased the sound himself. No, the pianist sat sideways to keyboard as if making a few more square inches was more important than a tune. As the landlord called time, Terry breathless as a landed fish, tried to explain a motor cycle accident he'd had. His attempt grew pathetic, with a wagging jaw unable to produce coherence, and hand parting the air to let a non-existent message swim through.

Fisher was sober, now, having drunk little in the past hour. So were the women, stiff, perhaps disapproving. Hollies' big face searched for sense from Terry. The neighbour shook hands, belching friendly inanities or promises, before taking the arm of a woman in a red straw hat, seashell with feather, whom he'd neglected all night. The pianist thumped Auld Lang Syne; some joined arms, but most sat, sodden-faced, staring ahead. Mrs Hollies' eyes were large with tears so that Fisher felt suddenly ashamed.

The other two men made a ceremony of finishing final drinks, chiding Lena for leaving a half-glass.

'Mr Fisher paid good money for that,' Hollies, threatening.

'Let Mr Fisher drink it, then.'

That summed the relationship.

Outside in the yard, Terry fell flat. Now he looked scared, hair unkempt, eye cocked for retribution. He had torn his trousers by his knee. Sandra's face seemed to shrink so that she could not, perhaps, cry out. Lena hummed to herself as they waited again for her husband's emergence from the lavatory.

They linked arms, filling the pavement. Fisher on the outside was glad that it was darkish now but they walked sedately enough. Even Hollies subdued himself, insisted on no dance-steps, shouted nothing, sang no songs, looked to his bed. Lena's arm through Fisher's hung soberly, chaste, even lethargically.

On the pavement outside the house Hollies began a speech which his wife interrupted.

'Don't wake the whole world.'

Hand-shaking ceremonies started quietly enough, though voices squeaked into excitement as Lena kissed Terry, then Fisher.

'Not me, you notice,' Hollies grumbled. Sandra made all well, embraced three.

'This is the best holiday I ever had,' Terry confided to Fisher, drunkenly, touching his arm, batting hair from his eyes.

Suddenly as they stood Fisher found himself detached, dispassionately in judgement. He wondered what his colleagues would make of this rite; they who would be hurtling round the motorways of Europe, tippling the wine, fighting the flies, flashing the phraseology, all, if they were to be believed, adept in bargains, cunning Europeans. Here in this mediocre street, nineteen thirties sunshine shoddy, he stood with a group of half-stoned people without culture or subtlety, chosen almost by chance not for their proclivities, listening, and weighing, sane enough, and yet puzzled how he'd arrived.

He touched a privet hedge, stroked its trimmed top.

Mountains, the high woods, fjords, glaciers, canyons, these he could afford, and yet he gawped over a hedge at a frilly curtained bow-window. These be your gods. Mind cool, he tried to work out if he were disappointed in himself, and why, and decided he was not. He had spent a week. That length gave away a secret; this was his parents' holiday, one week, no more, carefully planned, provided for. Again he condemned himself for loose thinking; he'd shot here in a hurry, because he'd no idea what to do, how to fill in his time now he'd walked out from his wife. Oddly, he felt no depression about Meg, but a calm, as if reason would prevail in the end, and tomorrow they'd shake hands, make it up, without flurry or fuss or passion, though with delays, demands, small demurs, before they started life over again with the new term in October. Not likely; not on. A vision of the Vernons taking a fortnight's rest in the glassy security of the Frankland Towers amused him, so that he laughed, said, 'God save us all.' They were great on abroad; Easter in Athens or Crete, Christmas in Morocco.

'What did you say?' Sandra pulled on his arm. They were all looking at him.

'God save us all.' Bold face on it.

'Go' save us all,' Terry repeated, swaying.

'And I think,' Hollies at his most deliberate, tonguing each word, 'sometimes as he needs to.'

'You'll have me crying next.' Lena.

'That'll be the day.' Her husband now rumbled without conviction. 'Roll on a big boat. And a Merry Christmas to all our readers.'

'If that's the case,' said Fisher tartly, 'then it's time we went inside.'

They obeyed meekly, negotiating the garden path, the short hall, the stairs without overmuch commotion. On the top landing they grouped themselves again, though Terry toppled off for the W.C. while his wife tiptoed to look at the boys.

'Come on in our room for a drink,' Hollies invited.

'As long as we're quiet,' Lena warned.

Fisher refused, but took Hollies' hand in both of his own.

'It's been a pleasure to meet you, and your wife.' They stood together, locked.

Terry emerged, a sheepish grin as he tugged his zip upwards.

'You'll join us.' Hollies turned to Fisher. 'A pleasure and a privilege, sir.'

'Thank you.' Fisher genuinely touched held his hand to Lena who shook it, quickly, like uninterested royalty. She had reservations, now, he could see, was ready to push him out of her mind without regret.

'I have been to some places,' Hollies said, not loudly, controlled and in command, 'at home and abroad, but I have never met a person that I would . . .' Syntax disintegrated. 'A man I appreciated. That's so, Lena?'

She did not answer. Sandra reappeared.

'Last drink,' Hollies told her, 'in my boudoir'.

That word surprised Fisher again, even though his father had exhibited curious knick-knacks of vocabulary from time to time. As the others trooped off, he felt deserted, sorry that he'd refused. Behind the closed doors, the others made no sound, but he wondered if they criticised him for unsociable behaviour. The men had drunk too much; the women did not care enough.

A note had been slipped into his bedroom.

Call on Mr Vernon, 10 a.m., Frankland T. Phone call. Important.

That summed the matter, for while they had been in cloud-cuckoo land at the 'Feathers', messages had been relayed, received; somebody had assumed responsibility. Life had progressed. He removed his shoes. The phrase, 'life had progressed', reiterated itself in his head, in the buzzing subdued activity, near words, that always spun, whirred there. He saw again the distant mountains, the snow peaks, the sage plains, the rising dust, föhn, tundra, the places he had never seen.

A startling laugh distantly burst the silence.

The gin bottle stood on his dressing table still. He put that away, completed his packing, strapping the cases. Then, sober, in his wrong mind, he went to bed.

Friday night. No thanks to God.

CHAPTER 12

Saturday's breakfast was business-like.
They'd paid their dues, and the staff
prepared to forget them. New faces that
afternoon when the rush of bundling sheets had
been scrambled through. Last corn-flakes, bacon,
for the zombies, final jokes as if the holiday were
still on, still provided pleasure.

Fisher felt a stiffness as he braced himself against
parting. It seemed entirely bodily, a matter of
nerves, not reasoned, not even imagined. The flesh,
the sense organs did not wish to lose contact with
these good people. The conceit slightly cheered
him for here was something to be pondered, some
innate method of feeling he did not want but could
not control.

Car boots were jampacked, slammed with twitters
of ill-temper; children assumed the expression of
boredom that was to characterize the day's travel
while fathers became important again, men, with
a status. The Hollies had decided to spend the
morning on the beach, to lunch out and then catch
their train and had therefore piled luggage on the
concrete square outside the front window ready

for the ordered taxi. They were subdued, not with hangover, but with the end of the holiday, said so. Lena cheered herself because in three weeks she was off again to stay with a married daughter in the country. Pathetically she described woods 'right behind the house', the slow existence amongst mud and animals, the vegetables, fresh, rich, the neighbourly greetings. It appeared that both daughter and husband worked, in Reading, and the holiday reduced itself to a thorough clean of the house between two spendthrift weekends but it served to bandage the smart of this parting.

Fisher shook hands all round. The proprietor and his wife spoke effusively, obviously puzzled why he should have patronised them, but determined to make something of it. The girls simpered over their tips, thanking him with blushes as they realised they lacked the correct form of wording for this man. Other guests pushed up, declared themselves pleased to meet him, hoped it would not be the last time, but signed the book in the hall, 'Made very welcome. Lovely food. Thanks. Mr and Mrs A Marriott and Susan, 23 Rice Avenue, etc.' with less panache, perhaps he suspected, fearing his schoolmaster's eye. 'There's a "c" in excellent, as I've told you often enough.' Terry Smith spoke offhandedly, looked pale, but Sandra putting a cool, damp palm into Fisher's, handed him a slip of paper on which she had written their address. 'It would be a shame if we never . . .' she said, not looking him in the face.

He was touched, dictated his own in return but warned that it would be only temporary; that was grudging, fobbing her off already. Outside one of the men lined the children for a group photograph. By eight tonight with the boys in bed, and a linen basket piled high with sandy clothes, Mrs Smith would have forgotten the holidays, be annoyed that her neighbours had neglected to order a loaf and the milkman had left bottles in the sun, would have started life again. Fisher indulged his imagination, saw Terry pulling out the three inches of sherry left over from Christmas, insisting that he and his wife had a celebratory drink on a 'first-class holiday, but I'm glad to be back.'

'You can always find me,' Fisher said, 'at the Department of Education.'

'Yes,' she shook her head, pushed further from him. What could she write to a scholar and a gentleman? Today I washed three pairs of Terry's socks and took Tony to the clinic. The doctor says he's slightly overweight, but nothing to worry about.

Fisher fingered her hand again, small and wet.

'Will you come here next year?' she asked, encouraged.

'I don't know.'

Silence, until the children broke from the garden, danced at their mother. Fisher followed them upstairs where he checked for the third time that he'd left nothing of his, stumbled round peering into mirrors, slightly disarranging curtains, nailing the insignificant pattern of the carpet into his memory.

He slipped quietly out to his already laden car, and drove towards the promenade, where he parked to stand by the railings peering at the distant, bright flatness of the sea. The sands gave an appearance of emptiness, but in fact plenty of families unpacked their belongings for the day. Carol and Tricia from behind wished him good morning. When he turned, he found their reddened faces uninteresting and honest; blue-eyed dolls ready for plastic-topped boxes.

'Not going home, today, then?' he asked.

'No. Another week.'

'Lucky girls.'

They smiled broadly, but hitched their shoulder bags and made for the concrete steps, with nothing to say to him this bright morning, nor he to them. He watched as they planted their well-fleshed legs solidly down, firm, well upholstered bosoms held steady. These were fine women, who offered him little, but who'd settle in Halifax or Batley or Bradford and bring up families and tend parents and know right answers occasionally at right times. He did not need them, did not despise them, but had chosen Meg who made her own erratic way, zigzagging through his sensibility until he lost sense of purpose or reason. That sounded wrong. He'd been drawn to Meg by a beauty which did not depend on her unstable ways. She and he, both, were father-fighters. Carol and Tricia, now at a distance, still stumped along the sands. If Meg flung herself naked into his naked arms, what would the consequence be? A few hours' peace, a transient sense of satisfaction, but no promise beyond that. As he stood here in the shine of a bright late summer's morning he could not clearly recall his wife's face. He envied those witnesses who could drag together identikit pictures of criminals they'd glimpsed in a fierce shortness of attack. He could not reimagine her right eye or nostril or chin, merely a darkened sketch of her features in a frock remembered in detail for its simplicity.

Yet the image was stored.

If Meg stepped from her car, here, he'd know her, would dwell with tenderness on this square inch of skin or that, not as a bit of design, a pattern, but as a deeply important part of reality fastening its fangs of attraction into him just so long as his eye rested on it, devoted its careful attention. He imagined the physical thump with which his body would respond to Meg's presence, and found again that he could give it no sort of precision. An ache here, a tingle, a breathlessness, a pained excitement in heart, shoulders, stomach. And had it happened, the effect would have reduced his powers of observation and thus hidden itself again, cocooned itself from the accurate words that would have pinned it down like a specimen for future inspection. Even that, he told himself, would not do. Those words did not exist; any description would be at best a rough sketch done across creased paper with blunt pencil on a dark night. His body would answer to her real presence with gland, nerve, muscle, but to the smudged word, a smudged thought. He acknowledged only physical reality, be it merely a line in her handwriting or a garment from her back, with any vibrancy.

Yet words, codes, signals were his business.

Carol and Tricia, small now, trudged on as if for the south coast. Why, if they intended walking so far, did they not stay on the promenade. They liked sand under their feet. Their exchange with him had jarred them. They'd no idea what they exactly intended. They were escaping from him.

He returned to his car, began to back out, but stopped to fling a short anger of words at another motorist who could not wait until he was clear.

'Keep out of the bloody way,' he shouted.

A white, middle-aged woman shrank from him, behind her protective glass, and whispered to her upright husband, who did as he was bid. Fisher felt the better for it.

In the great foyer of the Frankland Towers there was little overt flurry, though trunks were piled, and a few guests were escorted through the glass doors. The superior young woman on reception smiled, immediately rang for Vernon, hoped he'd make himself comfortable, pointed gracefully to seats. He had not long to wait.

His father-in-law stepped from the lift, wished him good-morning and said they'd talk upstairs. They exchanged no other words.

'Sit down.' Fisher was gestured into one of two armchairs by a window which overlooked three car parks, a main road and a row of bungalows. Immediately he began to work out the lie of the land, the name of the street, an impossibility, though he could tell by shadows that he was facing west. During this little exercise he paid no attention to Vernon, who waited, taking off his jacket, replaced it on a coathanger in the wardrobe when he saw Fisher had offered some token of interest. Then he took a position, that indicated the formality of his movements, opposite.

'This is the best place for privacy.'

'Is Irene not here?'

'No. She's leaving it to me.'

'Man to man?'

'If you please.' He did not seem to resent Fisher's tone. 'You're calling in on Meg later today?'

'She's told you.'

'I've spent a fortune,' Vernon said, pacifically, rubbing his hands flat palm to palm, 'this last few days on telephone calls. The latest not half an hour ago.'

Fisher said nothing.

'I can't claim to have made much progress. I've too much experience in these affairs to boast, but at least she and I can exchange rational sentences about you, which is more than was possible a fortnight ago.' Again he waited, but without exasperation as the son-in-law failed to answer. 'Whether such will be the case when she sees you this afternoon, I don't know. But she and I have discussed this at length. I want you to understand that.'

'Right.'

'One of the curious features is that she in no way blames you. That's hopeful.'

'Does she want me back?'

'Just take it easy, will you? This is no time for, no time . . . I'd have thought you'd . . .' He broke off, self-deprecating, handsome. 'I've spoken to her for a total of several hours, and yet I have to admit that I have not found out why you separated. Meg can't tell me. Can you?'

'We quarrelled.'

'Many people do.'

'I asked her if she wanted me to go. She said "yes". And she seemed serious. I thought it over, decided I'd had enough and packed my trunks.'

'Is that ever so sensible?' Vernon spoke slowly.

'It's how I felt.'

'I don't mean that. It's your account that I find unsatisfactory. "Take it or leave it" isn't very useful in negotiation. You see, Edwin, I want you to think hard about this, especially at this stage. I don't want you to close your mind.'

'Go on.'

'I'll accept that you and Meg were getting across one another, and to a considerable extent.

And, given this, I can see how attractive a break, a separation, might seem. Now you've had a few weeks apart you should begin to ask yourself if this is to be a permanent thing. Look, I don't think I'm maligning you when I say that I don't honestly believe you've worked really hard at this. Meg hadn't. That I can say.'

'Why do you . . . ?'

'One minute. There's an emotional block. You quarrel, nag, blow up and leave, and you're unwilling to, to probe any more deeply, because of the hurt.'

'I'll speak for myself,' Fisher said. 'I've done nothing else this last three weeks.'

'You think you have,' Vernon answered. 'You've felt the smart, the insults. If I can use a metaphor, you've not drawn back from the door of reconciliation. Not at all. But you've not tried to open it. You've padlocked it even closer.' He raised a hand. 'Even when you think you're doing the opposite. The trouble in these cases is that people are so tangled emotionally that they are incapable of seeing straight.'

'I don't think that's my case.'

'Maybe not, maybe not. It was certainly Meg's.' Vernon coughed slightly, as if to order, and ran a neat finger round the inside of his immaculate collar. 'And given this inability, this blindness, if I may so put it, a perfectly sensible means of therapy such as a fortnight apart becomes a permanent rift, by delay, by default, because the patients fail to see they are now cured, or at least convalescent.'

'Let's have the prescription, then.'

'You rush, Edwin, you rush. For a philosopher you're precipitate. Have you any feelings of guilt?'

'Of course.'

'Apart from your treatment of Meg? Have you been unfaithful?' Vernon looked up, blue eye mild, mouth almost at a simper. 'I know you want to tell me that it's no business of mine. And neither is it. But I've often found that one partner's feeling of guilt leads him, or her, to neglect, to torment, even to accuse the other, who may be quite innocent.'

'I've no qualms on that score.'

'I'm glad.' He did not appear so; the lips were thin with reproach. 'You're quite honest, Edwin? I'm sorry to press you.'

'I have not,' Fisher answered, grim now, 'committed adultery.'

'But you've thought about it?'

'Everybody thinks about it.'

'I doubt if that is so. But your admission may be important. To you. Not to me. I shall not sort this matter out. You must do that for yourself.'

Fisher considered a text. 'Whosoever looketh on a woman to lust after her hath committed adultery with her already in his heart.' He could hear his father's high-pitched voice whanging this pearl at the family when Arthur had been condemning the irregular life of one of the chapel congregation, a man Elsie had mildly defended. Edwin already knew what adultery was; grammar school education had seen to that, and his father's quotation had by no means seemed either apposite or clinching in the argument, but the odd words had stuck from that time in his mind. That whosoever . . . Might as well be hanged, then, for a sheep as a lamb.

He had looked at some of his students in that way, a colleague's wife, a secretary at the university club, but he'd done nothing. Risk did not appeal, and none of these women had gone out of her way, and thus temptation withered, and he went back to his wife, a superior catch. Opportunity had never been great; he might easily have slipped this week with Sandra Smith.

'I can also tell you,' Vernon preluded again, 'and I do so with some pleasure, that Meg has not misconducted herself in that way. That removes a complicating feature.'

Fisher shrugged, rudely.

'But as I am so uncertain how the pair of you will react, I would like, if I may without impropriety, to enquire how, no, perhaps what you intend to say to her this afternoon.'

'You've presumably asked her the same question?'

'I have.'

'What did she say?'

'She said that she'd listen to any proposal you made, and then think about it.'

'There was nothing positive from her?'

'No.' A long sound, repeated, echoed. 'No. No.

Not really. Of course, you know Meg. She gives the impression of working from the instant, playing it off the cuff. Not that I'm sure she's as spontaneous as she pretends. Her general mode of behaviour is often worked out.'

'Is it so, now?'

'Guessing, yes. I'd say it is. She's willing to have you back.'

'What makes you so sure?'

'Sure?' Vernon raised voice and chin. 'Sure? My dear boy. I am only surmising. I've talked to many women in her predicament. No one can be certain. But that's why I want to learn your line of approach. Not to warn her. To guide you. Do you want to go back to her?'

'Damned if I know.'

The answer burst from him, like a cough from a dust-choked man. His pride begged her return; he needed her body's beauty, but he'd shouted this little slogan of defiance because he did not know how he stood, felt himself belittled, found himself wanting.

'But you hope to find out this afternoon?' No hint of temper; urbanity all.

'I don't know what I want.'

'I see. I see.'

'Is that good or bad?'

'We are not scoring points in a debate, Edwin. I can't tell you. I wish I had the perfect solution, but I haven't.'

'I'm not your choice as a son-in-law, am I?'

'Nobody is good enough for a man's daughter. You're intelligent, and presentable. But headstrong sometimes, and at others hesitant, vacillating. I've been trying to work out all this week why you've taken this holiday here. I've no idea.'

'Neither have I.'

'I don't believe that.'

They both grinned, foxily, better pleased, and for the next half hour Vernon suggested approaches, made slow statements about Meg, enjoyed himself. At the end of the time, Fisher against his will believed that his wife wanted him back, and had expressed his own willingness to comply. Without dragooning, smarming oil or obvious hypocrisy, Vernon had managed all this, and as soon as his son-in-law had left the old rogue would be on the blower again reporting some comforting version to his daughter. Fisher said as much, watching the deepening wrinkles round Vernon's eyes, as smiles creased to chuckles, crashed to laughter.

'But, of course, of course.' Vernon crossed his legs. 'How would you describe out conference this morning?'

'Inconsequential. Haphazard.'

'That's about right.'

Fisher smirked agreement. That described the week here, among strangers, trotting on sand, riding the flat roads, eating the chops and chips, the tinned fruit and ice cream. Nor had he reached a conclusion about his marriage. He had not expected to. Meg was enigmatic only so far as he was obtuse, and the idea that this casual communication with chance-met individuals in this town should offer the possibility of marital peace approached the ridiculous. And yet.

His father.

That man he'd disliked, as an adolescent, who'd left him money, who worked and joked had now been elevated into a totem. Visit Dad's town and all will be healed. Put bluntly like that he could laugh the notion away, but when one staggered one neither saw nor spoke with honesty. And this man is now become a god. His father, Alfred, moustache and riddling questions, squeaky voice, certainty of right and wrong, presided over this week-long rite, the recapture of the bride.

Vernon talked again.

'We have got nowhere, Edwin. Perhaps it's as well. I can't decide for you. There is, however, one thing I should like to have said before you leave.'

'Say it, then.'

Vernon rubbed his hands, loudly, and when he spoke, did so blandly.

'This afternoon when you meet your wife you will see a frightened, disheartened, unhappy girl. However she appears to you. Please don't forget that. Frightened of the future. Uncertain. Needing help. Neglected.'

'How would you describe me, then?'

'Short of imagination. Self-regarding. In this matter, selfish.'

'Balls.'

'Be honest with yourself. Do you love her?'

'What's love?' Fisher asked, suddenly down in the mouth.

'You would not ask me that question if you loved her.'

'Sometimes,' Fisher said, 'I wonder if you can hear what you're saying. You tongue words like a tom-cat at the cream. Haven't you any concern with reality?'

'Now I've annoyed you. That is bad. You find me mealy-mouthed. Dripping unctuous Victorian orotundities. And yet they mean something. These words try to make you grasp what is happening. They wouldn't be those you choose. The picture they present are not the side of life you would see. And yet, Edwin, they represent a truth of sorts. Your temper's rising. You want to spit. You despise me as an oily hypocrite, and yet I am speaking truth, my truth, as I grasp it. That girl is certainly the same woman who plagued and taunted you into running away, who left you sore with her silences, or wounded with her barbs, but she does it from ignorance, and your neglect, and the lack of love, a simplicity of love that demonstrates itself in a kiss, a warm glance, a thoughtful . . .'

'Jesus.'

'I'm an atheist,' Vernon snapped. 'Human behaviour's my concern.'

'Nice blank verse, you mean.'

'Fathers usually dote on girl-children. Margaret

was the only child, and when she was small we were close. I mended her toys, or provided the treats. By the time she reached twelve she'd grown out of the stage. That's early, but she's odd. Now she regards anything I say as wrong just because I say it. She'll use me if she can. She can't despise my brains, so she takes it on herself to criticise my manner of life. I don't blame her. She has a point. She can hurt. But she's my daughter. It hardly seems five minutes since she used to sit on my knee begging me to put the doll's eye back or glue the felt to its board.' Vernon stood, histrionic, then statuesque. 'That was my finest hour.' He levelly took Fisher on, eye to eye, defying him to mock the cliché. 'I've built my practice up from near-beggary. I've won cases on my head-work and my industry. I've made some shrewd investments. But I don't forget that time when my girl depended on me. And I love her. She can act as savagely, as crudely, as vindictively, as unbalanced as she pleases, and she does, she does, but I still love her.'

It was impressive.

Fisher moved, troubled, determined to act justly, still smiled at the trite rhythms, the cunning play with worn words. He was reminded of an eminent judge, universally praised as a speaker, who used exactly this technique. When this jurist spoke he delivered with resonant clarity a series of slight variations on much-handled phrases; this perhaps, was necessary in the law court. The jury had no time for daggers of wit, or carefully ground neologisms. They needed the plain truth varnished with pulpit-rhythm and school-book words. Fair enough. Didn't Dr Johnson believe that contrite prayer was better without artifice? Repentance, trembling in the presence of the Judge, is not at leisure for cadence and epithets?

Did he speak with sincerity?

Who'd answer that?

'Thanks,' Fisher said.

'You don't mean that, do you?'

'I don't know what I mean. I don't know what I want. Or what to say this afternoon.'

'She's disturbed, Edwin.'

'Very likely.' Fisher thinned his lips. 'I won't forget, either, that she's your daughter.'

Vernon stood, shook his head, sighed so that he seemed shaggy, untidy, a rough diamond.

'And there's Irene.'

'What does she . . . ?' Fisher asked, harshly.

'Again I don't know. We've discussed it, but I don't know. But she looks on you as a suitable son-in-law.' He held up his hand to check the sarcasm. 'It's something. All we have are these bits and pieces.'

They did not part immediately, but juggled perhaps another quarter of an hour with words until Vernon advised his son-in-law to think of the journey home. They shook hands, and Fisher used the staircase, not the lift, stretching his legs in freedom.

273

In the vita-glass of the foyer, he stopped for a moment watching the small knot of guests arriving. He wondered if the place paid, a palace in an east-coast town. Who'd come here with sufficient money to pay for this entertainment? Those like the Vernons who did not wish to fly abroad more than twice a year, but had cash and leisure. The middle-aged who could step off the promenades, out of shouting crowds, amusement parks, piers, bobbing donkeys, candy-floss and body-odour into this deep-sea green of quietness and luxury. Or the young cutting a splendid dash for two days, three, not too far from home.

He smiled, raised a hand to the young woman at reception. Her return was dazzling, beyond his deserts.

Out of the air conditioning, on the courtyard, the sun was hot, dry, untempered. The flat sea gleamed. Human families jumped like fleas. A car engine raced, unsuitably, for the Frankland. He slid his key into lock, into ignition, made a start.

Oncoming traffic built up.

CHAPTER 13

He reached the flat a little after two, and on his colleague's written instruction helped himself to ham and salad from the 'fridge. The meal did not occupy him long enough, so he made coffee, opened a packet of chocolate biscuits.

Next, meticulously, he washed the dishes, cleaned his shoes, laid out a good dark suit, a clean shirt and underclothes. In the bath he scrubbed the traces of boot polish from his fingers, and sitting, shaved again, not cutting himself once. He decided against lotions, Meg liked men natural, she'd claimed once, not reeking with male perfumes.

Naked, he considered himself in the glass, was not displeased.

By three-thirty he parked on the arm of a chair, and toed the carpet. His colleague's note informed him that the flat was his alone until Wednesday. Fisher enjoyed the shabby symmetry of the place. Price-Jones hated mess, was a bit of an old woman, but decent, had brought food in for his friend, even a small joint for Sunday. Reader in physics, a dusty man, a widower without children, who'd let his house to the professor of surgery, and who moved in here, entirely happy, as far as one could judge, filling note-books with rows of mathematical symbols, and preparing, now, in these last three weeks, gastromomic treats for his refugee. He talked little, played the viola in the college orchestra, and was said to be up again for election by the Royal Society. Oddly, he'd no friend.

Fisher wondered why he wasted thought on Price-Jones instead of Meg, decided that he merely remapped known ground, reassured himself. He remembered the grandfather who'd come from Wales and made a pretty penny as a grocer in London, then the schoolmaster who'd added Price, his mother's maiden name, to the Jones and had begotten this one boy. Next year, Washbrook would retire and Bill P.-J. would succeed to the chair of physics, vice-chancellors, colleagues and the like keeping their heads. And if he did not?

'My best work's done Edwin. At thirty I was worth talking to.' The thin home-counties whine. 'Now I'm putting the frame round the picture.' The last sentence rang typical; odd in so dry a man, but indicative of his cleverness, his touch of the creative.

Fisher cleaned his teeth again.

He stood ready, wound his wristwatch, combed his hair for the third time.

Arriving at his old home, he parked in the street, though he knew there would be room in the drive.

The afternoon sky was dabbed with small clouds, and the privet hedge, well-trimmed, seemed dull with dust. Between stone-capped brick pillars the iron gates were shut and the one window he could see downstairs had its cream blind drawn. The Laurels. Stout, late Victorian, vicarage-style villa, double fronted with bow windows either side. Paintwork gleamed as if it had been washed that day, and the pointing between the handmade bricks was immaculate. In the middle of the arch of the front-door a head of a moustachioed gentleman, Kitchener or Stalin, craned forward under its cream paint.

Kathleen Twining, Meg's friend, invited him into his own house, placed him in the drawing room, where all was cool, half-shadowed, protected by blinds. He sat, inspected nervously.

'Meg will be in in a moment. Would you like a cup of tea?'

He said that he would. She closed the door without noise. Nothing had been changed; the same bibelots, including his grey Wembley Exhibition penknife, on the mantelpiece. On the walls, their reproductions of Vermeer, Chagall, Graham Sutherland, that Modigliani woman they'd argued about, Picasso doves, John Smith's honesty. Yet the room smelt feminine, as though they'd soaked, no, touched the solid furniture with scent, with tiny grains of sweet powder.

Was that bloody Kathleen to be a witness, then? Why was she so friendly?

He heard nothing from outside, in a room still as a dentist's, frightening. Shoes polished free of dust on trouser legs, shirt cuffs pulled to prominence. The top of a bookcase was crowded with Meg's glass paper-weights, huge gay marbles, cocky as clown's eyes, ridiculous but delightful. And her pot hen on the far table by the walnut fruitbowl she'd made on a lathe at night-class. In the corner behind him stood, he could not see, the tall bookcase with its Dickens, Scott, Hardy and George Eliot, bought in a sale, and on top of that, the slender vase in dark blue glass, white dotted, within a yard of the high ceiling. A huge bunch of lime-leaves filled the fire-place and a red biro lay on the hearth by the polished brass shell-case which held the irons. He peered over the arm of his chair to check that the small copper kettle was on its stand beneath him.

He trembled, cold across the shoulders.

Steps clipped on the terazzo of the hall-floor, voices hummed, faded, and the door handle turned.

He stood as his wife came in.

The entry was not impressive, for Meg stared, tripped the three or four steps then sat down fast, awkwardly on the far end of the settee, offering no hand. She wore a white blouse, and a maxi skirt, wide at the hem, in dark green, lightly lined in squares. An Edwardian governess on her first day. With a pang of pleasure he noticed that she wore both engagement and wedding rings, but her hair disappointed, swept up into neat dullness, false and prim.

'Sit down,' she said.

He almost expected her to burst into laughter, but she linked her fingers round her knees, not looking at him.

'Kathy will bring us a cup of tea in a moment.'

His thanks sounded thick.

'Did you have a good time at Bealthorpe? I was surprised when Daddy said he'd met you there.'

More easily than he thought possible, he strung sentences together about the weather, the digs, his fellow-lodgers. She turned her head as he spoke, smiled at him, as if genuinely savouring his clichés.

'Why did you go, Edwin?' Sometimes, usually on the telephone, her voice, cleared, freed itself from harmonics; so now.

'I don't know. I was at a loose end.'

'But Bealthorpe?'

'Your father went.'

'He says the service and meals at the Frankland are the best in England.' She giggled. 'I think he holds shares in it.'

The passage was unmalicious, and he unwound. He told her about his holidays as a child, while they conducted together a neat inquiry into the economics of so grand a hotel in so flat a resort.

Kathleen Twining knocked, laid down the copper-cornered tray, with crockery and cake, backed out to return with the large tea-pot.

'That's all,' she said.

Only two cups, the best china, from his mother's cabinet. Meg poured and as she moved after pot or kettle her skirt swung darkly about. The blouse seemed cheap, as if to disguise the full breasts, or crumple round them, clapped into lumpy elastic; the material faded, rummage-sale, handled.

The two stirred, clinked, sipped, knifed thin, buttered slices of currant bread. Fisher, not hungry, chewed smally, concentrated on the navy and gold ornamentation on the plate. When he refused more food, Meg described, in some detail, the diet that Kathleen had been following, and her success. She spoke as if that were important.

They'd gathered at this table after Donald's funeral, and laughed, in the early afternoon, over the fruit-cakes and sandwiches, people who would not have attended his birthday party. Meg had been attentive to them all, fussing over her mother, exchanging small grim jokes with Tina, Edwin's sister. The sun shone and the blinds had never been down. There all stood, in dark best, civilised people ready to resume important concerns when this ceremony, this teasing end to God's act of treachery was over. And Donald, with his ailments, was a small urnful of mortality. Today the Roman and his trouble / Are ashes under Uricon.

'I expect Daddy's been getting on to you,' she began.

'Yes. In his way.' Fisher determined to be serious.

'He's been on my back for a fortnight now, and when he found you at Bealthorpe, he took that as a portent. He's very superstitious.' She examined the palm of her right hand. 'A Methodist Druid.'

He acknowledged the remark, but refused to add to triviality.

'David thinks perhaps,' she did not hurry, concentrating on the finger-stretched hand, 'that I've been unfaithful.'

'Have you?'

'No.' She did not stress the word.

'Nor I. He pressed me about it.'

'We're very good, very well behaved, then, aren't we?' Now she looked at him, expecting anger, perhaps dislike. He did not answer; her blouse, buttoned high was secured at neck and wrists with black ribbon laces.

'Did he tell you what to say?' she asked.

'He said you were,' Fisher fumbled, 'damaged. Hurt.'

'He told me that I had to keep talking, that I mustn't sit here. I promised that I would.'

'Why?'

'Why what?'

'Did you promise?' Fisher cleared an obstruction in his throat.

'It seemed sensible. We don't just meet to look at one another. Or do we?'

'I find it not unpleasant.' He yielded to levity, at last, thus early.

'That's nice.'

She squared matters with these words and standing poured tea without more inquiry.

When both had settled again, they took their time, she asked muddily,

'What do you think?'

'About us?'

'Yes.'

'I don't know.'

She tapped the arm of the settee with long fingernails, as if vexed.

'That's how I feel,' she said, in the end. 'I think it's bloody silly, but I just don't know. Did you have any reaction coming into this house again?'

'Of course. I remembered things.'

'Was it, were they, important?'

'Some.'

'Donald? You remembered Donald?'

It was as if she'd clubbed him. That smashed the rules. The child should have been named as a last resort, in an extremity, not handed out with the currant-bread. He sat unnerved, a skin short, wounds oozing.

'The funeral. I thought of that. In here.' Strangulated, he gobbled, ashamed.

She wept.

Noiseless, tears grey on her blouse, she cried, small handkerchief clutched in her fist.

As he struggled up towards her, she signalled him away with her paws. Obediently he waited, as she dabbed, sobbed.

The door clicked open, and Miss Twining stood over her friend, tall and stooping.

'Oh, dear. Oh, dear,' she repeated. 'This won't do.'

She poured out a further inch of tea into a cup, and rummaged in Meg's handbag for a tablet. Without show, Meg swallowed, continued her crying.

'Put your legs up,' Twining ordered. She swung Meg to position on the settee, arranging pillows, spreading a tartan blanket. Had she brought that in? 'That's better. You look like a real invalid now.'

'I'd better go.' Fisher, now the fussing was done.

'You stop there. She'll be right enough. Just give her a minute. We shall be fine, shan't we, love?'

That sounded so condescending, directed at a childish fractiousness, that Fisher reddened, angry and disturbed.

'Perhaps I've upset her,' he said.

'Not at all. Not at all. Don't rush things. We're all right.'

The Twining had listened at the door, then. He did not mind because it meant there could be nothing final here today, or nothing with the appearance of finality. Miss Twining, with her Scottish voice and sharp nose, would preserve decorum, prevent blows, get the one used to the other, reinstate the habit of marriage. He straightened the flaps of his pockets, while, Kathleen, very leisurely, apparently talking to herself, though he'd no idea what she murmured, collected the cups and plates, stacked them.

'At a time like this', she faced Fisher squarely, and her small eyes were green, 'I'd recommend a cup of tea all round, but as you've just partaken it wouldn't be of much use.'

'No,' he said.

Both smiled; they could have shaken hands. Meg had recovered her composure, stared at the lampshade.

'Will you be all right, darling?'

'I think so.'

'I think so, too. So I'll leave you to your husband,' that stressed, rolled 'r' and sibilant prominent. 'To talk on. She's easily upset, as you'll imagine, Edwin.'

Christian name now; surprised she knew it. 'But she wants to speak to you.' Again, she deliberately reorganised the china, picked up the tray, and went, leaving the door ajar. Neither man nor wife moved. A minute or so later Twining closed the door, calling, 'I'm on the patio if you want me.'

'What was the tablet?' he asked.

'I don't know.' That sounded true.

'Librium? Valium? Something of the sort?'

'I suppose so.'

Meg was pale, but calm, with one white hand outside the blanket. Her eyes were shadowed with a pale violet.

'I think I ought to go,' he said.

'No. Please. They'll think we haven't tried.'

'They?'

'Daddy. Mummy. Kathleen.'

'Have we?' It seemed cruel, unnecessarily so.

He began to qualify. 'I mean. We've not said anything, have we? Important?'

'Would you come back if I asked you?'

'Yes.'

He did not know why he answered so eagerly. Politeness, a gesture towards her status as a patient. For the life of him, he did not seem able to feel. As a boy he'd once chewed a dog biscuit, tasteless and unappetising. He'd spat the mush into his hand.

'That's nice,' Meg said. 'Even if you don't mean it.'

She delivered without energy, as if the intelligence were there, but not the drive, the fire. It sounded more like a schoolgirl than his wife.

'It's the truth. Or the best I can do.' Why he made that graceless modification he did not know. 'Why did you cry just now? Because I mentioned Donald? Or you did?'

'Yes. In a way. I felt I owed something to you on Donald's account.'

'No, Meg. You don't.' Stern. 'You can put that right out of your head.'

'He was such a weakling, though.'

'That wasn't your fault.'

'It wasn't yours, was it?' She sounded petulant. 'He made such a poor start he never recovered. That's what they said at the hospital.'

'Nobody could have been a better mother.' Doggedly, like a man asserting what he barely believed. 'You did all possible.'

Without turning to him, in the same pinched voice, she asked,

'Do you ever look at photographs of him?'

'I've only the one in my wallet. Yes. I sometimes look at it.'

'What do you think . . . of? Then? When you . . . ? Her voice tailed off, not because she could not go further, but because her question was perfectly posed.

'Hard to say. I look. I remember him. I have a sort of pang. It's going. I wonder if it happened to me. He looks so healthy.'

'Which picture is it?'

He fetched out his wallet, opened it so that the photograph was revealed in its oval leather frame. The child sat in his push-chair, grinning, face chubby, arms up. She took the wallet, glanced down, away, down again thrusting her head back as if she had difficulty in focusing.

'Oh, yes. The one in the bobble-hat. You took it out here. He was so cross, strapped in. It was very cold.'

'Was it?'

'It snowed that evening. Not much. A few flakes.'

That scatter of snow he did not recall seemed as important to him now as the dead child. That lived in her mind. She closed the wallet and returned it, and as she did so, her face looked drained, bruised, deprived. They said no more for a few minutes, but sat in the warmth, not uncomfortably, but unrelaxed.

'Has what's-her-name been here long?'

He could not bring himself to name her.

'Kathleen? About a week after you left.'

'I didn't know you were so friendly.'

'We weren't.'

They'd worked together at the same school. Indeed, Twining was still there as deputy head. Meg played with her wedding ring.

'I rang her up one evening. I wanted to talk to somebody who'd not bully me. Daddy, oh, you know what he's like. Kathleen's nice, and full of ideas. If you're down in the mouth, she gets you on to making a complicated gâteau, that sort of thing.'

'It wouldn't suit me.'

'I would have said that. She comes Thursday morning and goes back to her flat just Tuesday and Wednesday.'

'Why?'

'To live her own life.'

He smiled, nearly laughed, thought better of it.

'I'm glad you've come to some sort of arrangement.'

'Are you all right with Dr Price-Jones?'

He put up a few interesting sentences, describing his host whom she did not know well. It seemed important that he should do his best, provide her with neat cameos for her entertainment, make her see that he was an interesting man exerting himself on her behalf. In return, she smiled at one or two of Bill's eccentricities and her husband's turns of phrase so that he found himself rewarded, enjoying his moment, putting himself out further. While embroidering Price-Jones's idiocies in his Rover, Edwin realised, with a cold start that she was not listening. He paused.

'You've not heard a word I've said.'

'I beg your pardon.' Startled by the new tone, she turned.

'Doesn't matter.'

'I was listening, Edwin.'

It sounded so pathetic that he thought of moving towards her, touching her, but she bunched herself in the corner of the settee as if shrinking from the liberty. Outside a car crunched gravel, the doorbell blasted; Twining tripped and there was subdued talk in the hall.

'You've got visitors,' he said.

'Yes.'

'Perhaps I'd better go.'

'You don't know who it is?' Her voice conveyed no liveliness. He waited, concentrating on the corner of a low cupboard, and beyond that to a corn-dolly, pert and straw-pale on the polished oak. 'Don't you recognise voices?'

'Usually.'

'My father and mother.'

Again, he decided on silence, squeezing her to speech, but this time she clasped her hands, rather malely, between her knees and sat forward, back bowed, ugly, awkward. A door was closed elsewhere, while these two protracted the pause, both edgy, half intent on advantage.

'Did you know they were coming?' At long last; generous.

'Yes, I did.'

'They'll . . . What do they expect?'

She puckered her forehead, pushed at her bright hair, as if she needed to concentrate on this, but smiled, gratefully, broadly.

'You know David,' she said. 'He's worked it out. First we're given the chance to straighten our affairs, but in the middle of it, he appears. A sort of spur. He's a very good opinion of himself. The voice of reason.'

'Is that right?'

Her account seemed intelligent, as if she suddenly livened herself, made the effort, but now she flagged, minutely expressing unconcern with her expression.

'I don't know.'

He should have pressed her.

'It seems likely enough.' Too late. He never repaired faults with Meg. Broken meant smashed irreparably. Though he was never sure.

On their honeymoon they'd been out for a walk, on a showery day, and though both were cold they hadn't the energy to strike out, warm themselves. They hugged each other, kissed in bleak fields, under wind-stunted trees, but seemed dazed, unable to find exhilaration in the weather, the whip of the gale, rain's slashing. They worked their way down to a valley where a muddy lane led between hawthorn hedges and through a farm yard.

Down there all stood quiet, with the air almost warm as they consulted their map. They differed over that; Meg wanted to climb back over the hill into the next valley where they'd meet a main road; he argued that they'd do better to move straight on past the farm on to a secondary road and back home that way. He was polite; meticulously he measured the distances, courteously asking her to check every calculation. By this way they saved a mile and a half and kept to moderately level ground. She yielded, grudgingly.

As soon as they set off he knew he'd done wrong to insist. It was not the superiority of his route, nor his proof of this she resented, but the mud on this lane. Puddles clouded brown, and the top half inch of the surface shone with moisture, as slippery as glass. She put her feet down gingerly; her stockings were already splattered black. As they trudged past the outhouses, dogs barked, fierce as wolves, while at the last gate, the ground stank with mud a foot deep, churned and pitted.

'Oh, to be in England,' he'd said.

The grey blackened, and for a few minutes hail raked their way, so they had to stand with their backs to the storm. His arm circled her, but she no longer responded, dabbed at her reddened face with a wet handkerchief.

'I can see blue sky,' he said. 'Won't last long.'

His trousers were soaked. She sniffed.

'We've more shelter here than we'd have up the hillside.'

Again she ignored him, shaking drops from her hood, shivering. Her face shone paler now, waxy with wet, as they set out again through a lane filthy as the yard.

'We'll walk in single file by the hedge-bottom,' he said, mounting a narrow bank above the level of the path. 'Shall I go first?'

She did not answer but he heard her behind him, plodding, uttering little gasps of displeasure as she slithered or brought a thrash of raindrops down from the twigs in the hedge.

'We're making good time,' he called back.

He did not believe it, fearing that his feet would go from under him and he'd be flat out in the sludge.

No reply, but the sniffs, the rustle of sleeve on anorak.

'We might have a bit of sunshine yet.'

A cloud mass was touched with gold once at its edges before the wind tore them into smoke.

Thud of feet, mud-soled; sullen silence; disgruntled breathing.

'When we get over this little ridge we should see the road,' he said. 'It can't be more than a mile off.'

Swish of coat, sleeve; toggle swing; dissatisfaction.

Here the surface was solider, grass-covered, and Fisher began to leg it, half to spite Meg. He heard her yelp of fright, the thump as she fell, but took three steps before he turned. She was down in the lane, on one knee and both her hands in the muck. Black water oozed over the silly pair of white gloves she wore, between and over the fingers. He took her under the left arm and heaved her to her feet. Without a word she stepped the six inches upwards to the bank.

'Are you all right?' he asked.

He could not see her face, turned from him in its darkening hood.

Savagely, clumsy, she dragged the gloves from her hands, squeezed the pair, black drop by drop, before she flung the ball of soiled cloth into the hedge bottom. Now she lifted her skirt. Her right knee was splashed with shining mud. Immediately he snatched at his handkerchief, wiped the stocking clean, then dashed his handkerchief to join her gloves.

She laughed.

He made her wear his heavy mittens, and soon they'd reached the road, arm in arm splashing. Her mood was light; he sang. Another shower did not stop them, merely caused them to walk faster and vie with each other in swearing at the weather. By the time they reached their lodgings, an hour and a half later, moderation had set in, they were temperate, but warmly friendly. That proved their best day as they talked by the sitting room fire, making subdued love in the vast creaking bed, dropping to sleep in an embrace. He remembered now the silver fat raindrops on the black hedges, bouncing, and flying, the wind's energy, the whirling débris of the disturbed sky and their walking, their strut, his proud 'Road to the Isles.'

She had laughed.

And as he'd wiped at that muddy knee, that sweet of sex, its juicy symbol, he'd known his role as husband. She'd fallen, without humiliation, switched from sulky anger to laughter which had saved him, cleansed his faults, sainted her, manned him in youth, crowned him, serf on the wrong track, lord of all.

Perhaps that would happen now.

'What are you smiling about?' she asked.

When he told her, she looked puzzled, had to be reminded grudging, admitted that it had happened, but offered no corroborative detail to encourage further reminiscence. As far as he could read her expression, it showed mild exasperation, embarrassment.

'You'd come back?' she asked again.

'Yes.'

She waited, in anticipation of qualifying clauses, but he left it there.

'I'm going away,' she said, distantly.

'From here?'

'Of course.' She frowned, without anger, at his stupidity.

'To live?'

Now she sat nursing clasped hands between her knees, in reverie. This annoyed him, because he knew now she was not trying, did not consider him, had some trick up her sleeve, but he forced himself to stay still, to rummage in his head for nothing in particular, to make a creative work of staring at the carpet.

'I shall go on holiday.'

'That's good.' A bonhomie he did not feel. 'Where will you go?'

'In September,' she said, 'I shall go to India.'

That flattened him.

'By air?' he said, gasping for it.

'Yes. The monsoon is over then, and I shall get the best of the weather.'

'Are you going on your own?'

'Yes.'

'Is it, is it a sort of, of package-deal?'

'Not really.'

'Isn't it very expensive?'

'Daddy will pay.'

That smacked down, reduced him in hope. Depression wrote his part. Daddy will pay. Edwin does not count. He poked a finger-end into his mouth and bit, gnawed the nail, the knuckle. He'd taken a week in Bealthorpe, in a boardinghouse, bed and breakfast with evening meal, h. and c. in bedroom, all mod. cons, while she made grandly for the gorgeous east, the Taj Mahal, Char Minah, Ajanta Caves, the Western Ghats, the Nilgiris. His geographical knowledge deserted him. Clive, Tipu Sahib, Akhbar, Warren Hastings, Zamindars, Gandhiji. History evaporated.

'Don't you think it's a good idea?' she asked.

He shook his head, sat rejected. Dejection

weakened the whole of his body so that he dare not speak for fear his voice collapsed into a hoarse cry, a howl, a sob, a hiccough of tears. He stumbled up to his feet, wagging an explanatory hand towards her, shambled across to the door.

'Where are you going?'

'Back.' The word barked, croaked.

'You haven't seen daddy, yet.'

He rested his forehead on the cool white paint of the door, with no attempt to disguise his distress. There, beaten, aware of his posture, doing nothing to correct it, he bent forward like a figure from a film, shot at the prison wall. Meg seemed not to notice, continued with her hand-hugging, until she said, sharply,

'Oh. Come and sit down, Edwin.'

The sentence was badly delivered. Oh. Come and sit. Down. Edwin.

'I'm going,' he said, forcing speech through his lips.

'Why should you? That's not reasonable.'

He moved so that he could see himself in the ornate mirror above the fireplace. Crumpled, but perfectly normal, tie slightly askew, he gloomed back at himself, diminished, but twinned now by the elongated Modigliani face behind him.

'I think Daddy wants to talk.'

'About what?'

'I'm not sure. I expect he feels the need to get us to express our minds, each before the other.' Precious.

'Did he know you were going to India? He must have.'

'He didn't suggest it, if that's what you mean.'

'Why did you?'

'Travel brochures. I'm very conventional, you know.'

He could have slapped her, though he realised she had not noticed his shocked defeat. He'd stood at that door, his manhood whacked out of him, and she'd not bothered to turn her head. Perhaps she had not dared; concerned with her own inadequacies, she carefully avoided his.

Now, not unhappy, she swung her legs, from the knees, almost girlishly, a child at exercise, in a pedal car.

'Are you angry with me?' he asked.

'No.'

'But you were glad when I left you. That's what you wanted, isn't it?'

'I don't know.'

'It's what you said.'

'I say a lot of things I don't mean. That's so, Teddy. It is.' She glared. 'You ought to know that it is. I was furious, and you were tired.'

'Won't,' he asked, without heat, 'the same thing happen again?'

'Very likely.'

'Then why should we bother? If we're going to break up, as soon now as in a month or two's time.'

'That's silly.' That dismissed him. 'We're married. Doesn't that mean anything?'

'What's it mean to you, then?'

'You asked me to marry you. And you wanted to. I thought about it, as hard as I could. And I wanted to marry you. I can think back exactly as I felt.'

'Can you?'

'I can think back, Edwin, think back. I know what I wanted . . .'

'When we were married, was that anything like you expected?'

'Yes, it was,' Meg said. 'Not in every particular, but it was. And I wasn't disappointed in you. You annoyed me, and you were childish, but you worked hard, and you considered me, and you did your utmost when Donald died. It's just like you now to ask all these awkward questions when we've almost settled things. You don't want to be bested. You don't want Daddy to trap you.'

'You've thought about it,' he said, 'and you've decided you want me back.'

'That's right.'

'On what terms?'

'On no terms.' She was crying, but in a flurry of anger as though she'd shake the tears to the far corners of the room. 'We're just spouting words. You aren't saying what you mean. You're making your side right for yourself, in your own little mind.'

He knew now, as well as such things could be known that Meg had been conditioned or bullied or cajoled into acceptance of the marriage, of his return, by her father and mother. Therefore this afternoon's tears meant little. She was to try him out, to assert herself with polemics, with a stately announcement of the oriental jaunt, and then take his hand, renew her vows.

That did not displease him.

He liked her tears, hated dangerous indifference.

When he was nearly eighteen, doing 'A' levels, he'd visited a girl in a mental hospital. She, Valerie Watson, two years older than he, was the daughter of a shopkeeper no wealthier than Arthur Fisher but who'd left the rooms over his business to live in a prosperous suburb. Valerie had been at Edwin's school, but it wasn't until she'd left that the pair of them struck up a friendship at a chapel social. She was shy, not unattractive, with beautifully white hands, blue-veined, and they settled at once to discuss Beethoven. Sometimes they exchanged letters, or visits and then they'd listen to records or play piano duets of Mozart Symphonies together. It would, be wrong to say there was nothing sexual in the relationship, for the young Fisher could not see women in any other way but they kissed hardly at all, barely touched fingers. At this time, he saw himself in love with two other girls, but not with Valerie.

His parents, as usual, displayed gawky concern.

Valerie was 'Ted's young lady' to them. They inquired about her, made a fuss of her when she came, reported that they had seen her in the street, described her character favourably as if he were incapable of making an assessment for himself. Looking back now, Fisher guessed they regarded her as a suitable match, in spite of the difference in age. Watson wasn't short, and Val an only child. But the boy himself did not know what to make of the arrangement. She was pretty in a straight-backed way, with wide eyes open at him, and possessed of a diffident intelligence; he bullied her, and she allowed it, though now and then she opposed his argument, sometimes beat him. She read widely, could contradict his facts, but still preferred a secondary, submissive role, and that pleased him. He could strut and lay law down, when he badly needed that confidence.

In her second year at the university she had been taken ill. He had seen her not a fortnight before his parents announced her nervous breakdown, and she had seemed no different from any other time. They had met less frequently since both were preparing for exams, but he'd been invited to tea, and they'd listened to the Beethoven Trio, Op. 70, No. 2 in Eb. They'd played it through twice, commenting favourably, and wondering why the composer had written so popular a work at this period. They'd squatted on the carpet in front of the gas fire and she had sat with her chin on her knees so that he could see her unstockinged thighs, a triangle of white knickers. This was unusual, and had excited him, but nothing came of it; they talked about William Cobbett and Spenser before she'd made him a cup of coffee at nine-thirty and sent him packing.

His parents gave no account of her breakdown. They questioned him about his last visit, and hinted that matters had not been normal for some months, that she had been under treatment. He could not say, honestly, that he had noticed the slightest difference, except for that careless exposure of underclothes, nor had her parents shown any anxiety.

This annoyed him. At eighteen he prided himself on his insight, often criticised friends for failing to notice small signs of distress and anger in others, announced that given those circumstances he would have had the nous to act otherwise. Yet Valerie had been normal, outwardly friendly and humble, listening, expressing approval of his theories about Keats's illness, Beethoven's professionalism.

In the next few weeks he had meant to visit the Watson house, but he was busy, with examinations, societies, games. He never admitted his fear to himself. Messages came through his parents; she was no better; consultants hovered, she had been admitted to a mental hospital; they tried bizarre treatments.

He received a summons through his mother. Mrs Watson had phoned to ask if he would accompany them one evening to the St Francis Hospital. He trembled.

As usually, he walked round to the house where the father spoke affably, even boisterously, shaking his hand, calling him Ted. The mother crept round the place, powdered white as death, drained of energy, but it was she who told him that Valerie had 'withdrawn.' He nodded, face arranged into seriousness, but dared not ask further. The drive to the hospital quietened the father, so that the three slunk across the car park.

As they approached the ward, a new one-storey annexe, built in the yard of the Victorian, dark-brick prison of the parent hospital, they braced themselves, put a front on, slapped feet on the coloured squares of lino in the passage, held heads up in the ward. First there was chair-sorting to be done, and Fisher made himself useful, carting not only a third for himself, but two for the elderly ladies visiting a plump, laughing matron in the next bed. When this chore was finished, he found the parents, either side of the bed, leaning over their daughter.

Valerie appeared to sleep.

Her hands were outside the sheets, but perhaps the parents, each holding one now, had rescued them. Mrs Watson talked feverishly, in a whisper, keeping it private, head down to her daughter's.

'Look who's come to see you, Valerie. Do you know him? Look who it is. It's Edwin. Edwin Fisher, y' know. Say hello to her, Edwin. She knows you. Look who it is, darling.'

Fisher mumbled.

Valerie's face lay pasty on the pillow, as she struggled to open her eyes, dark blue and unreal. After some moments, she murmured, sound like a sigh, and Mrs Watson jack-knifed over to catch the drift, arms astride the inert body, putting her husband away. The eyes closed; the voice died.

'What is it, Mother?'

'I don't know. I couldn't make out. I think she's pleased to see Edwin.'

The blatant lie annoyed him. One must face reality. He'd come here, and not for soft soap. For the next half-hour they tried to coax the girl into communication, and though she murmured, moaned, almost by chance, and once, a tear, a single tear, formed itself from the nearly closed eye. At the end of this time, and Fisher sat aghast at the energy of the mother, bending, willing her girl back into the wide awake world, Watson touched the young man on the sleeve to announce they were going out for a smoke.

Mrs Watson lifted her head.

'See the sister, will you?' she ordered, and returned to her vigilance.

Certainly they called in the small room at the end of the ward, but Watson seemed relieved rather than otherwise to find it empty.

'They can't tell you much,' he said. 'We'll look in on the way back.'

Outside it had rained, a brief shower which Fisher had not noticed, but the air blew spring-like, warm for late February. Watson flourished his case, offering his companion a cigarette which was refused. The lighting proceeded with ceremony, ritual gestures, set cupping of hands, but there was no mistaking the huge relief of that first inhaling breath.

They began to walk along the tarmac paths; touches of green decorated the winter bareness of the shrubs, spiraea, beauty-bush, while clumps of purple or orange crocuses opened to the flash of sunshine.

Watson made a remark or two about gardening, then led the boy to the car park where he praised or blamed vehicles like a salesman, lighting a second cigarette from the first. The man spoke strongly, but uncomfortably, clenching his hairy right fist to slap it in the palm of the left, pointing a finger, blubbering his lips, a strong man in weakness, bolstering himself, impressing his companion. When he finally announced that they had to return, he flung his dog-end violently into the bushes, and the pair returned without a word.

From the corridor Fisher could see Mrs Watson bent over Valerie, who had not apparently moved. The father touched his elbow, and the two went into the nurses' room where a dark woman sat at the desk, stirring tea with one hand and reading a large card she held in the other.

'Ah, Mr Watson.' Scots accent.

Watson placed himself in front of her desk, asserting himself, feet apart.

'Good afternoon, sister,'

'What can I do for you?' A wrinkling of eyes in a false smile.

'How is she, then?'

The woman shrugged, shrinking herself.

'It's a slow process, Mr Watson.' The word, 'slow'

dragged itself out. Dorically long. 'But I honestly think there's an improvement. It's slight, but it's there.' She laid down the card as if to stress her certainty. The father questioned her for some minutes more but got no further information, merely put back the time when they had to return to the bedside. As they left the office, Watson, blew a sigh, an involuntary sound, and walked with feet outspread on legs of sponge.

Valerie lay pale as her mother, but naturally so, skin smooth and delicate. Now her eyes were open, if not fully, but she made no attempt to greet them. Mrs Watson burst into a volley of words. 'Here's your father. Look at Daddy's new tie he's put on for you. You know Edwin, don't you? Isn't it kind of him to pay a visit? Now, I've brought you some lemon and barley and put it in the locker. Tell the nurse to let you have some, because it's always done you good, and it's very hot in here.' The garrulity was pitiful; its bright energy wasted itself, but cut Fisher deep.

When they left at the bell, Mrs Watson composed Valerie's limbs as if she were dead, darted at the pillow, kissed the still face. Watson bent, blowing; rose, rubbing the stretched cloth of his belly. Fisher, for a moment, grasped the white left hand; it was warm, in no way unpleasant.

He went once more, when Valerie was a little better, and spoke awkwardly to her, as she pulled her bedjacket across her chest. His mother reported to him later that she had recovered,

304

though she never returned to the university, and two years afterwards she married, some young man in business who lived in Watford. He did not visit her while she was convalescent, nor write. After his 'A' levels, he made for France, worked there, until he returned for a term to prepare for Oxford. His part in the affair was inconclusive, if not shameful, and when he listened to the third movement of Op. 70, No 2, he hated its simplicity of happiness which mocked his self-approbation.

Now, this summer afternoon, he recalled the incident as Meg sat, face wooden as Valerie's, as incommunicative as she flung words at him. His wife had not withdrawn, but had seceded from decision, left it to her father to order this part of her life. He had no time for her as a zombie, preferring her moody volatility to this flabby acquiescence. Should he say so? Should he worry her now back into her own mind?

'I'm making it right for myself, I agree,' he said. It sounded patronising. 'It's a failing of mine, as well you know. But there is one thing worrying me.'

She made a slight gesture of interrogation.

'It's this. Do you want me back?'

'I've said so.' Quick, firm.

'You've not been pushed into it by your father?'

'No, I haven't.'

The answers lacked enthusiasm, delivered however promptly.

'I want to be sure, Meg. You sit there as if you didn't care either way. No, that's wrong. You sit

305

as if you're so badly damaged that nothing matters any more.'

'I can't help it.'

'You're not like yourself. There's no go about you. You look as if you're waiting for your father or Kathleen or somebody to push in and rescue you.'

'What do you look like, then?'

'Good question. I'm undecided. I've had this silly week's holiday. I've got plenty of work to do. I think I might start my play. I promised your father I'd come back to look at you, at least.'

'So you like what you see?' No devil.

'I don't understand it. You act as if you're ill, or drugged.'

'And that makes you frightened to come back?'

'I've said I would.' He tried to infuse warmth into the words. She, after a second or so, dropped her hands as if at some culmination of expected idiocy. They closed mouths, hearts.

In the end, surprisingly, it was she who spoke.

'I'm scared,' she said. 'You see, when we broke up, though I was only too glad to see you go, it seemed wrong. If I couldn't make a marriage with you, then who could I with?' Words dropped like awkwardly kicked pebbles on a cliff face.

'I don't know about that.' He felt he must stick his chest out with honesty.

'It's not rational. There may be men better suited. At least with them I don't suppose I'd have crippled the marriage for a start. I'd be on the look-out for snags.' She seemed to have lost control of language, but her meaning stood powerfully obvious. 'But you're my type of man. I think so.'

'What type's that?' Dry, he accepted no olive-branches. The words seemed to make love which her flat tone denied.

'I don't know. When we married I thought I'd chosen the right man. He'd chosen me.'

'You may have been mistaken?'

'That's what you think?'

'No, Meg, it isn't. I want to be sure that you're not taking me back because you've been told to, or because, oh, God, I don't know, the neighbours might gossip.'

If her new tone roused nothing but suspicion in him, it concealed no wish to quarrel. Before, she'd have flared at this, sworn, told him to piss off, cried, thrown something, banged the room door damned near off its hinges.

'I've thought,' she began, 'about this for days on end. Commonsense says we should chuck it up, try with somebody else. We're not kids. We had a fair time. Perhaps we should start again with somebody else before we're too old and set in our ways to mess that up. I don't want common sense. We were married. We had Donald. We had some good times.'

'I wiped your knee with my handkerchief.'

That was not immediately applicable, not at the forepoint of her mind. She searched for it, groped, found, remembered, smiled.

'Rationally, there's nothing in this. Marriage is no more a legal contract. I don't believe it was made in heaven. I don't believe in heaven.'

'But.' He made a big sound of it, boomed.

'But . . .' She laughed, tentatively. 'Upbringing makes me think otherwise.'

'While I've been away from you, I've considered you,' he said. 'And I decided I'd rather be married to you than anyone else.' He did not even know if this was the truth, but he spoke forcefully. 'I hated the idea that we'd never live together again.'

'Why didn't you tell me?'

'I don't trust myself. I don't like change for a start. Then it may have been pride. "He's been turfed out by his wife, you know." And we were getting on each other's tits.'

'You can say that again.' Warmer.

'Odd,' Fisher said. 'We should take up the marriage again. We're agreed. We haven't the faintest notion why. And we haven't mentioned love.'

'If you had . . .'

'Yes?'

'I'd have been suspicious.'

'Don't believe that,' he said. 'Everybody likes being told he's loved. I do.'

She paused, patting her forehead.

'I'm not sure that I could, quite, say, that, now.' The last words plopped separate.

'You will, Oscar, you will.' She smiled again, nervous yet. 'I like you Meg. I admit it. There's something about . . .' He broke off. One could overshoot the mark, and she still stared at the carpet dumbly, again without expression. 'We're not talking sentimentalities, are we?'

'Very likely.'

'We'll try again.'

'I don't think, really, that much good comes of talking. Daddy argues it does, and you. Or do you? I don't. We're not rational creatures. Not you and I.'

'I know. But if we don't act with reason, where are we? What standards can we apply? We'd go about knocking one another out with knuckle-dusters or bombs.'

'That mightn't be any worse.'

'You know damn well it would. Blow a man's hands or legs off, where is he? What is he?'

That exchange sounded livelier, so that a spot of colour burnt on Meg's cheekbone, as she sat with a straighter back, but at the sharp knock on the door, she started, glanced wildly round.

David Vernon breezed in, smile deeply etched at his mouth, his eyes. 'Do I intrude?' His voice had a rich quality, a velvet, an actor's thrust so that to Fisher the breathy sentence he and Meg had bartered during the last hour seemed thin, without life. 'Come in, Irene.' His wife wore purple to match his voice, managing to look pretentious and pathetic, yet scrupulously clean. A smile twitched on Fisher's lips for this toga, from which he felt benefit. 'Kathleen is preparing further cups of tea.'

'We've eaten,' Meg said. Certainly her tone lacked resonance.

'Then eat again.'

He showed his wife to an armchair, stood in mid-room hands in pockets, face rugged with pleasure.

'What's the news, Margaret?' Very Welsh.

Meg looked at her husband.

'We're making it up,' she said.

'You are?' He turned a forensic expression towards Fisher.

'We are.'

'You have talked this matter through? It's what you want, is it? It's not to oblige me or your mother or some abstract principle.'

'No. Entirely selfish.' Meg seemed to grow in intelligence whenever she talked to her father.

'That's so, Edwin?'

'Of course.'

He and Irene smiled across at each other.

'I do not like these matters rushed. To me you are important people. What you decide affects your mother and myself. And that is the reason why I do not want any haste, any skimping, any neglect or . . .'

'Dereliction,' Meg suggested, merry almost.

'You joke, my young lady.' He leaned over. 'Two weeks ago it was tears, depression, desperation.'

'Were they any more real?' Fisher asked, supporting his wife.

Vernon frowned, clenched fists in pockets, as though the question needed thrashing out.

'They were real enough for me.' He threw out his arms. 'Let us offer you our congratulations, then.'

Irene made appropriate noises, but did not get up.

'You've worked pretty hard at this,' Fisher said.

'I do not deny it.' He took both Meg's hands. 'Sufficiently for me to risk a pose or two here, a striking of attitudes. We slaved, did we not, Irene, after our fashion?' He retained one hand holding it at arm's length to declaim,

> '"I would not with swift winged zeal
> On the world's errands go,
> And labour up the heavenly hill
> With weary feet and slow."'

'What's that?' Meg asked.

'Thomas Hornblower Gill.'

Steeply, in Lincoln.

'Is it relevant?'

'The only verse I know is from the hymn books, and a smattering of Palgrave. And we deserve some heightening of language, do we not?'

Kathleen burst in with a larger tray, more stacked cups, a second plate of buttered currant slices. She gushed inanities.

'Come in. Pour the tea. Then sit yourself down,' Vernon said. 'Dance with them that dance.'

Fisher had not touched his wife, who sat beautiful, some three yards from him now. They'd not

311

arranged the day or time of his return. Whatever she felt, he was not convinced that anything beyond a verbal agreement had been reached. Kathleen Twining pushed a cup into his hand, shouting about sugar. He, the man from holiday, who'd met Jack and Lena Hollies, Terry and Sandra Smith, Carol and Tricia, who'd thought of his father, filled his shoes with east-coast sand, talked to strangers, but at a loose-end for a week, had now, could claim, a wife again. He did not know what it meant. He felt a sexual stirring; in the brightness of the room it seemed proper. Meg did not move much, but looked pleased with her cup held high. The Twining dodged about, serving. Fisher wanted to talk to her, hear her troubles, if she had any, or her pleasures. His father used to say as he went upstairs to bed, 'That's enough of that day, then.' Now the son had tired himself.

'They should sit together,' Irene said, gesturing with her plate.

'Of course.' Vernon leapt.

Obediently, Edwin did as he was bid, parked himself by Meg, who acknowledged his arrival. He shivered, pleased and uncertain. Vernon held his empty cup to the light. Irene inquired about the brand of the tea. There seemed nowhere obvious for Kathleen to sit, so she took a chair in the corner of the room.

'That's better,' Vernon said, pointing to the couple. 'Much more like it.' What banality would Arthur Fisher have managed?

Edwin touched Meg's hand, almost expecting a rebuff.

She smiled, reciprocated.

'Tea, Kathleen my love,' Vernon boomed.

Nobody knew anything, Fisher decided. He and his wife held hands as a sign of the new bond, bondage.

'We're all ignorant,' he said aloud, not meaning to.

'That's just like you,' Meg whispered.

Nothing had been settled, but he would gladly return that evening. As soon as Arthur Fisher had dumped the holiday suitcases in the hall for his wife to empty, he importantly picked up the post, usually no more than a couple of postcards from travelling friends, and the morning's newspaper, and announced, waving his small handful,

'I'm glad to be home.'